DOUBLE CROSS RANCH

Ty narrowed his eyes. "You're a liar, Duggins."

The man smiled, and with a black cheroot smoldering between two yellow-stained fingers, he patted the air, as if feeling the back of a beef. "Easy, boys, easy. I'm sure what Mr. Farraday meant was that I am mistaken. Perhaps I heard Mr. Winstead incorrectly."

"Nope," said Ty. "I called you a liar." It was a calculated choice of words—and the truth.

"What makes you say such a thing, Mr. Farraday?" said the man.

"Because it's the truth. Me and Winstead, we got along about as well as two rabid marmots in a sack. If you knew Winstead, he'd surely have mentioned that. Maybe even warned you about me."

"Warned? Hmm, that sounds as though you have the potential to be . . . dangerous, Mr. Farraday. Could that be a thinly veiled threat you are offering me?"

"Nothing could be further from the truth," said Ty. Then he leaned forward, the saddle leather creaking. "Unless there's some reason I should be threatening you. Is there, Mr. Duggins?"

Ralph Compton

DOUBLE CROSS RANCH

A Ralph Compton Novel
by Matthew P. Mayo

A SIGNET BOOK

SIGNET
Published by the Penguin Group
Penguin Group (USA) LLC, 375 Hudson Street,
New York, New York 10014

USA | Canada | UK | Ireland | Australia | New Zealand | India | South Africa | China
penguin.com
A Penguin Random House Company

First published by Signet, an imprint of New American Library,
a division of Penguin Group (USA) LLC

First Printing, May 2014

ISBN 978-0-451-46823-9

Printed in the United States of America
10 9 8 7 6 5 4 3 2 1

THE IMMORTAL COWBOY

This is respectfully dedicated to the "American Cowboy." His was the saga sparked by the turmoil that followed the Civil War, and the passing of more than a century has by no means diminished the flame.

True, the old days and the old ways are but treasured memories, and the old trails have grown dim with the ravages of time, but the spirit of the cowboy lives on.

In my travels—to Texas, Oklahoma, Kansas, Nebraska, Colorado, Wyoming, New Mexico, and Arizona—I always find something that reminds me of the Old West. While I am walking these plains and mountains for the first time, there is this feeling that a part of me is eternal, that I have known these old trails before. I believe it is the undying spirit of the frontier calling me, through the mind's eye, to step back into time. What is the appeal of the Old West of the American frontier?

It has been epitomized by some as the dark and bloody period in American history. Its heroes—Crockett, Bowie, Hickok, Earp—have been reviled and criticized. Yet the Old West lives on, larger than life.

It has become a symbol of freedom, when there was always another mountain to climb and another river to cross; when a dispute between two men was settled not with expensive lawyers, but with fists, knives, or guns. Barbaric? Maybe. But some things never change. When the cowboy rode into the pages of American history, he left behind a legacy that lives within the hearts of us all.

—*Ralph Compton*

Chapter 1

•

It was the yips, snarls, and growls of the coyotes that first drew Ty's attention to the little draw. Otherwise he'd have ridden right by, never having seen the bloating corpse of Alton Winstead, his closest neighbor and a man he held in no great regard.

Such was the deceiving terrain of the foothill country of the western slope of the Sierra Nevada, laid out like a rumpled blanket. Ty Farraday, mounted atop Stub, his sure-footed Morgan gelding, rode close and caught sight of the three cur coyotes, which looked up from their recent discovery. The three yippers sported thickening fur, though in mange-riddled clumps, the clinging sign of a hard summer and sure sign of a harder winter to come.

It appeared to Ty they weren't quite sure what to make of what they'd found, circling and snapping at one another as they were. No doubt they were lured by the stink of decomposition, something about the stench of death triggering the ever-present impulse to feed that he'd never seen a wild creature without. Only man and anything man had domesticated could afford to pass up the opportunity of a meal.

Breath left Ty's solid frame in a quick sigh of shock once he recognized the green worsted-wool waistcoat with its gold buttons, and the outer gray wool coat over it, the entire ensemble stretched tight and fixing to grow tighter with every hour the day's heat increased; then he knew for certain who the dead man was. And despite how he felt, seeing the man, once so powerful, self-confident, and cocky, so full of swagger in his various local dealings, Ty felt a twinge of sadness.

That the man was dead, and had been for at least a day, was apparent from the bloating and the drawn, pasty look of his face, despite the lateness of the season and thus the coolness of the air. And, reasoned Ty, anything bothered so by coyotes would surely flinch. Nonetheless as soon as he saw the ragged creatures slinking and darting in on the dead man, he slid his rifle from its boot beneath his right leg and levered a round. The smooth, clean "tang" sound of steel sliding over steel sliced the still air and the three curs, as one, jerked their narrow heads toward the sound. It proved all they needed to hear, and they kicked up trails of dust thinner than their own flicking feet.

Maybe it was the effect of seeing the man astride a mount, perhaps the same man who had drawn down on them in the past for chasing his calves? Ty suspected it was the critters' deep sense of mistrust and fear of man—in them since birth— that caused them to scamper away with such vigor.

He stepped down from Stub, keeping the rifle leveled toward the direction the coyotes had scampered. If they were as hungry as they appeared, they might dart back in and lunge at him. He'd seen it happen before.

Only when he stepped cautiously around the body to the far side did he see the blackened, dried clot of bloodied hair on the back of Winstead's head. Since he lay faceup, it almost didn't catch Ty's attention.

"Did you tumble from your mount, Winstead?" said Ty in a low voice, squinting and hunkering down close to the man. He'd not yet begun to smell too bad, though Ty knew that if he could detect even a slight smell, the coyotes could surely detect the scent of the body from a long way off. And if coyotes could, other critters would soon be along as well.

Ty sighed and eased the hammer back down, then laid the rifle at his side—still close at hand. "Let's flip you over, see if I can hoist you up and take you back to . . . Mrs. Winstead." The taste of that name on his tongue curdled and stung like flecks of salt. Through the fabric of the man's clothes, Ty felt the stiffness of the body, the flesh flattened on the bottom. A day? More, he guessed.

Ty Farraday was a tall, lean man who looked almost as if he were hewn from a block of rocky bone. He bore a perpetual haggard but determined look about him, common to hard-laboring men—as if no matter his pursuits, he would let nothing stop him from making it a success. Sandy hair, cut short and trimmed neatly about the edges, could barely be seen from under his low-crown, funnel-brim fawn rancher's hat, slight sweat stains ringing the leather band.

His clear green eyes had taken on a natural squint from years of range riding, and they scanned everything before him from under sun-bleached brows. His angled jawlines were clean-shaven, save for moderate sideburns that defined the sides of his lean face. His tall, lean frame had been bedecked in worn but well-tended rancher's gear since after the war.

He'd seen much death in the war, on the range, and on his own small spread, the Rocking T, which lay not far to the south. But there was no way a man could ever fully grow comfortable with the presence of that one sure thing in the world, the inevitable that everyone could expect, sooner or later. He skinned his clean-shaven lips tight to his teeth, gritting them against the grisly edge of the task. As he lifted the man, he caught movement in the husky gray scrub brush off to his left. A fawn gray face peered at him, a pink-and-black mottled tongue wagging with a panting effort.

"Get outta here," barked Ty. "Git!"

The cur retreated without sound, though not far. Not far at all. Good thing it wasn't a big cat. Might be one along soon, though. He had to get a move on.

As he shifted his gaze back to the task at hand, he saw more of the clotted, bloodied mess the back of Winstead's head had become. Ty glanced quickly once again at the earth around the body, saw as he had before he dismounted that there were the hoofprints of at least one horse. They were difficult to read in the graveled surface. Maybe Winstead had fallen? He'd never struck Ty as the sort of man to become unseated, but it could happen to the best of riders, especially if a horse got spooked by a rattler, or even its own shadow. Horses could be fickle creatures. Then again, Ty recalled that he'd rarely seen the man ride, remembering instead that Winstead often favored that fancy barouche.

Ty cursed himself for stomping all over the place with his own boots. Might be he'd have discovered more footprints than just his own. As if to verify his budding suspicion that maybe Winstead met his end by means other than a horse-throwing, Ty felt with a fingertip beneath the man something crusty, close by a hole in the back of his dead neighbor's coat. A bullet hole?

"Well, hellfire, Alton Winstead. You and me, we never did get along in life, but I'll be darned if I ever wanted anything such as this to befall you."

Ty grunted as he moved the body of the portly dead man higher onto its left side and nodded his head at what he saw— several close-bunched ragged holes punched in the gray wool fabric, an expensive coat doing its owner no good at all. And now he knew for sure this was no accidental fall from a spooked mount. This was a killing, a back-shooting, at that.

Ty shifted his weight onto his right knee, looked over the man's right side and glanced at the swelling belly, but there didn't appear to be exit wounds. He didn't think there would be. Those holes looked to be made close-in and from a small-caliber weapon, maybe a .22. But they had been close enough to have ignited the fabric, causing it to singe the puckered threads. What blood had leaked out had hardened and crusted on the surface, but Ty felt the softening wetness sticking beneath his fingertips. He lowered Winstead to his accustomed spot.

Then a sudden thought jerked his head upright, eyes wide, scanning northeastward, as if he could see through the landscape, straight to the very image in his mind's eye. "Sue Ellen!" he said, rising to his feet and snatching up the rifle at the same time. He mounted up on Stub, then glanced back once at the dead man.

As he reined Stub northeastward he said, "Sorry, Winstead, but I've no time to keep those critters from gnawing your stubborn hide. I'll do for you what I can, when I can. Right now I have to see to your widow."

Ty set Stub off at a lope in that direction, and for the somewhat hidden spot that he knew would put him within glassing distance of the ranch house of the Double Cross, Winstead's spread. He let Stub have his head and they thundered down the steep embankment of an arroyo, then switchbacked up the other side, which was equally steep. The late-fall air marked their breaths, man's and beast's, as plumes of dissipating smoke as they rode.

Clumps of dried grasses, like phantom heads poking from the knobby earth, rattled and scratched as they rode by, the brown stalks' slender, harmless fingers caressing Stub's legs as he ran through. Stub only ever balked when he saw a snake, and once on a bull thistle, just about this time of year, mused Ty, scanning the terrain ahead for the hard, brown tell-tale sign of the sticking culprits.

One more slight valley, down then up, and there was the

Winstead spread, the Double Cross, an impressive, if hollow, set of buildings that fit in out here no better than had their owner. What exactly had Alton Winstead had in mind when he came into the region ten years before? He'd promptly bought up the land that Ty had a handshake deal on with the previous owner, old Regis Horkins. Bad enough that Winstead had made Horkins an offer the scrimy old buzzard couldn't refuse, but that land had been Ty's ace in the hole.

He'd been counting on buying it and expanding his own small spread. But just like that, one day he was headed in that very direction, lifewise, with thoughts of marriage on his mind and a vast spread on which he could ranch right, and the next thing he knew, Alton Winstead, in his slick black barouche, rolled in and bought all manner of local land, including the very acreage that Horkins had promised to Ty.

But it had been the theft of his intended, his one and only girl, Sue Ellen, that had stung Ty the hardest. Even after all this time, the memory still set his teeth to grinding.

Ty reined up and had to jerk the reins hard once to keep Stub from fidgeting while he scanned. There was always something moving on that horse, an ear flicking, a swish of the tail, hooves dancing, a shake of the head. Ty had never quite gotten used to it and mostly found it annoying, but he also knew it was as much a part of Stub's nature as was Ty's perpetual hard stare.

He'd been told often enough that people found it offputting, enough so that he'd been approached a time or two in the nearest town, Ripley Flats, by men who thought he'd been trying, as one scarred character had called it, to "put the fear" into them. He'd laughed then, walked away shaking his head, but he knew what they meant. And he didn't much care what people thought.

"Why don't you smile?" Sue Ellen had said more than once.

"Why would I?"

"You seem so serious, maybe unhappy."

That had made him smile. "But I'm not."

She sighed. "I know, but you . . . oh, Ty. You look as if you are always angry."

"Nope. Just thinking. I can't imagine anyone would make a stink about that, now would they?"

He'd winked at her and she'd finally smiled, her eyes crinkling like they did when she'd give in to his way of thinking, even if she didn't buy what he was selling. That look on her face used to make it downright impossible to look away from her.

Even after all these years, he could still recall that look, which made it more difficult than ever to put her out of his mind. He thought he'd succeeded. Heck, he'd have bet that he'd succeeded, but then he'd come across old Alton Winstead dead, already being savaged by critters who didn't know any better. If they'd bothered to ask Ty his opinion, he'd have told those fool creatures that pecking and nipping flesh off that particular man would only lead to gut ache.

As he crested a rise, the last before Winstead's Double Cross Ranch, and the one that would give him a sightline on down to the buildings, Ty reined up and rummaged in a saddlebag for his telescoping spyglass. He worked the focusing rings on it, zeroing in left, then right, on the impressive main house, and there was Sue Ellen Winstead, lugging a galvanized pail from what must be the kitchen of the house over to the well. She looked a little tired, wisps of hair hung in her face, her cheeks were in high color and her dress, skirt, and work apron wrinkled and soiled. Beyond stood and sat several men in the yard and on the porch, looking to be doing little more than ogling Sue Ellen and loafing.

As Ty spied on them, one man planted in a rocking chair on the porch swung his mustached face in Ty's direction. Ty immediately lowered his spyglass, but knew the effort was too late—men had already begun bustling into action. He'd been seen, probably because of light glinting off the glass.

"Curse the sun," he muttered, sighing. He collapsed the brass spyglass and slipped it back into his saddlebag. Then he nudged Stub higher upslope so he'd be fully skylined. In for a penny, he thought as he pulled out his makings and built himself a smoke. He'd wait them out, not run like a child, since it was obvious that two riders had been dispatched to his direction.

At least Sue Ellen was alive, if haggard looking. But even at this distance and even though she looked to have been worked hard, he had to admit Sue Ellen was still a fetching woman. He was a fool for her, always had been, always would be. Even on his wildest day of imagining Ty couldn't conjure a time when he'd not been attracted to the woman he'd known all those long years ago.

He finished drizzling the fine-chopped tobacco into the trough of creased paper and smoothed the thin smoke, dragging it through his lips twice to seal it. He always took his time in such matters, found that most anything in life that was rushed more often than not turned out poorly. Just a fact. He reckoned he'd learned that from his mother, bless her Irish heart. And also from good ol' Uncle Hob. Certainly wasn't from the old man, a rascal more concerned with his next bottle of tanglefoot than in finishing a task well, on time, and happily.

Other than to slip off the rawhide thong looped over the hammer of his Colt Navy, Ty kept still, his hands resting on the saddle horn as puffs of dust from the riders bloomed ever closer. Soon he made out the horses' coats—a chestnut and some sort of roan. Stub had marked their progress and now nickered, tossing his head slightly at their approach.

"Okay, boy. We'll know something soon enough."

And within a minute more, the two thundered upslope and into sight, no weapons drawn. They reached the top of the rise at which Ty sat atop Stub. The first horse's rider sat tall in the saddle but only because he was a tall man, his obvious height accentuated by a black felt hat with a crown that ranged skyward. The man's rounded shoulders gave him a look of defeat that warred with a flinty look of deviltry in his reddened eyes. He also sported a long, beaklike nose, red around the nostrils with quivering drips hanging from them.

The roan's rider, a shorter, wider man, looked solidly built. Bandoliers layered a sweat-stained peasant shirt that, from the looks of it, had ranged a far piece from its days as a white garment.

A tall-crowned wide-brimmed woven hat with a large curling brim adorned the man's head, which itself was a dark-skinned affair, all snagged teeth and shocks of thick, raw hair jutting as badly as his teeth. His efforts at working up a mustache looked to have been doomed for some time, as the entire affair was little more than a haphazard series of spidery hairs that, if possible, detracted further from the man's scant looks.

But it was the eyes under thick black, beetling brows that caused Ty's jaw muscles to bunch. They were the dark, dead eyes of a man who cared little for his own life, and so would gladly take the lives of others—and Ty wagered with himself that the man probably had, numerous times—as easily as a scythe lays low stalks of grain.

The two men paused, assessing him and he them, each in turn. Then they split and flanked him. Ty tightened on the Morgan's reins and walked the horse backward briskly. "Whoa, now, gents. Hold up." And the two riders did just that.

"You and me, we're not getting off to a cordial start. Usually such meetings go something like, 'Hi there, I'm so-

and-so and you're riding on my home range. Who be you?'
That sort of chatter. But when you two ride up bold as brass
and think to outflank me, why, a man will become suspicious, don't you think?"

This appeared to confuse the strangers. The tall one finally spoke. "You ought to come with us." He dragged a
sleeve across his drippy nose, jerked his head back
downslope, toward the Double Cross, his tall hat wagging as
if it might topple from its lofty perch.

"Was that a question or an order?" said Ty, careful to keep
one hand on the bunched and taut reins, one resting on his
leg, poised for snatching his Colt from its holster.

"Come on. Don't want to keep the boss waiting."

Ty wondered who that might be, and what he came up
with was that these men and the others were strangers to him
and carried more than a whiff of wrongness about them. But
not knowing this as a certainty, Ty merely nodded at them
and waited.

They regarded him, looked at each other; then the smaller,
swarthy-faced man made a low growling noise deep in his
throat and gave what Ty was sure was the man's orneriest
glare.

Ty pulled in a long, slow draft of air through his nostrils,
keeping his hand close by the Colt. "I got to tell you, fellas,
I don't scare easy." The entire time he spoke he eyed them,
kept their hands in view, making sure any sudden movement
was met with one of greater speed and force. He would brook
no foolishness from these two ill-born wastrels.

"Come on, then," sighed the tall, slump-shouldered man.
He jerked his head downslope once again and the smaller man
growled once more, giving his glare a last squinty effort, then
nudged his horse into a slow walk beside Ty. It was obvious
they intended to keep him just ahead of them. But since he
was pretty sure these two and whoever else lurked at the Win-

stead home place were probably responsible for Alton's death, a back-shooting and bludgeoning, to boot—no accident there— then he was not about to let them behind him.

He held Stub to a halting slow walk, and had to admit to enjoying seeing the muscles of the smaller man's homely face and stalky neck tense and his veins throb. It's a wonder the runty short-fuse of a man had any teeth left. Under such hard treatment, Ty suspected they'd have long since powdered. Still he kept a lid on his grin, no need to push the little man over the edge. Just up to it would do nicely.

They proceeded on down the last slope, then onto the long flat that led to the ranch. The roughs flanking ahead of him gave up their flagging attempts to drop back and heeled their mounts into a jog, though they were still careful to glance at Ty every few seconds. He kept up with them, though he hung back a few paces.

As they neared the ranch entrance, he glanced up at its ironwork archway. It depicted a doubled cross that looked, Ty supposed, somewhat like a fanciful letter "W." To his knowledge, Winstead had never bothered to make official the mark as a brand, at least not with the local cattlemen's association. More and more as time wore on it became apparent to Ty and everyone else locally that Alton Winstead was anything but a rancher. And if he intended to be, as he kept on telling everyone he was, then he had sure taken his time about it. And now it looked as though he'd never get there. But maybe Sue Ellen would.

They passed under the arch and Ty nudged Stub into a quick gallop that caught the two strange men by surprise as he passed between them and beyond, making a beeline directly for the house, where a handful of men clustered. As he approached he saw three on the long porch of the place, loafing, and another man lazily easing forward and back in Winstead's ornately carved rocking chair.

The two riders caught up to him, doing their best to flank him like skulking wolves, just as he reined up a half dozen yards from the porch. Stub fidgeted, dancing in place, eyes beginning to whiten and roll. The horse was a good judge of situations and men and he sensed all that and more of what Ty also felt.

"Whoa, boy," murmured Ty in a low command. He cut his gaze to Sue Ellen. She stood halfway between the porch and the water trough. A galvanized pail, still glistening wet inside, hung from a work-reddened hand. She looked at him with wide eyes filled with warning—that much was plain. He forced himself to keep his own eyes level, no flinching or twitching. That one in the rocking chair had the look of boss hoss about him. Any sign of recognition or weakness would tip him off about something that Ty wasn't even aware of yet.

He had to admit that Sue Ellen looked worse up close than she had from a distance through the spyglass. Worn and flushed, those green eyes wore dark rings and sweat caused long strings of hair to cling to her face. He kept his face stern, looked down at her, touched his hat brim. "Mrs. Winstead," he said, his voice grave, his face revealing nothing, yet his eye jounced, betraying him in some small way, of that he was sure.

Half a dozen hard cases, a couple with a Mexican-bandit look to them, made a show of leaning about the place. They bore the same general appearance as the two who had escorted him. To a man they looked dirty and showed signs that they drank too much, and their hard glances and gritted teeth revealed them to be as designing as starving wolves in a chicken coop. They looked to Ty to be bad men.

Those on the long, low, shade-giving overhang were tough characters sporting various scars, ratty, much-patched articles of clothing, and worn boots and hats. What they did each carry that gave Ty pause even for his own safety, though

more for Sue Ellen's, was weaponry. All manner of killing
devices bristled visibly on their persons. They did not look
much like ranch hands. But then again, what business was it
of his? Alton Winstead was an odd piece of work, so it stood
to reason he'd be chummy with odd characters, maybe even
hire them.

A russet-haired, bloodshot-eyed man in a bowler an-
chored an edge of the broad steps and flashed a one-sided
grin as Ty's eyes raked over him. He took in a pepperbox
revolver wedged in the man's waistband, a chip-handled ma-
chete stuck in the other side of the same waist sash, and two
mismatched cross-draw pistols snugged oddly above the
man's belly, just under his chest.

Two more men stood on either end of the porch, and
looked as if they could well be brothers close in age. Nut-
brown skin shone with sweat and the oil of poor living, a
rough diet, and lack of good sweat-labor—a trait they all
seemed to share. Their personal arsenals consisted of Bowie
knives and six-guns, and they each cradled a longer gun, one
a sawed-off, the other a rifle. They did not share the bowler-
wearing, Irish-looking fellow's penchant for grinning.

The man seated in the rocker still worked that piece of
furniture ever so slowly, all the while eyeing Ty as keenly as
Ty had his men. Ty's gaze rested on this man for a moment.

Each man wondered why the other was really there. Ty
eyeballed the slowly rocking man. Already he knew not to
trust the look of what had to be his gang of men. But this one,
he looked at once to be the best and worst of the lot. He had
a dark look about him, maybe Italian, maybe Mexican,
though none of that mattered. From what Ty could see, the
man was all cold and ornery behind those bright, inquisitive
eyes. What was this one's story? Why was he here?

One of the man's legs was outstretched, the boot canted at
an odd angle. Ty noted that the sole on that boot, somewhat

facing him, bore the marks of hard use, particularly along the outer edge. As if it had been held for a time on a spinning grindstone.

The man's face was hard, homely, and it was full, just shy of thin, so he ate regularly, and didn't have that scurvy, hungry look his fellows wore. The others looked as if they were the human counterparts of those coyotes up back in the hills who'd been nipping and snapping at the corpse of Alton Winstead.

"What brings you to the Double Cross, sir?"

The question took Ty by surprise. It was precisely the thing he was set to ask this arrogant man. No, arrogant wasn't quite the word for him, much closer to bold and self-confident. He looked like a cat that had just filled its belly on a bawling new calf and lazily watched as its kits snarled and fought over the carcass.

Ty sucked in a quick breath through his front teeth, straightened in the saddle. He wanted to play this calm and cool. If these gents caught on that he had seen the body of Winstead—and that he knew they'd done him in—then he might as well let them drill him in the back, too. And that wouldn't help Sue Ellen. He didn't dare glance her way again.

"I was about to ask you that same thing, fella." Ty softened this with a head nod. "You chums with Winstead?"

The man laughed softly, a dry, papery sound. "And I could ask you that same thing . . . *fella*." He closed his eyes lazily, almost as if he were in the midst of an enjoyable drinking jag. "As it happens, yes, I am an old acquaintance of Alton Winstead. My name is Clewt Duggins."

Ty noticed that a few of the men started at the man's mention of his name, as if they didn't want him to say who he was. Curious.

"Winstead kindly invited me and my crew here"—he waved a finger left and right—"to mind the ranch while he's away."

Ty regarded him a moment. "Away, huh?" That was a plausible response, considering he knew that Winstead often took trips of a week or more, sometimes taking Sue Ellen, sometimes not.

The man nodded, looked almost as if he wasn't about to reply, then said, "He's gone on an extended business trip, buying cattle, primarily. He hired us to set up the spread, so to speak. Get it ready for the first herd to arrive." He leaned forward, rested his palms on his knees, as if warming to his topic. But he focused his eyes on Sue Ellen Winstead, who had yet to move. She stared from Ty to the man, back to Ty.

"Mr. Winstead," continued the man in the rocker, "he has a whole lot of good ideas where this ranch is concerned. Lots of planning, I've been told, has taken place since he arrived in these parts. Would you agree, Mr., ah . . . ?"

"You say Winstead has gone to buy cattle."

The man's smile faded as he shifted his gaze back to Ty. "Yes, that's what I said."

"I don't believe you," said Ty, not altering his gaze.

The men loafing on the porch all tensed as if pulled from behind by a common wire. The man in the rocking chair lost his smug smile, but patted the air to either side of him, calming his men. They resumed their former positions, though all remained tight and tense. A few moments passed. Then the man in the rocking chair stood, his extended leg remained rigid, and he swung awkwardly forward, pivoting on it over to a porch upright. He squinted his eyes and poked his head forward, as if really paying attention to Ty Farraday for the first time since they began talking.

"You come right to a thing, don't you . . . Ah, what's your name again?"

"I reckon I do, yep. No sense playing games. And no, not 'again,' because I haven't said my name yet. But it's Farraday. I own a neighboring rancho, the Rocking T."

"Ah, yes, yes. Alton—that is"—the man smiled—"Mr. Winstead—he spoke of your place, said you were quite a rancher, good stockman, had lots of good things to say about you."

Ty narrowed his eyes. "You're a liar, Duggins."

It was as if he'd drawn down on the lot of them. Each of the men—and he suspected there were a couple more he hadn't yet seen—squared off on him, readying for a blazing minute of fast gun action. In such a circumstance as this, he decided mentioning that he'd found Winstead's body being gnawed on by coyotes was not in his best interest. These men sported all the outward markings of killers. No need to offer himself up as the next notch on their grips.

"Seems like your men are a mite touchy."

The man smiled, and with a black cheroot smoldering between two yellow-stained fingers, he patted the air again, as if feeling the back of a beef. "Easy, boys, easy. I'm sure what Mr. Farraday meant was that I am mistaken. Perhaps I heard Mr. Winstead incorrectly."

"Nope," said Ty. "I called you a liar." It was a calculated choice of words—and the truth.

"What makes you say such a thing, Mr. Farraday?" said the man.

"Because it's the truth. Me and Winstead, we got along about as well as two rabid marmots in a sack. If you knew Winstead, he'd surely have mentioned that. Maybe even warned you about me."

"Warned? Hmm, that sounds as though you have the potential to be . . . dangerous, Mr. Farraday. Could that be a thinly veiled threat you are offering me?"

"Nothing could be further from the truth," said Ty. Then he leaned forward, the saddle leather creaking. "Unless there's some reason I should be threatening you. Is there, Mr. Duggins?"

Duggins had puffed his cheroot down to the nub, then dropped it and mashed it into the plank floor at his feet with one scuffed boot toe. He let thick streams of gauzy black-gray smoke leak from his nostrils. They carried over, clouding at Sue Ellen's face, before breaking up and away. When he spoke smoke continued to drift from his mouth. "I can only tell you what I was told, Mr. Farraday." He raised his empty hands, let them fall by his side, two weathered, leathery claws curved close by the butt ends of his six-guns.

Ty regarded him a moment, aware that he could be drawn down on any second and no one here would care. Except Sue Ellen. Maybe. He looked at her. "Mrs. Winstead, how are you faring? You look . . . tired. Do you need anything?"

A rare tremor of fear passed over her face. She parted her lips to speak but Clewt Duggins cut her off.

"The ranch is well in hand, Mr. Farraday. Well in hand, I assure you. We have been entrusted by Mr. Winstead with the care of his most precious gem." Duggins smiled, indicated his joke to come. "And also his wife."

Ty didn't take his eyes from Sue Ellen's face while the man spoke. He knew something was wrong, very wrong. She was not a fearful woman, and though life with Alton Winstead had to have made her many things, Ty was sure that fearful of the man she'd chosen for a husband wasn't one of them. To Winstead's credit, it had seemed he'd fairly doted on Sue Ellen, a fact that had long galled Ty. Though he knew, too, that it could easily have been the other way, Winstead could have been an abuser in much the way he was a blowhard.

So why was she so fearful now? Did they intend to kill her next? Had he ridden in on the moments before her death? Something told him no, something told him they needed her, for whatever reason. He hated to think about that. He was on the verge of doing something rash, something foolish, and she must have sensed it, because Sue Ellen spoke up.

"Mr. Farraday, I can assure you that what these men say is the truth and you are interrupting the progress on the corrals and fences we must have built before Alton and the others arrive with the new herd."

Ty listened and nodded slowly, not believing a word of it. She'd said the words, yes, but her voice trembled ever so slightly. And her hands, reddened from scrubbing something, knotted and unknotted the soiled apron-front of her dress. This nervousness was not a trait of the Sue Ellen he knew, but he knew for certain that she needed his help.

"The lady is correct, Mr. Farraday," said Duggins. "It is time you left us to get on with our work. Time is of the essence, as a smart man once said."

"Time is what a man makes of it, Duggins. Nothing more, nothing less."

Ty nodded to Sue Ellen, touched his hat brim with a finger, then tugged Stub around, not once granting Duggins or any of his men the expected courtesy of a glance or a nod. Ty guessed she would be able to hang on—she was scrappy and these men needed something. He had to devise a plan. He felt sure she would have found some way to tell him had she been in mortal danger. Maybe she didn't even know about her husband's death?

How long had she been tending to the band of killers and thieves? How long had Winstead been dead? And how far had they gone in abusing her good graces? They had killed her husband, after all, and with a shot to the back, too. He didn't think they would treat her with any amount of respect. But there were too many of them for him to take on just yet. Getting himself shot would not help Sue Ellen one bit.

Chapter 2

He took the more traveled ranch road back to his place, in part to avoid trailing back toward the direction he'd found Winstead's body. It would not do to have Duggins suspect he'd actually seen the body or that he might accidentally see it on his way home. Bad enough he'd been somewhat near the body when he'd been caught glassing the ranch.

After a while he noticed the same two riders who'd been sent to escort him down out of the hills fogged his back trail all the way back to the Rocking T. It set Ty's teeth tight, but he could do little more than glance their way now and again. He figured they didn't take any pains to hide themselves, so why should he? Besides, there was not much he could do about it for the time being. He had to get back home and feed the stock.

Ty reached a long, low cluster of well-tended ranch buildings, walked Stub past a barn, a smokehouse, a chicken coop, and a small eating hall and kitchen before coming to a stop in front of a small, tidy log ranch house. It had been the first structure he and Uncle Hob had built when they settled the land.

He sat atop Stub for a moment, listening for signs of the two men's horses, but they were far off, having turned back at the entrance to the Rocking T. He needed a bit of time to think, had to reason out his next move. From inside the house he heard a rangy voice draw closer to the door, accompanied by a clunking sound.

"Well, look what finally decided to drag itself on in here. After being gone all day!"

Ty felt his usual twinge of relief and comfort at the sight of his old "uncle," Selkirk "Hob" Jones, ex-lawman and general crank, leaning in the open doorway. He had a monstrous wooden spoon gripped in his left hand and an equally odd-looking wooden knob balancing the other, lower corner of him. He was called "Hob," short for "Hobble," because his right leg, from the knee down, was less of a leg and more of a barely carved length of ash stove wood, somewhat rounded on the smooth-worn end.

It was unsettling to most folks who met the old curmudgeon for the first time, but he had never cared what others thought of him in all the years Ty had known him—which had been much of Ty's life. His father had met his end because of Marshal Jones, so Selkirk had taken it upon himself to make sure young Ty and his mother were taken care of. Ty reckoned he'd not have the Rocking T had it not been for Jones's steady, if not quiet, presence in his life.

He also knew that the old goat had been sweet on Ty's mother, though whether the two of them ever did anything about it remained a mystery to Ty. Fine with him; he figured that such things were a man and a woman's own business.

He climbed down off Stub and looped the reins loosely around the rail by the steps. The horse canted a leg, stood hipshot, and appeared to settle in for a wait. Jones's reedy voice, which hadn't stopped since Ty rode up, continued yammering at him as he mounted the steps, pulled off his hat, and ran a hand through his thatch of sweat-curled hair.

". . . to think I been reduced to working on a dirt farm instead of doing what I was put on this green earth to do—chase women and outlaws, in that order!"

Ty nodded to Uncle Hob and walked into the kitchen, the familiar *clump ka-clump ka-clump* sound of the old man following him, the voice ceaseless in its assault. Ty almost smiled for the first time that day.

"And to top it all off, I'm still stuck nursemaiding a . . . a tall galoot like you!"

That failed to elicit any response from Ty, who poured himself a cup of the thick-as-axle-grease coffee the old man kept bubbling on the back of the stove, day and night, for as long as Ty could remember. In fact, he'd never seen him empty grounds out of it, just add another handful of them, along with water, whenever the mood suited him.

Hob rattled his wooden spoon on the top of the hot stove. "You wanna know what I been up to whilst you been gallivanting all over God's biggest section-and-a-half?"

Ty glanced up at him, didn't change his expression, looked down at a plate of cold biscuits on the table. "Nope. But I reckon you're about to tell me."

"And don't you think you're going to wrap one of them claws you call a hand around one of them biscuits, neither. 'Cause I didn't spend all morning hunkered over that blasted stove so you could come on in here without a by-your-leave and muckle onto anything you have a mind to. . . ."

Ty watched the aproned, one-legged old lawdog sputter and churn in an erratic half circle in the midst of the low-roofed ranch house's open kitchen. He threatened the very air of the place with that favorite blackened wooden spoon in much the same way an Apache would wave a war lance at a camp of whites intruding on his sacred lands.

"You about done, old man?"

His question had the effect he'd hoped for—he loved riling Hob—much as he'd seen a full henhouse react when a fox appeared in their midst.

"Who in the blazes are you calling old? I may be longer

in the tooth than you, but that's only because I was born a ways back. It don't mean I'm old! Why, I had a mind to, I could whup you up one side of this raw knob of dirt you call a ranch and down the other. You got me?"

Ty waited for the dust to settle. Finally a red-faced Hob looked at him.

"Yep," said Ty as he snapped up a pair of biscuits, and bolted from the room. He just made it through the front door when he felt a slight breeze by the side of his head and the wooden spoon *whang*ed into the log wall beside him. It was accompanied with a fresh flurry of howled words, some of which he'd never heard before. Ty smiled and strode from the porch. He'd put the horse up, give himself time to figure out what to do about Sue Ellen.

He was halfway to the stable, Stub stepping easy behind him, before Ty remembered to look to the long, low rise to the east. He wasn't surprised by what he saw. In the afternoon's waning light, two riders were skylined. As if they had seen him, they quickly drifted back down behind the ridgeline and out of sight. But Ty had seen them, and he knew for certain they'd been watching him closely. And anytime anyone watched Ty Farraday was too much watching. He was a free man who didn't like the notion of being fettered by anyone or anything. He could only imagine what Sue Ellen was feeling.

He moved in his long-legged, easy gait to the stable, finally remembering he had two of Hob's tasty biscuits in his work-hardened hand. He munched one, and when he got Stub stalled, he fed bits of the other biscuit on the flat of his palm to the bold Morgan.

"If ol' Hob saw me feeding you this biscuit, he'd pitch another of his fits. But you and I both know he feeds you plenty when I'm not around, right boy?"

The next half hour was spent in the barn, feeding a few

straggly, bawling young stock and tending the half a dozen horses in the corral, two of which he'd only begun to break. Then he found himself uncharacteristically climbing the corral and staring at the snubbing post. He sat on the top rail as the sun continued its slow crawl downward to the Pacific Ocean, the cold bulk of the Sierra Nevada range at his back, forming the terrain of his ranch, hard-earned land on the sometimes-verdant slopes of the foothills.

And he fell to thinking about Sue Ellen and everything that had brought him to this point. He knew this was not productive, knew he should reveal all to Hob, maybe send the old lawdog to ride for the law himself, and bring back a posse of men. But something told him to hold off. That there was time. Just what did he know?

Alton Winstead had been shot in the back, that much was certain. But who's to say the law wouldn't think Ty did that to the man? After all, it was well known in Ripley Flats that Ty held no kind thoughts for Winstead. Not that most folks could blame him, considering the way Winstead usurped the land he'd had his mind and heart set on. But the wealthy newcomer had endeared himself to one and all in town by donating substantial sums to the church, to the school, helping various business owners by offering little loans, and by chumming up to the old town marshal.

None of that mattered a whit to Ty. Buying his coveted land out from under him would have been one thing, but turning the head of Ty's longtime girl, Sue Ellen, and then marrying her. . . . Well, that was the roughest blow of all. Folks didn't blame Winstead wholly for that, for as was said, it takes two to make a couple.

After that, when most men would have sunk into a bottle and run their personal and business affairs into the ground, there was Ty Farraday, along with grouchy old Uncle Hob, doggedly working, day after day, month on month, year following year, to build up his meager spread into something more than it could ever hope to be. No one could fault the man for his efforts, but he never seemed to get to that next plateau, not for lack of trying. They all knew it was largely because he needed more cattle, more horses, and he couldn't get those unless he had more land.

And all that rangeland and grassland, which should have been his—would have been his—until it was sold out from under Ty's nose, and on the very week he was fixing to make the final installment of the down payment. And that day he'd set aside to ask Sue Ellen to be his wife. But the irony was that all that fine land that Winstead bought had since lain fallow and unused.

Well-intentioned people had gone out of their way to tell Ty just what they thought of the situation, that he should just eat a big slice of humble pie and ask Winstead to allow him to use that land. But Ty merely stared them down, one after another, his eyes narrowing and his jaw muscles working reflexively.

Even old Hob had long since given up on his seething anger toward Winstead and had come around to dropping hints that Ty should make the rich man a plain old business deal and lease that land, build up a fine herd, then buy him out. Ty had merely stared the old man down until Hob, normally a tough nut to crack, had turned away with a groan and tended to his stew. Neither man spoke for a week afterward.

But all of that water under the bridge hardly mattered anymore. Less so now that Winstead was murdered. And that one fact did not bode well for Ty Farraday.

Before he knew what was happening, a rifle shot sliced the air, whistling by his ear with the intensity of a thousand angry bees. Ty pitched himself forward off the rail, landing on his face in the dust of the corral. He held there, face down, hands planted flat in the dirt, boot toes dug in, paused in the near-dark for a few heartbeats, assessing the situation. Was it a warning shot? Or intended as a killing shot? Either way, he had to tell Hob right away about his afternoon now, for the old man's life could be in as much danger as his, merely by association with Ty.

The shot had come in from the northeast, just where he'd expect such a shot to come from. He rolled over to the darker, shaded edge of the corral, a good six feet away, and gained his feet there in the shadows. With the corral to his back, he pulled his Colt Navy, eased the hammer back to the deadly position, and scanned the far side of the yard.

Since it was too early for fall roundup, the only ones here were he and Uncle Hob. The men he regularly hired, mostly young, roving ranch hands from nearby spreads who hired out to make a bit of winter spending money and to keep up their cowboying skills, wouldn't be there for a few weeks yet.

As Ty cat-footed, low and hunched, around the perimeter of the corral, he heard another set of steps, slow and cautious, off to his right by the house. But the cursed loafing shed was between him and the house. He held up in the dark interior and listened. Presently he heard it again, an odd, uneven sound. Maybe the footfalls of someone unfamiliar with the layout of the place. Probably be those two he'd dealt with earlier. Maybe one of them had crept down close in order to ambush while the other shot from a distance?

Then he heard a hissing whisper from the closest corner of the house. "Ty! Hey, boy! What was that shot all about?"

Ty exhaled slowly in relief. Of course, with that uneven sound, it was Uncle Hob and his wooden leg. But now he had to warn the old man to keep well back out of any lingering light. "Hob!" he whispered. "Hob, it's me, Ty. I'm fine. Keep back, get back in the house and stay low. I'm coming!"

He listened for sign of the old man's retreat. Hob might be

a curmudgeon of the first order, but he was also an old war-horse who knew by instinct, honed in the heat of a hundred close-call battles, when a situation called for silent action and no argument. He listened to the soft retreating scuffing sounds, satisfied that Hob had reached the relative safety of the house; then Ty scuttled like a man-beetle around the far side of the loafing shed and beelined to the house himself. He had a feeling that whoever had shot had intended it as a warning. Otherwise he would probably be dead instead of worrying about such things.

Chapter 3

Cuthbert Henry Atwood, a man as ordinary in appearance as his name was odd and unlikely, wiped the fingers of his blood-pasted left hand on the shirt of the man he'd just shot. His sigh was a long, lingering thing that trailed out of him like steam from a worn relief valve. Not for the first time that day, nor the last, did he think of how very welcome a day away from his job might be. He didn't dare let that line of thinking unspool, for it might lead to bigger, bolder thoughts, such as how would a week or a month away from Dane Creek feel? How about an entire year? How about never returning?

He'd been in this sinkhole of crime for nigh on to two decades and it never got easier. In fact, in addition to the various gold and more recent copper strikes, since the cattle drives began to make the settlement a regular stop, his headaches as its sole full-time lawdog had only increased, to the point where he had had to hire a deputy. That man, Lemuel Cleveland, had been a local, lured to the job by promise of steady money. Not good or particularly safely earned money, but the paltry sum could at least be counted on to put food in his wife's belly.

Unfortunately, not but a few months into the position, Lemuel had become a widower when his wife had been found slit open like a market fish in an alleyway behind the Horizon Saloon one too-bright morning. Rumor had it she'd been selling off what her husband had always gotten for free, telling him her extra money came from taking in washing and sewing. What he didn't know, she figured, wouldn't hurt him. What she didn't know was that it might not have killed him, but it sure did crush him. That had been the previous year.

Since then, Marshal Atwood felt he'd been doing a pretty good job at building the man back up again, and Lem's role as deputy had begun to earn him threads of self-confidence. Atwood's own family—his young wife, a pretty Mexican girl, Maria, nearly twenty years his junior, as well as their young son, Henry Jr., nearly six years old—had been helpful, too, in bringing life back to the deputy. They often had him over for a warm meal of a night.

But then Clewt Duggins and his boys had ridden in hard, ransacked the town on their way to somewhere else—north, he figured. And in their haste to have fun and then leave Dane Creek behind, they looted, pillaged, burned, and shot their way out of town.

Unfortunately for Marshal Atwood, of the things they shot, in addition to a number of buildings, one piano, a series of nearly full spittoons, and two cur dogs, were a number of people, among them his sole sad deputy, Lem Cleveland. The rangy green lawman had been caught merely doing his job, trying to prevent the bloodthirsty south-of-the-border gang of drunken drifters from shooting, intentionally or otherwise, citizens of the hard-bitten little mining and cattle town. In the process, Cleveland had instead gotten shot himself. Gut shot, but not before one of the weasels shot him in the back, close-up by the looks of it, with a small-caliber piece, maybe a pepperbox.

Poor Lem had taken a good many hours to die. The only saving grace to the drawn-out process had been that something in Henry Atwood's mind finally became decided that he'd reached the end of his rope, so to speak. If he wanted to live to see his own boy become a man, he'd better get his family out of harm's way, and that included quitting the law-dog line.

"You don't mind me saying so, looks to me like you could use a hand in this town, Marshal."

Atwood looked up from the face of the latest man he'd shot to see a bearded gent looking down at him, blocking out the sun. The marshal squinted up at the man's face, at the wide-brimmed hat. "Do I know you?"

"Not yet, but I have a feeling we'll become fast friends."

"Oh? How's that?" Atwood's extra sense, that thing that warned him by the tightening of his scalp when he might be in danger, had now begun to tingle.

The man laughed and extended a hand. "I'm US District Court Judge Sam Mulholland."

Marshal Atwood continued to eye him, so the man kept speaking. "Got my papers in my saddlebag." It wasn't a question, but an offer. Atwood softened and shook the still-proffered hand.

"I'm Cuthbert Atwood, though I go by Henry. I'm marshal of this"—he waved a hand wearily at the dusty little burg, let it drop to his side—"this place."

"I know. And I am here to help. My superiors received word from you—in the form of a petition to the state, I believe—that you needed more law and order down this way. After hearing about the crimes hereabouts, and seeing that you are but one man against a sea of border trash, we naturally . . ."

"Decided to finally pay attention to my little town, huh? Finally just decided to ride on down here and see what all the fuss was about?" Atwood knew he should be grateful that his constant efforts at getting attention from a higher municipal power than themselves had finally fruited, but dang if he wasn't steamed.

"What's this all really about, Mulholland? Don't get me wrong—I'm happy to have the help, but I'd rather have a dozen men handy with weaponry of any sort than a man with a bunch of books and papers in a saddlebag. No offense, but we need guns, not gavels, sir."

Henry turned back to the body in the street, bent to lift the man by the shoulders. "Now, if you want to be useful to me, you'll grab hold of this dead fool by the boots and help me lug him over to Chauncy's. He'll welcome the chance to build another coffin. It's been nearly a week since we've had a shooting and I expect he's running low on whiskey money."

The portly man in the black suit, coal black stovepipe boots, black silk string tie, white shirt, and matching black boss-o'-the-plains hat bent at once and scooped up the dead man by the heels. "Of course, of course." They crossed the nearly empty street in silence before Mulholland spoke again. "None taken, by the way."

"How's that?" said Henry Atwood.

"Offense. You didn't offend me, sir. In fact, I quite agree with you. There's a time for gavels, as you so succinctly put my line of work, and there's a time for guns."

"My line?" Atwood smiled grimly. "And which do you think we have here, Judge?"

"As it happens, I saw what happened back there in the street. This drunk had been terrorizing that woman, wherever she's gone to now, and you braced him. What you didn't see, Marshal, but I did, was that before he spun on you, and no doubt emboldened and dumbed down by the drink in his belly, he actually smiled the world's most confident smile. He looked to me as if he knew he was going to shoot you dead, Marshal."

"So you're saying my shooting him was justified, at least

in your eyes, is that it?" Atwood offered a half smile as he stepped up on the boardwalk's creaking, sun-popped boards.

"Well, yes, that's exactly it."

"Well that's good to know, judge. Seeing as how you are a judge and all."

"Now, see here, Marshal. I came here in good faith and—"

"I know, I know, Mulholland. Don't get your knickers bunched. I only meant a little fun is all. And maybe I'm a little bit rankled that you had the nerve to tell me what I did was justified, seeing as how I've been forced to be the judge, jury, and executioner of far too many people for far too long here in this fine upstanding town of Dane Creek."

"Point taken, Marshal. I do hope you'll forgive my brash enthusiasm."

"You got it. Now, let's get this poor sap taken care of. Then what say I stand you a beer at Nell's? Then you can tell me all about these guns you hinted at earlier."

Within five minutes they were seated at a small, sticky-topped round table in a back corner of the quietest drinking house in Dane Creek. Nell herself, a busy and busty older woman, resembled a rain barrel more than she did a bar matron—save for the knot of high-piled hair, wisps straying from it in all directions like attendant birds, showing more silver than Nell's former chestnut tones. Somewhere just below her hair resided two rosy-apple cheeks and just below those a smile that never failed to show itself.

She and her husband, a miner of no great claim, large or small, which had never mattered to either of them, had all but settled the town nearly two decades before. Others had found the gold and silver that Nell's husband, Gareth, a Dane from the old country, and the man from whom the town drew its name, had known should be there, somewhere in or around the dried-up old creek beds veining the region.

He'd never had a knack for finding it, but Nell had found

a knack for distilling her own popskull and brewing her own beer, staples for any burgeoning mine camp. And so she stayed on, long after her beloved Gareth died on the trail but a few miles from town. His old donkey, also named Nell, was found staring down at his two-day-old corpse, braying in misery, and baring her teeth and kicking up a minor dust storm anytime a buzzard dared descend on the toothsome treat that had been Gareth.

"Gents, I can bring you beer or whiskey, or beer and whiskey. What'll it be?"

"Hmm," said Henry, rubbing a callused hand in great thoughtful gestures all over his thinly bearded face. "I'm feeling partial to a . . . glass of beer. Yes, that's what I'll have. And you, judge?" He nodded at Nell as he said the man's title. It had the effect he'd intended on Nell.

She leaned close to the newcomer and as the marshal knew she would, laid a pudgy, work-reddened hand on his sleeve. "Is that true, sir? You are a"—she leaned even closer and whispered the word—"judge?"

Mulholland smiled back, patted her hand, and said, "Not completely."

Henry's own smile slipped and Nell backed up a step.

Mulholland continued. "I am a judge"—he leaned toward her this time—"with a mighty thirst for a cool glass of beer!"

Nell's rippling laugh filled the nearly empty room, and she waddled back to the bar, waving a limp old tea towel at them and shaking her head as if she'd just been called the prettiest girl at the dance.

"You've made our Nell a happy little gossip, Judge," said Atwood.

"She's a peach. I'm glad to have been introduced. Now"— Mulholland steepled his fingers just below his serious gaze—"I have, as you say, brought guns. Or rather, they will be here soon. A contingent of men from Fort Nickersby, some two dozen in all, with more promised me should the need arise. They will arrive by no later than tomorrow at midday."

Nell brought the beers and set them down before each man, said nothing, but fluttered her lashes at Mulholland and backed away, barely stifling a schoolgirl giggle before she made it back to the bar.

"You've made a friend there, judge," said Atwood, quaffing the frothy top of his beer. "Now, I know I should be surprised by this news of men soon to arrive in my town. But I suspect it's not caused by the spate of killings we've undergone here in recent months, is it? On second thought, it wouldn't have anything to do with the recent discovery of a rich vein of copper, now would it?"

Judge Mulholland paused in sipping his beer, froth bubbling on the bristles of his mustache. He stared at the marshal over his glass. "You are an astute man, Marshal. And, yes, sadly it is not in direct response to your pleas for help in taming the criminal element. That will be handled as well, but in a rather, shall we say, roundabout fashion. In an effort to get to the meat of the matter, the powers that be in Washington have, shall we say, discovered a need for copper that far exceeds their current needs for gold. I am not privy to the finer points of that assessment, but have been instructed to see to it that anyone holding claim to a promising copper strike be offered more than fair value for their ore. In return, they will be given protection—protection, and please don't take this the wrong way—that you are at present unable to offer."

Marshal Atwood eyed the judge coolly a moment, then tipped his hat back and smiled. "That, mister, is the best news I've had all day."

"I'm so relieved to hear you say that. I didn't want to step on your toes."

"No, no worries there. My feet are tough. Besides, I'll be

moving on and you can have this town, lock, stock, and barrel."

"But, Marshal, I . . . I believe there's been some misunderstanding. We still need you here, I'm sure of it. I have so many questions."

"Nothing the rest of the townsfolk can't answer." He sipped his beer, still smiling. "I have a family, judge. A young wife and a little boy. I never thought I'd be that lucky, especially in my line of work. This town has dealt us all a hard set of circumstances and there's no way I'm going to keep pounding my head against the same old wall like I have done for far too many years now to count. I'd only get depressed if I did tally them up. Now drink up, we're late on that second round."

Henry Atwood let his almost cheerful tone unspool in conversation, but all the while he was thinking of the brute carnage Clewt Duggins had unleashed on his town, and of the fact that he'd been unable to do anything to stop it. Worse than that, he'd made the biggest mistake of his career, thinking that he could prevent yet another night of drunken violence in Dane Creek by trying to keep the peace. It had worked in the past, but he'd never come up against anyone like Clewt Duggins and his boys. Never.

And if Cuthbert Henry Atwood had any say in the matter, the final thing he would do in defense of keeping the peace would be to hunt down Duggins and put an end to it. Otherwise he would never be able to live with himself as an ex-lawman. Never.

Chapter 4

"Don't tell me those two idiots aren't back yet?" Clewt said, a tin cup of tepid coffee paused halfway to his mouth. It was nearing dinnertime, and he'd walked over to the bunkhouse from the main house at the Double Cross, musing on the name of the ranch that Winstead had chosen.

The unspoken but implied meaning of the name meant only one thing to him—it meant that Winstead was fully aware of what he'd done to Clewt Duggins and his boys. He was aware of it and had named the ranch after what he'd done to them, after the very way he'd managed to use them, promise them the moon and the stars, then leave them holding their hands up in the air at gunpoint of the law while Winstead rode off howling with laughter with that wagon full of priceless loot. At least that's what Clewt imagined Winstead had looked like when he'd left them to swing for his plan.

A plan, Clewt admitted, he and the boys had gone along with. But that was exactly why they deserved most of the treasure. Not ten years of hard labor. And that was exactly why they were here, at Winstead's ranch, after tracking that foul leech all this way, from Mexico all the way up here to the mountains of California.

And now here he was, this close to having it all, finally,

and his hired fools were, it seemed, about to blow it for them all. Perfect.

"They're doin' just what you said to, boss."

"Oh?" said Clewt. "And just what's that, Paddy?" Clewt leaned in the doorway, eyeing the men seated around the table. It was Paddy's turn to ladle up the god-awful-smelling concoction he'd been burning all afternoon in the big tin pot on the cookstove. His reply was almost a challenge to Clewt, not a surprising development since Paddy had been that way from the start, though even he was wearing thin on Clewt's nerves. He'd use him up, then slice him up. Just as planned. But just not yet. Didn't mean he couldn't have a little fun with him in the meantime.

Paddy dumped another ladleful of bean goop into a bowl, the recipient wrinkling his nose at it, and said, "Just that you told them to fog that rawhider's trail back to his place."

"Yep, as it happens, I recall telling them that. What's your point?"

Paddy sighed, as if he were exasperated with having to explain things to the boss.

Clearly, thought Clewt, the Irishman is testy, which means he hasn't had anything to drink in the last hour.

"No point, boss. Just that it might be a further piece than they expected."

"Good, Paddy. Good. I expect we can wait a while longer. But I wanna know when they get back. I wanna talk to them. You hear?"

All the men murmured in the affirmative, unsure which of them he had said that to.

All except Paddy, who continued around the gable, doling out beans to men who were hungry, but from the looks of their reactions, Clewt decided they were not that hungry. A couple of them skipped the food altogether and began rolling after-meal quirlies.

"Tell you what, boys. I sure am glad I have Winstead's woman in the house cooking me up a fine meal. I surely am glad."

"You trust her, boss? I mean, you did kill her husband and all."

It looked to Clewt that Paddy regretted saying that as soon as it fell out of his mouth. Clewt couldn't let this stand, not in front of the other men. He shucked his stag-handled Bowie and tossed it up in the air. It arced up, end over end, and the smooth gray-black handle landed thump in his palm, glistening blade out, slick as you please. All the men sat still, half-built smokes paused in their mitts, others protruding from pooched lips. They knew what the knife could do, and they knew that Clewt wasn't afraid to do it—to anyone or anything that got in his way. Even Paddy.

"You wanna keep flapping your gums about that, you go right ahead, Paddy. I'll show you just what that sort of palaver will earn you, you hear?"

For once, the bucket-mouthed man serving up his burnt beans just nodded, unsure if the boss was about to gut him right there and then. But Clewt did see the sneer on his *segundo's* face.

Clewt slipped the knife back in its sheath on his belt. "Fine, then." He sipped his coffee, letting a few seconds pass. Then to the room he said, "I will be sure to bring you all back something edible, maybe a fine pie."

With that parting shot, he turned and clomped down off the short porch of the cook shack. He heard Paddy say, none too carefully, "I've about had enough of him. I'll tell you that."

In the nearing dark, as he strolled back to Winstead's fancy ranch house, he sipped the last of his coffee, and smiled to himself. You and me both, Paddy. Not going to have to wait too much longer, though. And time enough tomorrow to

worry about those two idiots he sent to trail that nosy man,
Ty Farraday, back to his paltry spread.

Clewt even let out a low, dry chuckle as he mounted the
steps. Now, he thought, let's just see if this widow—who
doesn't know she's a widow—can cook. And maybe do a few
other things, while I'm at it.

Chapter 5

Sue Ellen Winstead watched as the tall, stiff-legged, scar-faced man strolled slowly around the long, cherrywood table, using the knurled tops of the high-back chairs to guide him as he stepped. In the low light of the room, he almost looked regal, his back as rigid and upright as the chairs that Alton had prized, along with everything else Winstead had filled the house with. All these . . . things it seemed that Winstead had felt he had to have.

Duggins smiled. It was a funny thing, wasn't it? Work so hard to acquire all these things and now Winstead was as dead as dead could be. Duggins snorted back a laugh.

And yet Clewt Duggins didn't know that for all Winstead's talk the house he had built had still been fairly modest, at least by the standards to which he constantly measured success and wealth. And the furnishings, while nice, were hardly museum pieces. They were far lovelier and often more impractical than their counterparts in most local ranch homes.

And that's what Sue Ellen found curious, especially early on in their marriage. But what had really puzzled her, about which her frequent questioning of Alton yielded no result, was that he had no intentions, it had become apparent, of buying cattle. Then why buy all the land? She'd asked him that a number of times, but gotten no useful answers.

"It's pretty," was all he would say. Pretty.

And so, after a few years, Sue Ellen grew to understand that her husband wanted only to be a man of leisure, to live a quiet life, though to be regarded locally as a wealthy man. But as time passed, it became increasingly apparent that he was not one. She'd never asked him where his money came from, only asked where it was going and why couldn't they run cattle on their perfectly useful land to make more money. Ranching, she had argued, was a perfectly respectable business, one that would ensure the money wouldn't just run out one day. But he remained unmoved.

And now here was this man and nowhere to be found was her Alton. All here and all gone within the same day. She was no fool. Alton and these men had known one another, but from how far back? And what did they want? "What did you do with my husband?"

"Do?" The tall man turned on her as if shocked by the question. "Do, Mrs. Winstead? We haven't done a thing with him. As to his whereabouts, I can't speak for the man. Except to say that anyone willing to leave a spouse so, if you will allow me, so very handsome as yourself, why he deserves to be . . . *shot.*" With that last word his mouth corners drooped into a frown, and firelight danced sharp flames in the centers of his dark eyes.

Clewt Duggins resumed his strolling about the table, stopped to sip from the aperitif glass, smacked his lips, and ran the tip of his tongue round them in appreciation. "You're sure you won't care for a sip of . . . your own liqueur, my dear?"

Sue Ellen stood and walked to the fireplace, put her hands out to warm them. "If all this is leading up to something, I wish you'd get to it."

"Mrs. Winstead," said Duggins, pooching out his lips in a mock frown. "You wound me. And please, sit back down in that chair. I do insist." His last words were hard and convincing.

Sue Ellen returned to the seat, feeling that coil of fear in her gut again. This man was all show but only an eggshell-thin crust. Inside he was as savage as a hydrophobic wolf.

As if to prove her right, Clewt Duggins, despite his stiff-legged amble, lunged to her side and snatched the woman by her shoulders. Sue Ellen struggled and bucked, feeling for certain this time that one of these coyotes would finally have their way with her. A cold clot of revulsion lurched in her belly and she thrashed against his tightening grip.

"No! I won't let you!"

"Won't let me?" Duggins hissed, his face so close that their nose-tips touched. His lips pulled across his tight-set teeth and she smelled his breath, a blend of musky tobacco odor tinged with a sweet edge of the cherry liqueur. She jerked her face to the side and he pushed his mouth to her ear. "I will do anything I please; do you hear, you foolish harlot? And the first thing I will do is make sure you don't interrupt me again."

What was behind his threat, Sue Ellen couldn't tell, but she didn't like the quaver in his voice. Up until then he had been cool as a full-bellied cat, seemingly unable, or at least unwilling, to lose his temper. But belief in that, she realized, had been mere folly on her part.

Leaning in even closer, he slid his hand down her left arm, and she felt something tightening around her wrist.

"What are you doing?" She hated the fear in her voice, but she couldn't help it.

"Relax, I am merely going to . . ." He spun the chair, its feet squawking on the polished wood floor. Before she knew what was happening, he had grabbed both her flailing hands again, clamped them tight in one of his, long enough to lash a rawhide thong about her wrists. ". . . tie you up, my dear. I cannot stress how important it is that you pay close attention to what I have to tell you. And I cannot"—he tugged the two ends and her wrists cinched tight together—"do that if you keep rising from your chair, interrupting me with your chatter and complaints." He stood and spun the chair back around, so that she once again faced the finely laid table, and the sumptuous feast she had prepared at his request.

"Now, I would like to believe you would accommodate me and share this fine meal, but I cannot trust you. So, I will forge on ahead without you."

With that, he smiled, offered her a slight nod, and returned to the table. He made quite a show out of dragging the chair back from the table, sitting down, shaking out the linen napkin, and finally, commencing to eat.

Despite her best efforts, Sue Ellen found herself running her tongue tip over her lips. It had been what . . . a day? Two days since she'd eaten? Even though she'd fed this jackal and his pack of men almost on a nonstop basis. She wanted more than anything to know what it was they wanted, the one question she had repeatedly asked since they'd arrived. Their appearance just so happened to coincide with Alton's disappearance.

She wanted to scream the question at him while he guzzled her husband's wine and gnashed his big teeth into their chicken, the chicken she had prepared. The squash, carrots, potatoes, all of it, he drizzled with fatty gravy. His demeanor had changed from a seeming gentleman, at least in speech, to that of a ravenous wolf. She wanted to tell him that with an appetite such as that, he would soon grow obese. And she would laugh at him the entire time she said it.

She wanted to scream and howl in his face, but his chilling voice cracked into her thoughts like a pry bar. She had no doubt that he could—and would, eventually—keep his promise to somehow abuse her, and that was something she didn't dare risk. But she stared at him, glared, hoping she would somehow convey her anger. It was all she could do.

Finally, after so much sucking and biting, chewing and snorting, probing his own mouth with a grimy fingertip, he drew the cloth napkin from his lap, thoroughly wiped his mouth, and sighed. Then he balled the soiled cloth and tossed it on his plate. During the meal he did not look at, nor once address her. Finally, he said, "That was a superb meal, my dear. You'll make someone a fine wife one day." Duggins threw back his head and laughed loudly.

Sue Ellen gritted her teeth and cut her eyes to the fireplace, tried to concentrate on the dancing flames, on the coals glowing beneath in the brazier, on anything but the million things she couldn't help feeling: her emotions about her missing husband, seeing Ty today, then being abandoned by him. Why hadn't she tried harder to tip him off? Why hadn't he made some indication that he knew her, that he was going to save her from what obviously was a pack of ravenous, bloodthirsty killers?

The scent of chicken, the sound of Clewt Duggins sucking food bits from his teeth repulsed her, and yet her own stomach betrayed her with a long, low growl.

Duggins paused, but still did not look at her. Then he reached for his wineglass, which he had filled at the start of the meal, and sipped loudly. He smacked his lips, smiled, and still not looking at her, said, "You must forgive me for pointing out the obvious, my dear, but you really are rude."

It was the last thing she had expected to hear.

Now he looked at her. "Oh, yes, you see, staring at a person is considered bad form."

"What would you have me do?" she said, speaking before she remembered his threats should she speak.

But he merely smiled. "Why, my dear, if you were more civil, I would have you join me."

"I would not join you in anything if you were the last man on earth, you . . ." Her face bunched in anger.

"Yes? Do go on, my dear. You are so pretty when your blood is up. No? Well, I can tell you that the pretty scenario you paint is not likely to happen. The world is filled with people, many of them men. The others . . . women. But I am only concerned with a handful of them right now." He turned his chair, with some little effort, the fullness of his belly having slowed him down. He belched and looked at her. "Oh, my dear, what you must think of me."

She snorted, looked away. "I don't think of you."

"Ah," he said, scratching a match alight on his pants' leg and touching flame to one of Alton's cigars. "But you will. You will when you listen to the story I am about to tell you."

"Does it always take you this long to come to a point?"

He puffed thoughtfully, looked at the cigar, then said, "Only when it's a matter of life, death, revenge . . . and much, much money."

Despite herself, Sue Ellen looked Clewt Duggins in the eyes.

"Ah-ha," he said in a low, stone-on-steel voice.

Through a veil of smoke Sue Ellen saw that his smile had vanished, and his eyes had settled back into their deadly dark stare, one brow arched.

Chapter 6

"Last time I was in Chihuahua was nearly eleven years ago. More precisely me and the boys—oh, you've met the boys, my dear, so you know who I mean. Well, most of them aren't the boys from back then, but close enough.

"Anyway, we were down there, me and the boys, cooling our heels south of the border, doing as little as possible, save for drinking mescal and dallying with the little *putas* down there. The entire place is brimming with them, filthy with them, and who are we to deny such lovely creatures our company? Of course, the only reason they showed interest in any of us was because we had money. Oh, yes, my dear, we had, as an Englishman I once met said, gobs of it.

"The worst part of being in Mexico to me is the heat. Oh, but I was made for fairer climes, I will admit. So I did the only thing I could do in such circumstances, I drank. I frequented one cantina in particular; the name was some Mexican phrase I have forgotten. I went mostly because there was a certain barmaid who worked there. She was a curious creature, not at all like other Mexican girls. This one was taller, more slender than the rest. She was also half-German, or some such thing. But that lent her an exotic edge that she played to great effect to charm men from all over who came through town. But she rarely indulged in . . . sport with these men. That is, until I came along."

"What makes you think I want to hear about this?"

"Oh, but you will, my dear. You will. Besides, it's not like you have anywhere better to go." Duggins's coarse laughter hacked out of him, chilling Sue Ellen to the bone.

"Now, where was I? Oh, yes, the cantina. So you see, I cannot say that the girl, with her long chestnut hair, her high cheekbones and wide, angular face, with those luscious full lips, with legs that went all the way to the ground, and those eyes, oh, let me tell you . . ."

"Please don't," said Sue Ellen.

"But I insist," said Duggins, that smile still twitching his mouth. "They were the color of blue ice with light shining through."

"How poetic."

He ignored her and continued with his story. "One day I happened to become bored with the usual round of games with the boys at their favorite bar, so I wandered to my place, where I knew Inga worked in the afternoons. And as I pushed in through the swinging doors, I stood there waiting for my eyes to adjust to the dimmer interior. And when they did, do you know what I saw? No? My dear, I saw a gringo you might well recognize.

"Yes, yes." He nodded. "It was the very same man you married. In truth, though he was much thinner, a harder man in all ways, rougher around the edges, more hair on his head, certainly young—"

"How do you know how much hair Alton has now? How do you know what he looks like now? What have you done with my husband?" Sue Ellen began kicking, lashing out, the chair lurching and scraping the floor.

She struggled against the rawhide, but Clewt had already made it to her side. He snatched up two napkins from a stack on the sideboard and, braving an assault by her flailing leather shoes, he managed to lash her ankles to the chair legs.

Sue Ellen's shouts grew louder, but gained her nothing but sore wrists and ankles and rough treatment by Duggins. She knew no one was around who could or would help her. Certainly not that weak-spined Ty Farraday.

Yet even as she thought this, in her frenzy of anger, she knew she was wrong. She knew Ty pined for her as he had since the day she broke his heart at the tumbledown of boulders beside which flowed the Olefine River, which pooled there at the bottom of the falls. They had called them Lucky Falls in honor of the ranch they were going to build up together—they were going to call it the Lucky Cross, because they agreed they were lucky to have found each other. And they had vowed in those sillier, youthful, quiet moments that they would always celebrate special times there at the falls.

Those days seemed a million years in the past. And yet she knew, just by being near Ty the few times they had been forced together, found themselves in each other's presence through sheer happenstance over the years, that he still burned for her, still longed for her. It was a flattering feeling, but painful, too, for she was a married woman. Married to a kind man, though a slightly older and much more formal man. One who had built a way of life on pretense, of maintaining a facade of importance of wealth and worldliness and intelligence. And though he had some of each of those attributes, to be sure, they were in far lower measures than he wished others to believe.

Alton was also a nervous man with a bitter edge that rose to the top when discussing the shortcomings of others. Sue Ellen avoided the topic of her old love, Ty Farraday, like the plague. But somehow when Alton was in the mood, often after he'd had a few drinks, she found herself defending Ty's reputation and honor to Alton. She hated that he put her in that position, but over the years it became obvious to her, ironically because of Alton's wheedling, and his probing of the topic, that he was jealous of Ty because although Ty had far less material wealth than Alton, Ty really was a better man. It had hurt Sue Ellen to finally admit it, but it was the truth. And as some wise person once said, the truth stings.

Ty had his faults, to be sure. He could be a pensive, moody man, sullen at times and prone to not sharing what was troubling him. He was overly protective of those he loved and of his privacy. He also worked too hard, driving himself beyond the bounds of reasonable limits. But he was also one of the most generous people she'd ever known. Giving of his time to others, as well as his expertise, which was considerable, about horses and cattle. He was good with his hands, able to fix most anything with few supplies and a considerable amount of gumption and self-confidence.

And he had Uncle Hob, a cantankerous old rooster, but one who Sue Ellen liked very much. And she believed that he had felt the same way. When Sue Ellen had broken off her engagement with Ty, she felt as though she had lost not one but two family members that day.

All these thoughts and more flooded back to Sue Ellen when Duggins lashed her legs to the chair and bound her shouting mouth with another napkin. She seethed then, eyes red and crying and not caring that the foul man saw her tears. She had not cried outwardly since Duggins and his filthy gang had descended on the ranch not long after Alton had left on a quick trip to town.

She had heard the pounding of many hooves, a few yips and crude laughs: then before she could draw back the curtains, these unwashed, hard-faced men had swarmed up onto the sitting porch, and pushed their way into her kitchen. They surrounded her, made themselves at home, all the while eyeing her, making lewd comments. Duggins had assured her that should she do anything that might tip off others who might visit the ranch, the life of someone she loved dearly might well be forfeit.

"What have you done to Alton?" she'd demanded, but he just laughed, and never outright admitted he'd seen Alton, but if she deviated from his directions, she knew what he meant by his threat. It was Alton's life that would be forfeit. She had asked scores of questions but received no answers, no replies but threats and lascivious winks.

In the end, she did what Duggins said, wary the entire time, sleeping little, tending to their every whim, fending off a nearly constant onslaught of unwanted advances from Duggins's men. Only when he'd caught two of them, having cornered her in the kitchen, ripping at her clothes as though they were long-penned wild animals—which she supposed they were—did Duggins take action and forbid them from associating with her.

She knew this probably only meant that he was saving her for himself. That had been her life for two days, and then Ty had shown up earlier today and his unexpected presence had given her hope. It was the first glimmer of it she'd felt in days. She hadn't seen him in nearly eight months, since they'd passed each other in the tightly packed aisles of Hathaway's Mercantile in Ripley Flats. He looked gaunt but as solid as ever then, perhaps a little grayer, a few more lines around the eyes and mouth, those of a man unused to smiling frequently. He'd looked much the same today.

"Are you listening, my dear Mrs. Winstead?" Clewt Duggins leaned close to her face, spoke in his low, husky growl, his voice made that way, she'd come to know, through his constant smoking of foul-smelling little black cigars.

"You'd better pay attention, because it concerns you. Oh, yes, it concerns you mightily. Now, where was I? Yes, yes, the cantina. By the time my eyes adjusted to the dim interior of the cantina, I saw a lanky, though not overly tall fellow with sandy hair leaning against the bar. He didn't wear the usual dusty trail clothes, worn boots, grimy spurs, and sweat-stained hat of most folks from north of the border who found themselves down Chihuahua way. Instead this man sported low-heeled black dandy boots, narrow black-striped trousers, and I'll be darned if he wasn't wearing what looked to be one of those smoking jackets, wine red in color, and a black felt derby topping it all off. But all of it was a mite dusty, as if he'd ridden on a long, hard trail and someone had fogged it the entire time.

"Now, I hadn't noticed any tired-looking mounts out front. Come to think on it, I hadn't noticed any mounts out there at all. Nor any local nags. It was, after all, a hot day. I figured he probably had the sense to lead the beast to the stable.

"Inga flashed a pretty eye at me and I strode forward, eager to meet this new man who appeared to be making a play on her. Though we had no formal arrangement, I considered this dusky, half-Mex maiden my own. And I didn't appreciate this smile-flashing interloper scooping on in and sweeping her from me. Not just yet, anyway. Me and the boys had plans to stay in town a few more weeks as yet. We figured that was enough time to cool our heels; then we'd be moving on.

"The son-of-a-gun must have read my thoughts, for he spun and in his hand appeared a firearm so small I had to look twice. But the bore wasn't tiny-looking—it was a pepperbox, .22 caliber, and it could deliver enough pain to my innards in such close quarters that I determined to get out of its range, and quick. I dropped to my right knee and rolled down onto my right shoulder. At the same time, with my left hand I shucked my Colt, thumbing back the hammer. We held like that, me having come up some feet away to one side, back by a table. I had half a mind to knock down that table in front of me as a shield from flying lead pills from that homely little pepperbox. That stranger crouched there, holding that little spitter outstretched as if he were going to lob it underhanded to me. I am sure neither of us knew what to make of the other.

"For my part I am confident that I didn't have a hand in any provocation of the man's sudden and unfriendly actions. However, there was a part of me that would have gladly put one or two to the man's forehead just to be rid of him, such was my fast-burning wick of hatred at seeing him talking with my lovely girl at the bar." Duggins thumbnailed another match alight and puffed a fresh cigarillo to life. He replenished the wine in his glass and looked at Sue Ellen.

Despite her discomfort, and the foul situation in general, she found herself silent, actually listening, wanting to hear what happened next between the two men. He had to be talking of her Alton. Who else could he be talking of? Obviously they both lived through it, for here was one man now and she was married to the other, unbelievable as Alton's actions sounded to her. Then again, these events, if they happened, had taken place eleven years before now. He may well have been a different, more daring man back then. What had changed him?

Duggins drew on his cigar, plumed a channel of thick smoke at the fireplace, and continued his story. "I see by the light in your pretty eyes that you are wondering just what happened next in that dusty little cantina south of the border so long ago." He smiled. "So I will tell you. I got him."

Sue Ellen's eyes widened for a moment. What? How could this be?

Duggins laughed, head thrown back as if he'd heard the mother of all windies. "No, no, I mean that I saw in his eyes that he was a blowhard. So I got up off my knee, walked right up to him, pulled my gun-hand backward over my right shoulder, and slammed him upside the temple. Gave him a scar above his left eye, on the high side of his cheek. You know the spot, I know you do."

Sue Ellen knew the scar well. Alton had told her he received it in childhood, something about playing rough with other boys, swinging sticks like swords at each other.

"That was my contribution to his pretty-boy looks. Well, sir, when ol' Delbert Hawkins came around to consciousness again—what? Wait. You mean you didn't know that Alton Winstead's real name was—is—Delbert Hawkins? Well, sakes alive, yes, indeed, my dear. At least, now that I come to think on it, that was the name he went by back then." Duggins fixed her with a steady gaze, looking as if he were mustering an attempt to look serious. "Perhaps no one but Delbert, also known as Alton, knows how many names he's had and just which is his true and given name. Heck, maybe he doesn't even know anymore." Again Duggins laughed.

Sue Ellen tried to swallow, sniff back the fresh wave of hot tears that ran down her face, annoying her. Delbert Hawkins? She'd never heard that name before. He'd shown her his Union Army discharge papers with the name Alton Winstead on them, for all to read.

"When he came to, I asked him just what it was he thought he was doing drawing down on me when I was a stranger. 'You were coming up behind me' was his answer. Well, you can imagine my surprise. 'Coming up behind you? Why, I wasn't aware of any other way to get into the cantina to purchase a beer to soothe my parched throat, you itinerant dandy,' says I. Well, once again we stared hard at each other, trying to figure out the other man. For my part, I still wanted to hit him, now for a number of reasons and not just for nibbling on my girl. But I tell you what . . ." Duggins shook his head and sucked deep on his cigar.

When he resumed speaking, the blue-gray smoke chased the words from his mouth. "There was something about him, something that made you want to help him. He looked both bold and hollow, brash and weak, all at once. But he had some sort of sand, I will give him that much. He told me I was a worthless cur and that he would fight me in a duel, since I had bested him and besmirched his honor in front of a lady. Can you imagine? Those were his words; I've never forgotten them, I swear. I suspect Delbert was feeling emboldened by his foofaraw chatter, but I was ready to let him have another clout, just for insolence. And then he smiled and broke down in a full-body laugh. I swear I have only seen a few people laugh like that in my entire life. And never in the face of such potential danger. I reckoned he was either crazy or fearless. And I didn't think he was fearless. So he had to be the other one.

"At first I was offended, as he'd been looking at me when he set off to laughing in such a manner. But then I realized it was genuine. That got me mad all over again. So I clouted him again and it made me feel good to see him crumple at my feet in his soiled finery. My happiness was short-lived, though, as I looked up at Inga. She was hurrying around the end of the bar, if you can believe it, fluttering to help her fallen little gambler. Curse his gentrified hide! So I snatched up his pepperbox, searched him for any other weapons, and came up with a long wallet filled with nothing, a watch fob with a handless watch attached, and a pocketknife with half a blade. And that half was dull. The man was next to useless. But this woman still wanted him. I ask you, as a woman yourself, does that make any sort of sense at all?"

He looked at Sue Ellen and it seemed to her that he was

genuinely still miffed and puzzled by the barmaid's swooning reaction. But Sue Ellen could understand. After all, she had fallen for him in much the same way. Duggins was right—there was something about Alton that made people want to help him.

"A long story short, that's how I came to meet Delbert Hawkins. Or Alton Winstead. Whatever name you care to call him by, why that's it." He smiled and shook his head. "Those were good times. Me and the boys and a town full of women and liquor. And"—Duggins turned from the fire and stared right at Sue Ellen—"a new compadre with a plan to make us all very, very rich."

She swore his eyes were afire. That it wasn't just the reflected flames from the fireplace. Once again all pretense of a smile had disappeared and he said, "I wish with all my heart that I had shot him dead that day instead of befriending him."

Chapter 7

"Oh, you probably want to know why I said I wished I had killed old Alton back then when I first met him—I'll call him Alton so you don't get all confused, my dear. Well, I will tell you, but as with all good things in life, it comes with a price. And that price is waiting to hear the rest of the story. And it's a doozy, I can assure you, Miss Sue Ellen. But first, I suspect you are getting dry in the throat, so I will indulge that and offer you a sip or three of wine, okay?"

Sue Ellen dearly wanted to tell him to keep his wine, difficult since her mouth was gagged. But she was dry, and the gag hurt her mouth terribly. Maybe he'd leave it off after she drank. And he did—though not without pretending in feint a couple of times to cover her mouth again. She'd jerked her head to the side each time, and he finally nodded as if relenting to her superior power. "Okay, okay, you win. Now, back to my story. Your interruptions are slowing my momentum."

"The very next day, a contingent of *federales* was spied heading to town—returning to town, I should say, for that is where they were based. Did I mention that when we got to town the week before, we had— How do you say politely, dispatched? Yes, that's the word Delbert—excuse me, Alton— would have used. We dispatched the men left behind to guard the town and their barracks. This was no easy job, as they had superior weapons and a whole lot of walls to hide behind. But me and my boys, back then it was easier for us to sneak in and out of places. We were leaner then." He smacked a hand against his solid, though not paunchy, belly, and smiled. "But we are no less hungry now than we were then.

"Eventually we wore them down and the townspeople were mostly happy about this because they were no longer under the thumb of the corrupt *jefe*. Little did they know that they were now under the thumb of me! When word came to us that we were about to be greeted by a whole lot of returning soldiers, soldiers who would not be pleased to know that their fellows they had left behind to guard the barracks outside of town had been . . . dispatched, well, you can imagine how that put the wheels in motion." Duggins made a twirling motion beside his head, with a finger.

"And the most curious part of it all? It was your Alton who tipped us off. After that strange meeting with him in the cantina, you can be sure I was not willing to listen to much the man had to say, much less look at him. But he had been ranging in the hills near the town, doing who knows what, when he spied them. I thanked him for the information and since it looked as though we were going to need every hand on deck, as the sailors say, I gave him back his silly little pepperbox. I told him that if he tried to pull it on me again, he had better use it or be prepared to bleed to death, because my gun was bigger than his. I made sure to say this in front of the pretty barmaid, Inga.

"We positioned ourselves around the town, not having the ability or the time or the inclination to flee, intent on picking them off one at a time. They rode in grouped and gabbling together like stupid chickens in a penned yard. We wanted to at least even the odds, you see, so that we might reduce the number of people chasing us when we left."

Sue Ellen could restrain herself no longer. "Alton would never be part of anything like that. Never!"

"Oh, you mean the man who lied to you, his own wife, about his very name? You mean the man who wanted to shoot me, a stranger, on our very first meeting? You are correct, of course, he didn't do much shooting that bloody day. No, no, dear Alton was much better with the up-close work. He borrowed a Bowie knife off one of my men and . . . well, let us just say that never since then have I seen a man behave in so savage a fashion."

Sue Ellen gasped, sputtered for breath.

Duggins spun from the fire. "Yes, you might well be surprised. I know I was. But as hardened as we were, he was a brute. We only found out later, of course, just what his motives really were." Duggins turned back to the fireplace, prodded it with the iron poker, then laid two more lengths of wood atop the coals. In moments, their smoky fragrance and the sounds of crackling dry bark filled the room. He strode, stiff-legged, to the sideboard and rattled the cut crystal top off the decanter.

He splashed a liberal amount of Alton's expensive bourbon into a glass and looked over to Sue Ellen with raised eyebrows.

"No, thank you."

"I get a thank-you, at least. That's nice. But come now, I have so much to tell you, and believe me, you'll want a drink to take the burred edges off some of it. Trust me, dearie."

She shook her head no, so he topped the decanter and returned to his place by the fire, sipped. "Ahh, nice. So, where was I?"

"Lying to me about my husband."

"*Telling* you all about your vicious husband, that's right."

Sue Ellen snorted and looked away, but she couldn't prevent herself from hearing him. And he kept right on talking, curse him. And curse her, she thought, for listening. For wanting to listen to every word. Somehow she believed what he was telling her. At some level, in some deep place, she knew her husband had been something . . . different in a former life, in those times before they were married that he'd not wanted to talk about.

And when he did speak of it, he'd only begrudgingly offered weak, vague information to her. Nothing satisfying. Very little about family. Just that he'd been orphaned by a random act of violence and set adrift, his words, at a young age, left to fend for himself in the world. That alone had endeared him to her. And he'd built their courtship and subsequent marriage on such sad truths. She saw that now.

"We watched him as he advanced on the line of unsuspecting soldiers, creeping out of the shadows, looking for all the world as if he'd done this sort of thing for years—maybe he had, at that—and I determined that Alton must have an ulterior motive, as the smart people call it. And by golly, he did. And a doozy it was. I'd noticed that the soldiers had taken a long time to get to town from the time they were first seen, and determined that they were not the regulars. In fact, the men we'd . . . dealt with earlier . . . had been the only regulars. These men were a special transport troop escorting . . ." He turned to Sue Ellen and smiled, waggled his eyebrows. "Can you guess? No? Okay, I'll tell you, but only because you are one pretty lady."

Sue Ellen's fears increased. As Duggins drank, he became more open with his rank remarks to the point where she was quite uncomfortable, but there wasn't a thing she could do about it—she was completely in his control.

"Turns out they were transporting looted religious artifacts, worth, and I kid you not, millions of dollars. The gold alone would be enough to cripple ten donkeys. That's why they had a massive ore wagon loaded and covered with canvas tarpaulins. And the jewels? Oh, I could choke on them for a month of Sundays and still not meet my end!" He turned, smiling, his eyes shining at the notion. "They were . . . stunning, delicious. A sight to behold, so . . . so much! Don't you see!" He waved his arms, sloshing the whiskey. For a moment, Sue Ellen thought he might actually break into tears, so excited had he become. Then his sly reptilian smile crept back onto his leering scarred face.

"So what did you do about it?"

"What did we do about it, the lady wants to know."

Faster than she thought possible, given his state of increasing inebriation and his leg's obvious affliction, he lurched to her side and once again pressed his face close to her ear.

In a deep, husky voice that purred like silk sliding over rusted steel, and with breath that stank of food and whiskey, he said, "What do you think we did? How else would I know what it is they were carrying?" He stood and brayed a drunken laugh, obviously reliving his past glories. "We relieved them of their burden, of course. But it was not so easy. No, no, no. It took many days and many hours of planning and much help, I will say, from the man who knew this load of happy goods was coming our way. You see, he had no choice but to cut us in on the action. I speak of course of your fine, upstanding husband, Alton Winstead or whatever he called himself lately." He waved his arms and the bourbon splashed, but he didn't seem to notice or care.

"It seems that he came to Chihuahua knowing they would be there. And he had convinced himself that he would be alone and would do what he had to to liberate—that was a word he used—as much of this bountiful treasure as he was able to, as a lone operative, and make his getaway. Imagine the confidence on this man? Here he was, alone, poorly dressed, armed with a broken pocketknife and a paltry little pepperbox pistol that I'm not sure ever fired properly. Truth be told, I don't even know if it was fully loaded, and no money, and yet there he was, an American in Mexico, dead set on liberating much of, if not all of, a vast treasure of looted holy gold relics from an entire Mexican army regiment. Now that takes guts. Me and my men? We just lucked into the right place at the right time."

He paused, slung his head back, and took a long drink, realized his glass was empty, and wobbled over to the sideboard. "Sure I can't offer you a tipple, m'lady?"

"I don't believe a word you're telling me."

"Oh, it's all true, I swear it."

"I don't doubt that it happened, but my Alton was never involved. If you knew him as you say you do, you'd know there's no way he could ever have been involved in something so awful as that."

Duggins closed his eyes, leaned his head back. Sue Ellen saw that the wine, heavy meal, and whiskey were finally having an effect on the man. He weaved slightly in place, his stiff leg held to one side, as a leaning post of sorts. He sniffed. "Perhaps you are correct, Mrs. Winstead." He opened his eyes and looked at her. "Perhaps I am a fool. Perhaps I imagined that story I just told you. It is, after all, rather a fanciful tale, don't you think?" His canted head told her he was once again toying with her.

"But then again, something tells me"—Duggins once again bent low over her, his whiskey-tinged, tobacco breath clouding her face—"that you know I am telling the truth." He smiled a wide, long smile, then stood. "Otherwise, how would I account for this?" With that he rapped his knuckle hard against his leg.

The sound was the same Sue Ellen heard every time someone knocked on a table for luck, or a door, begging entry. "Yes, my dear. It's a wooden thing. All the way up to here." He rapped the dead-sounding thing higher, halfway up his thigh, to within a hand-length of his waist.

"Perhaps later I will invite you to see just how much of this limb I have lost, eh?"

Sue Ellen felt ill. None of this made any sense. Where was Alton? Why wasn't he here? What had they done to him? She'd asked them so many times, receiving nothing but leers and laughs and confusing stories. And as much as it pained her to admit it, she had almost lost her curiosity. Almost.

Chapter 8

Ty thumbed the cabin's front door latch and hustled in low, then shut it swiftly behind him. Uncle Hob, his head down, growled from the far side of the bulky, work-scarred kitchen table. "You mind telling me just why we're being shot at, and who in the world is doing the shooting?"

But Ty was too busy low-walking over to the pair of waist-high single windows—a rare extravagance for which he'd ordered the glass at no small expense back in the days when he'd thought Sue Ellen would be coming to the ranch as his wife. Now they were a spot by which he and Hob could sit on a snowy evening and watch the sun set.

Though in truth, Ty would prefer to keep them shuttered in the cold weather. But he knew the old man liked to sit there in his ramshackle rocker, clucking at the empty house, stroking his flea-bitten rangy tomcat, No Ears, so named because, like most toms, he couldn't keep from getting into scrapes with anything that looked as if it might need a limbing. As a result, the cat sported ragged nubs for ears.

Through the windows, from his low vantage point in one corner, Ty scanned the yard through squinted eyes. He had no intention of answering the whispered sputters of Uncle Hob just yet. Someone, perhaps a couple of someones, had shot at them and though Ty suspected he knew who'd done so, he wanted to know for sure the who, the why, and from where. If he couldn't catch them alive, he'd gladly drill them where the cowardly bums hid.

"Boy, you'd best come clean with me." Uncle Hob had somehow crawled over behind Ty. That unnerved the big rancher. He didn't like the idea of drifting so far into his own thoughts that he wasn't aware of what was going on around him. Seeing Sue Ellen again, and in such dire straits, had affected him mightily, and in ways he didn't much like, and which weren't proving especially useful.

"Uncle Hob," whispered Ty. "You want to make yourself useful, I'd appreciate a hand—or rather a couple more eyeballs—scouting from the far end of the house toward the north. I have a feeling we have two visitors, one closer up, one hanging back up there. Maybe we can catch him skylined up there before the light leaves us wanting."

The old man grunted and presently Ty heard him low-crawl back to the bedroom at the far end of the small house. The bedroom would be the safest place for him. Hob could play heck with a man on a daily basis, wearing his nerves down like rain on a rock, but he was the best man Ty could ask for in a pinch. Unquestioning, decisive, and with a long history as a lawdog, Uncle Hob was one of the best, especially in a situation where they were pretty much cornered in their own shack.

"Was me," came Hob's raspy whisper from the back room, "I'd chuck a torch in this direction. I only hope whoever it is out there ain't half as smart as me." His soft cackle brought a momentary smile to Ty's face. This was a long, strange day, and he had a feeling they were in for a long, stranger night to come.

As if on cue, Ty heard the rush of running boots grinding on gravel out front. From the sound, someone was running out of sight, between the south end of the horse barn and the loafing shed, pretty much the path Ty had taken a few minutes before. He cursed himself for building them as he had done, with a blind spot big enough to block out a freighter wagon towed by oxen and piled high with goods, kids, and barking dogs.

The running sound resumed; then whoever it was slammed into boards, as if reaching their cover and not caring who or what heard them, confident that they were not able to be seen easily, given the waning daylight and the hiding place they'd found.

Good one, too, mused Ty. The bum could draw a sight on the house without much being seen.

"Hey . . . gringo!"

Ty's eyes sharpened, strained toward the dark mass of the loafing shed. He wasn't about to answer, and he knew Hob had no intention of doing so. Tipping off a viper to your whereabouts was no way to get the drop on him. He looked toward Hob at the far end of the house, saw the old man's outline, facing him, crouched low on his knees with a long gun held crosswise, cocked and ready to deliver its goods.

Ty nodded, set his own weapon down, and quickly tugged off his boots. Then he gestured toward Hob, then to the floor—*stay put*—and he jerked his thumb at his own chest, then pointed across from himself, toward the back door off the kitchen. He arced the finger around in a semicircle, indicating his intentions. Hob nodded and readjusted his grip on his weapon.

With sagged, well-worn stovepipe boot tops gripped in one hand and a Colt Navy in the other, ready to thumb it back at a moment's notice, Ty got down on his hands and knees. He wasn't about to crabwalk across this room, risking potential exposure through the window, with a weapon on full cock. Not yet anyway. First thing he had to do was get to that back door. The worn floorboards, full of poking knots and protruding nail heads, poked unmercifully into his kneecaps, but Ty made it to the door without drawing fire.

Moment of truth, he had to hurry, not sure if the man in the shadows who'd shouted, would oblige Ty by waiting much longer where he was—the ideal spot for Farraday to catwalk around the end of the house and get the drop on him.

Ty was sure it was one of, and likely both of, the two stumblebums who had escorted him down out of the hills to the Double Cross today. Had to be—who else? But the question was, why did they want to ambush him? Not much of a head-scratcher, Ty, he told himself. They had to know that he'd found Winstead's body. And anybody who didn't suspect those packrats of the deed was not the thinking sort.

He didn't bother looking back toward Hob before cracking the door. He knew the old man would eagle-eye both directions as much as humanly possible. Ty poked his boots out the door, waited. Nothing. He glanced out the crack, nothing. He'd not heard a sound from behind the house, and the gate back there around Hob's little garden was a squawker, and it was the only way back in behind the house. Unless somebody was hiding out in the entry to the root cellar, gouged into the slope behind the house, there was little chance he'd be seen snaking out the door. In for a penny, he told himself, and slipped out the door.

The bottom step of the three-step rise let out its squeak when he put his weight on it. Curse that thing! He ground his teeth, but took his weight off it slow enough that it barely made the sound again. Knowing the walkway was stone-cobbled around the house toward the loafing shed where the raider was waiting, and thus prone to giving him away were he wearing his boots, Ty stuck to his stocking feet. Still crouching, he made his way quick and low to the end of the house. As he scooted, he cautiously thumbed back the hammer all the way on the Colt.

He peered around the corner and saw the small, low roof-line of the shed beyond. Nothing moved. The man would no doubt be eyeing the front of the house and hopefully not ex-pecting a backdoor attack. Ty pulled in a quick, deep breath, let it out slowly, and bolted as fast as his socked feet would carry him along the rocky path.

His feet barely made a swish of a sound as he scooted low to the shed. He waited there at the far corner. The night was far too quiet—always the way when it would have been use-ful for the calves to bawl or some critter to kick up a fuss. What to do? He'd never make it the last ten feet to get the drop on the man without a distraction. The night air smelled of dust and leather.

He caught a whiff of his own smells—the strong tang of horse, and his own sweat, rank and sour from a day's hard labor in and out of the saddle. Only thing he really wanted to smell was a big bowl of Hob's divine beef stew, bubbling so dark it looked black in the pot, aswim with carrots, potatoes, and onions, and topped with dumplings, piping hot and gummy to the bite. Time enough, Ty, he told himself. Or else it means you've judged this little situation all wrong and then you'll be in such a spot you'll be beyond caring about food and peace and quiet, and women, and cattle, and crabby old uncles.

He wished Hob could read his mind, set up some sort of commotion. That's it—Ty almost smiled as he reached in the dark by his feet, his long, work-hardened fingers scrabbling in the dirt for a rock. They closed around one, egg-sized. It would have to do. He lobbed it underhand out toward the middle of the yard, where it thunked, rolled. And didn't, to Ty's ears, sound much like a noise a man might make. As he'd just told himself, it would have to do.

It was dark enough that the ambusher wouldn't be able to see it was nothing more than a tossed object. Ahead, beyond the corner of the shed, Ty heard the man shift position, heard a boot, maybe, lift, then plant again. Good, might mean the man was looking toward the yard. Now or never, Ty Farraday.

Cat-footing once more, he made the corner, aware of the touchy hammer peeled back on the Colt, lined it up with the intruder's body, a dark, irregular shape at the other corner of the shed, not but ten feet from him.

Ty kept his crouch, and in a low, even voice said, "Do not turn around, mister."

The man tensed but held the pose, faced away from Ty.

"Raise those arms, drop that rifle. Now!" Careful to keep his voice low, lest the man's companion lurked nearby, Ty kept the Colt's dealing end poised squarely on the man's bulk.

The intruder sighed and slowly raised his arms.

Going to happen now if it happens at all. . . . And Ty wasn't disappointed. The rascal dove to one side, while at the same time pulling the rifle back in tight to his body, and working the trigger. Ty squeezed the Colt's trigger, saw the gout of bursting light match that of the culprit's rifle, and was already on the move, tucking and rolling down onto his left shoulder. He felt something pop deep in his shoulder, bone, muscle—he didn't know and didn't care. Ty was acting on pure animal instinct now, a defensive, protective feral beast with a raw urge to kill or be killed. He'd been hunted before, he'd been the hunter, and he'd been successful every time. But that knowledge gave him no satisfaction now, merely an edge of cautious confidence.

He knew that back in the house Hob would be working himself into a lather, probably crossing the kitchen floor himself and following Ty's path. He had to wrap this up before the old man got in the midst of things.

From his temporary cover on the opposite side of the open

shed doorway, Ty peeked between the vertical boards and saw a shadow that didn't seem familiar. He knew to trust his gut at such times. He also knew the man was quick, nimble, and ready to kill. So am I, thought Ty. "I'll give you one more chance, mister."

The shadow shifted as the man spun silently in the dark to level on Ty's rough position.

"Oh, gringo, now you die." The man's voice was low, a raspy purr, and Ty knew for certain it was the shorter of the two men from earlier. The swarthy, stocky Mexican-looking rider.

That moving shadow, the position of the man's voice, was all Ty needed, all he'd hoped to draw out. He sent a shot a flash of a second before the stranger fired, and was grimly rewarded with a clipped shriek, following by a sound like a sack of meal hitting a stockroom floor. As he waited out the next few seconds, he heard a wet, gagging sound.

Good, thought Ty. Good that I struck bloody gold, but bad for that fool. He waited a few moments more as the man's labored breathing became even more of a struggled, wet noise. It sounded as if the man were drowning from the inside out.

"Boy?"

It was Hob's voice, a higher-pitched whisper than he was used to hearing from the man. Ty wanted to wait out the man. One guessed shot was rarely enough to kill a man. And a wounded man, especially one who knows he's dying, may have no trouble in delivering a wild shot or two. Ty had no idea if this man had a pistol or two or ten, in addition to his rifle.

He'd have to risk a quick shout or the old man would keep on coming, sick with worry. "Hob—stay back!"

"You okay?"

Less worry, good. "Yep. Stay back."

To the wounded man in the shed, Ty said, "Mister, you are in a bad way. Give it up and we'll do our level best for you."

Two, three heartbeats passed; then Ty heard a wet cough. So the man was still alive, though Ty could no longer hear his breathing. And if that was a laugh, then he was likely as hard a case as he'd seemed earlier. "Why did you come here?"

Again, a few seconds passed before Ty heard a similar wet sound as before. Then he realized the man was trying to speak. Could be he caught him in the neck, though he'd sworn he shot the brute in the breadbasket.

There was a shuffling then from inside the shed, a slight dragging sound. The man was probably repositioning himself. Ty heard the throaty clicks of a hammer ratcheting back. Here we go again, he thought, tightening back against the relative safety of the wood planking that separated him from whatever this man had planned.

But in the next moment, it all became decided. Another shot split the dead air.

Seconds passed as the rifle shot echoed quickly and dwindled away, fracturing into silence with each passing second.

"Boy?"

"Okay, Hob. Stay there."

"What's going on, Ty?" The old man was annoyed.

Ty waited a moment. "Man just did our job for us."

"Well don't that beat all. Hard against it, I'd say."

"I'd say." Ty ventured into the dark shed, crept low, his Colt thumbed and straight out in front of him. But in the dim light he saw nearly nothing. Silence all around. He kept the Colt aimed where he thought he should, plucked a lucifer from his jacket breast pocket, and picked it with a thumb nail. The matchstick bloomed alight and Ty tensed even more, but instantly he knew his guess was dead-on.

There lay the Mexican on his back in the chaff-covered dirt of the loafing shed. One arm lay over his chest as if he were snoozing, the other stretched alongside his body. The rifle lay just beyond. His right leg lay bent under his left.

As Ty suspected, the man's throat was a ravaged mess, more a ragged wound where his Adam's apple had been. That must have been where Ty's bullet found its mark. But the killing wound had been from the rifle's snout poked in the man's mouth, for above his right eye was now a raw, pulpy mess.

The burning match stung his thumb and he shook it out but held it, working the hot tip between his callused fingertips out of reflex, an almost natural reaction to anything that might cause a fire in what, at times, was dry country.

A sound behind him spun Ty, ducking low and pitching to one side. His actions fully on instinct once again, his Colt thrust at the doorway behind.

"Easy, boy. Easy. It's just me. Just ol' Hob." Uncle Hob's uncharacteristically soothing voice floated in before he ventured a step into the open doorway himself, his gun still gripped in his gnarled hands.

Ty let out a long, stuttering breath and stood. Hob clapped a hand on his shoulder. "I seen him by your match light. Rum thing, that."

Ty nodded. "Yep. But he wasn't alone."

Hob bent low. "What? Now you tell me?" He whispered. "I been paradin' around out here like a big-city dandy and now you tell me that?"

"Relax," said Ty, his turn to be the soother. "I'm pretty sure his partner stayed up in the hills, keeping watch, or some such thing."

"Oh," said Hob, straightening.

Ty thumbed another match alight, bent low and checked the Mexican. "Dead as he'll ever get."

Hob nodded knowingly. He'd seen enough dead men to not doubt that. "Grab his weapons," he said, turning to go. "And we'll deal with him in the morning."

Ty smiled, shaking his head. Ever the general, he thought. Nonetheless, he retrieved the rifle and found a long knife and a battered, much-used and empty small-caliber pistol tucked into the Mexican's waistband.

Hob made his way back behind the house to the kitchen. Ty held back, looking toward the north, thinking. Then he laid the Mexican's weapons down and stood in the middle of the packed-dirt dooryard, between the house and barn. He looked again to the now-dark hills to the north. There was no danger of him being seen, since he was near no lights himself.

Ty cupped his big hands around his mouth and bellowed loud and slow, sending a message to the hills: "Your partner is dead! You hear me? The Mexican is dead! You tell that to Clewt Duggins!"

He let his arms drop to his sides, suddenly more tired than he could remember being in a long, long time. Far off, in the hills, from the direction toward where he just shouted, Ty heard the hammering of hooves. Someone was hell-bent homeward, delivering a message.

Ty sighed and made his way back toward the porch and the kitchen, where Uncle Hob had just lit an oil lamp. Soon, he hoped, they'd tuck into bowls of stew. He felt almost guilty thinking of food when he'd just shot a man. But he couldn't deny it, he was tired and hungry . . . and angry.

"Almost forgot to tell you," Ty glanced toward Hob, fussing and slamming pots and pans on the warming stovetop. Once Ty was inside, he crossed to the back door of the kitchen and paused there. "Saw a one-legged man today. And he wasn't you."

For once, Uncle Hob was speechless. His old gray eyes pierced like daggers, the wiry brows above them beetling as if they were angry insect legs, bristling. Finally he grabbed a word. "What? What's that you said?"

But Ty had already ducked out the back door, now relatively assured there wasn't someone waiting in the gloom to peel off a shot at him. He was almost smiling as he groped for his boots. Tomorrow would bring plenty more strange goings-on, but he doubted anything more would happen tonight. They'd spell each other and take what rest they could get. He was in no mood to rehash the day's events for Hob, even though the old man deserved to hear why he'd been shot at.

Chapter 9

Sue Ellen jerked awake, pulled in a sharp breath, and looked around the dimly lit room. It was as if someone had tugged a string attached directly to her core. Her heart thudded hard in her chest as she took in her surroundings. It slowly became familiar, recognizable as her own drawing room, just off the dining room. Through the open door between the two she could just make out one half of a chair draped with limp rawhide wraps. And then the evening before came back to her. She sat up, feeling her dress, her face. How had she gotten in here, laid out on the divan?

She swung her feet to the floor and smoothed her dress in her lap with shaking hands, unsure of what to do next. At least she was no longer tied.

"Relax, my dear."

Sue Ellen turned to see Clewt Duggins, looking freshly washed and wearing clean clothes. He looked fitter and sprightlier than he had a right to. And he was smiling.

"You were exhausted, my dear. No other way to put it. I'm afraid my chatter in the past has had that effect on some folks. Sadly, I will now have to add you to that list." He sighed theatrically and disappeared back into the kitchen. Moments later he returned with a steaming cup of coffee and carried it to her.

She reluctantly accepted it, sipped. The strong brew helped clear her head. "How long was I asleep?"

Duggins lifted a pocket watch from his vest pocket, clicked it open. "It's nearly ten o'clock. You have slept the night away and then some." He smiled, clicked shut the watch and returned it to the pocket.

A chilling blade of warning stabbed up Sue Ellen's middle, tightened her throat. "Where did you get that watch?" She recognized it, but wished she didn't.

"I think you know the answer to that." Duggins's voice was flat, cold, and reptilian, just like it had been when he spoke with Ty the day before. "I also think you know he won't be needing it." He turned away, then stopped. "And make sure you eat something today. I won't have any wilting flowers working for me." He headed for the kitchen.

Sue Ellen was halfway to her feet when she let fly with the cup. As if slowed in a dream, she watched the delicate china vessel turn, end for end, through the air, the hot black liquid gouting outward in a slow arc. At the same time, Clewt turned his head and with finger-snap speed the cup drove straight into his scarred, pockmarked cheek. It split into a number of pieces, exploding on contact with his face.

The coffee spattered him, and Sue Ellen saw in his already hard-set eyes sparks, his surprise turning into a delicious anger.

Sue Ellen felt sudden satisfaction. She would no longer submit to this foul beast and his men. She would fight or die, as she was now sure her Alton had. There was no one else on God's green earth who cared for her. Seeing Ty's emotionless reaction to her desperate plight had proven to her that she was alone. If she wanted salvation, she would have to provide it.

Although she could not claim she had ever truly been *in* love with him, she had *loved* Alton. And now that she knew without doubt that he was dead by their hands, and for reasons she didn't understand—perhaps never would—at least the veil of hope she had drawn over herself, the veil that had kept her a simpering, quivering wreck these past few days, was now gone. In its place stood a woman who gritted her teeth and offered a grim smile to her captor, come what may.

And that didn't take long in coming. Clewt Duggins swatted at his face, now bleeding from a deep slash and several smaller cuts just under the eye and along his temple, all welling red blood down the length of his pocked cheek. The hot coffee had an equally raw effect, leaving puffy splotches on his face and neck.

He lunged for her, his stiff leg barely slowing his efforts. But Sue Ellen was already on the move. She pivoted from her crouch and ran, barefooted, into the dining room, her one thought to get something substantial between herself and the madman, now looking almost comic as he stiff-legged toward her.

"You cur!" he shrieked, his now-homely face a mask of blood, reddened welting skin, and wet gray-black hair. He didn't slow as he approached the long dining table that just the night before he had dined at and on which still sat the leftovers. Fat congealed on the plate where the rest of the chicken and potatoes sat.

The room was darker than the sitting room, the curtains having been drawn.

Duggins swung left and right with abandon, thrashing his arms and sending the fancy, press-back chairs clattering, scudding across the floor and knocking into other pieces of furniture, pieces Alton would have been sickened to see treated in such a rough way.

A pretty milk-glass oil lamp with green-and-rose-colored flowers painted on its globe tottered, then toppled to the floor. Shards of glass sprayed and skittered, and the stink of lamp oil filled the stagnant air in the room.

"What did you expect?" screamed Sue Ellen. "That I'd just forgive you for murdering my husband? Isn't that what you and those other foul animals have done?" Sue Ellen trembled from the opposite side of the table, spitting the words at him. She could have ranted all day, but he was on the move. He did not circle the table as she thought he might, but bent low and began shoving the heavy table her way. He intended to trap her in the corner!

She groaned and pushed back against the table. And the vicious, howling man actually began laughing at her efforts. It only made her angrier. And in the midst of this struggle, from outside, Sue Ellen heard popping noises from far off, then shouts from men in the yard, close by the house, as if they had been just outside, listening to the struggles taking place inside.

Even Duggins turned his head toward the front of the house, sneering at the intrusion, his white teeth set tight together beneath his sopping, bloodied mustache.

"What? What is it?" he shouted, but none of his men responded.

Sue Ellen made a quick and rash decision then, whether to be trapped in the corner or run toward the far end of the kitchen while she still had a gap between the shoved table and the sideboard. She took the chance and dashed forward.

But Duggins was faster than she thought he might be, and less distracted by the sounds outside than she hoped. He caught her by the waist with one rugged arm and she kicked and flailed even as he lifted her from the floor and slammed her backward on the table. Her head hit hard and she felt a blackness like a veil lower over her. No, no, no! Sue Ellen begged herself not to give in to this. The room spun as she forced her eyes wide.

But he was too heavy, leaning over her, forcing her arms flat to the tabletop. And then she heard another voice even as she looked up, trying to focus, seeing only Duggins's leering, teeth-clenched face.

"Boss? Boss! You got to come quick!" The voice was one of his men, the tall, thin one who didn't say much, just looked askance at everyone, as if he were confused all the time. And now he was looking at Duggins with a very confused look. "Boss, what happened to your face?"

That seemed to snap Clewt from his reverie of rage. He looked to his side at the tall, thin cowboy, spittle dribbling from his mouth, and growled. Then he released one of Sue Ellen's wrists and delivered a quick snapping backhand to the tall cowboy's face.

"When I want you to interrupt me, I will tell you so. Now get out of here."

The tall cowboy held a hand to his face, confusion and hurt that would look much more suitable on the face of a child warring on his brow. He backed away, saying, "Sorry, boss, but . . . you . . . you should come on out here. We got ourselves something you need to see." With that, the tall cowboy turned on his heel and legged it out of the room, glancing back once as if to make sure the man who'd just smacked him hadn't followed too closely.

The interruption had served to give Sue Ellen time to somewhat recover from the knock to the head she'd taken. It also apparently gave Duggins pause. He made no effort to grab Sue Ellen's wrist again, but stared at the spot where his underling had stood. Presently he snorted and shoved Sue Ellen's other arm away from him, pushed off and away from the table.

"You are lucky I have a situation that requires my attention. Elsewise, we would be having an entirely different discussion right now. You understand me, woman?" He pointed a meaty finger at her face, glared at her a moment longer, said, "But this changes everything." Then he ambled from the room. Soon she heard the front door slam.

Sue Ellen struggled to sit up, ended up sliding off the end of the table. Hurry up, she told herself. This might be your only chance to be alone in the house long enough to figure out some way of besting them. She fought dizziness and a rising sick feeling spiraling upward from her gut, filling her windpipe, her throat. She dropped to her knees, holding the sides of her head as if it might crack like an egg, convinced at any second she was going to vomit.

She held that position for a few moments, aware that every second she spent not moving forward, trying to escape, was a wasted second of effort, a tiny gift to the evil men who had descended on her quiet, ordered world and blasted it apart. And that thought made her angry, angry enough to rise to her feet, steadying herself with the edge of the table. From outside she heard more shouts, from the front of the house. What was happening out there?

Chapter 10

"What was so important out here that you are shooting the morning sky full of holes?" Clewt held a dish towel to his bleeding, throbbing face. That vile woman would pay for this attack, and dearly. But for now he would tend to these buffoons. Teach them all a lesson first.

"There, boss. You see? A man's coming in—looks to be Barn Cat. I bet he has some good news for us, eh?"

"That's what you brought me out here for? That's what you're out here wasting bullets for?"

"No, we were answering his shots, letting them know we are still here, see?" The man shrugged, eyebrows knitted together.

"Still here? Where else would we be, you moron!" He turned to a man in a dusty, dented bowler. "I expect better from you, Paddy. Next time, rein in these fools."

The man in the bowler sighed and shrugged, but said nothing.

Clewt turned back to looking toward the incoming rider. But he'd seen the rheumy-eyed look on Paddy, his *segundo*. Man was reliable when he wasn't drinking. Problem was, he was always drinking.

This had better be good, Clewt thought, or I will begin gutting these fools like fish even sooner than I had planned to. He visored his eyes with a hand and watched as the rider drew closer. Perhaps he would bring good news; perhaps he had killed that nosy neighbor rancher. But why was there only one? He'd sent two men. "It does look like Barn Cat. If that's the case, then where's Paco? Oh, I can't tell from this distance who that is. Is that one horse or two?"

Clewt bet with himself that one of those fools had got himself killed. But he needed money first, in order to bet it. And the only place he could get money was here, with whatever was left of the treasure that Winstead had squirreled away, buried deep somewhere on this cursed ranch of his.

A ranch? Of all the foolish things Winstead could have spent money on, he up and buys a ranch. If it were me, thought Clewt, I would have kept on riding, taken all that money and hit the trail hard, stopping long enough to drink and whore and gamble, leaving a trail of winnings or losings all over the place. Maybe I would have bought a fancy train car or two to haul me and my wealth around the country. He smiled at his momentary mental folly. Of course he could still do with a train car. He just needed to find Winstead's stolen loot.

As if reading his mind, Paddy said, "Boss? That neighbor rancher. You don't think he found Delbert's body yesterday, do you?"

Clewt turned with a sigh and regarded Paddy again, verified the man was somewhat drunk, could smell the booze on his breath. This was the man who was, sadly, his second in command. Not a bad sort, and even clever at times when sober. But drunk, he was not the sharpest knife in the kitchen. Still, Paddy had been with him through it all, the only one of the boys left from the old days, and so, the only logical choice for a shotgun rider.

But the Irishman had a bad habit of talking too much once he was in his cups, and as an Irishman, that happened frequently. Paddy's drunken chatter had forced Clewt to slice the throat of that pretty young whore in that flophouse in Reno. The dumb Irishman had blathered about them and their coming fortunes to her, and Clewt had felt bad about having to kill her off.

She was anything but dim, and she hadn't been in the trade all that long, not long enough to have become a diseased thing like the other women in the place, old crones all. But she had been told things she shouldn't know. He could tell, could see the glint of greed in her eyes. Would she play him for it? Blackmail him with what she hoped would be leverage enough to gain her a cut of the fortune? Ha. Easier to kill her and be done with it. Sadly, he didn't think her death had taught Paddy one bit of a lesson.

Be that as it may, Clewt knew he would do to them all eventually what he'd done to the greedy young whore, just as soon as he didn't need them anymore. And that day would come soon, very soon. He could feel it.

"It was a shame we had to kill ol' Delbert, or Alton Winstead, or whatever else he called himself, eh, boss?" Paddy said this as he, too, shaded his eyes and looked toward the approaching rider. "Might be we could have gotten that information out of him some other way."

Clewt felt his teeth grit together tight, despite the throbbing pain in his newly cut cheek. "Don't you think," he said in a barely controlled hiss of a whisper so that the other morons clustered about the yard would not hear, "I would have avoided that if I could have? From now on, Paddy, you keep your mouth shut about that, you hear me?"

The Irishman looked at his boss and nodded. He knew what the boss was capable of, had seen it plenty of times. That stag-handled slicing tool of his, one of the meanest Bowies he'd ever seen, always gleamed with a fresh sharpening. For a one-legged, scar-faced, old-looking fella, Paddy had to admit the boss sure could put the scare into a man. And now he was turning that same killer look on him—the very man whom he'd shared a cell with for ten years. Paddy nodded again. "Yeah, boss. I meant nothing by it. I will keep so quiet you'll have to—"

"Paddy?"

"Yeah, boss?"

"You're talking again. A whole lot. And after I told you how it grates on my worn nerves, too."

"Yes, bo—"

Clewt jerked his hand up between their faces, a long scarred finger of warning standing like a lone, wind-stripped fencepost poised between them. "Shut up, Paddy."

Paddy swallowed hard and nodded, his yellowed, blood-shot eyes shifting back toward the rider, certain now that it was Barn Cat, and with no sign of Paco. Which likely meant that the two men had gotten into a skirmish with the nosy rancher and Paco didn't make it. The boss was not going to like this.

Clewt knew Paddy was right. So help him, he hated to admit it, but Winstead hadn't given up the location of his secret treasure as easily as Clewt had expected he would, hoped he would. Delbert had even withstood the pain he'd inflicted, the beating and little nicking slices all over his body. How could a man stand up to that and still grit his teeth, even smiling around gritted teeth? It mystified Clewt.

Finally, and though Clewt had known it was the dead wrong thing to do, even as he did it, he had hit the worthless, no-talking, cheating, son-of-a-scoundrel on the head with a rock. Only meant it to coldcock him. But it had worked almost too well. Winstead had wobbled, spun on him, his eyes glazing, blood streaming into one from somewhere inside the man's head. And still Winstead had smiled at him. "I'll tell you . . ." he'd said.

Clewt had leaned in close, also smiling himself, put his ear closer to the wobbling Winstead's face, and said, "Good, good, you tell me and we'll lay off you. You have my word."

"I'll tell you . . . nothing." Winstead straightened then and smiled, blood drooling out one side of his mouth, his left eye completely red, as if someone had poured blood straight on it. Still smiling, he turned from Clewt, showed him his back, and he made a dignified if feeble effort at lifting a foot and walking away.

Clewt had been holding Winstead's pepperbox, that same old thing Winstead had pulled on him when they'd met in the cantina over a decade before in Chihuahua. Only this time the weapon was in working order and loaded. And had been in a fancy leather holster worn high on the side of Winstead's now-fat belly.

Clewt could not contain his rage. He bit together so hard that his head shivered and his vision blurred. All those years, all that jail time chipping big rocks into smaller rocks, wearing chains and humiliating rags in the vicious heat of the rank Mexican desert. All that to finally find the man who did it to them, who was solely responsible for the most hellish time of their lives, and he smiles and turns his back on them?

"No! You turn your double-crossing hide around, Winstead!"

Alton Winstead laughed, a wet sound that ended in a sudden coughing fit as he stumbled slowly forward, still upright, but now bringing up gouts of bloody phlegm.

"Turn around and face me!" Clewt strangled out the words, his seething rage shaking him to his core, the pepperbox quivering but gripped firmly in his hand.

The reply was another wet laugh from the man whose back was but five feet before him.

The pepperbox snapped and popped in his hand as it spit one, two, three, four bullets, like tiny, angry lead bees, straight into Alton Winstead's back, close enough that the black wool of his jacket smoked and bubbled. Blood welled outward from the freshly savaged fabric and the men who stood before Winstead saw on his face quick, wide-eyed surprise, then an even wider smile and slow nod, as if he had been waiting for it, as if he had expected nothing less than that outcome.

The group stood silent for long moments as they all watched Winstead, dead and not yet knowing it, weave in place, one leg slightly forward, as if he were in midstep. Then, as if time had been slowed somehow, the portly man with the fresh haircut and fine boiled wool suit and green cloth vest and gold pocket watch gagged, still smiling, and pitched forward. Right there on the top of a pretty knoll on his own ranchland in the western foothills of the northern Sierra Nevada of California.

All these little facts bubbled through Alton Winstead's frantic dying mind as he withered like a pinched-out candle flame, far-off, surrounded by beauty, but closer in, surrounded by men the likes of whom he had hoped never to see again, but secretly guessed he would one day. And he had known the inevitable outcome. Had predicted in his mind that it would likely end just as it had.

Did he feel remorse for leaving a pretty wife? Yes, yes, indeed. She was a good, good person. Did he feel bad for not telling her about the rest of the fortune? Maybe, maybe he'd decide that in the hereafter. Ha. That was a laugh. If there was something like heaven, then Winstead knew where he was headed, and it wasn't filled with people in robes playing celestial harps.

No, all in all he had few regrets. Except maybe for not killing these fools when he'd had the chance eleven years before. And now it was all too late. He hoped they didn't hurt

Sue Ellen. Hoped they would somehow leave her be to enjoy the ranch, the land, maybe even resume a life with Ty Farraday. But he knew as he pitched facedown onto the gritty hilltop soil that Sue Ellen would not give in to them, these men would not leave her be, they would upend every single stone on the ranch looking for that fortune, and none of them would ever find a thing. And that is what left him with a smile stretched wide on his face as he died, hearing the seething shouts of anger from just behind him, unfurling from Clewt Duggins's revenge-addled body. Never, never, never. . . .

"Boss! What in blue blazes did you do?"

Clewt blinked himself out of the daze he found himself in, the little pistol still smoking from the snout of its barrels. "I . . ." He narrowed his eyes and spun on the man, Paddy, who'd uttered that reproachful question. Then he raised the little pistol. "You know well what I've just done. And you'd be wise to keep in mind that I will do the same to any of you fools should you dare to question me again. You hear me?"

To a man they all nodded. A few murmured, "Yeah, boss."

"Now I know what you all are worried about. You think that because this worthless corpse here"—he toed his stiff leg against Winstead's flopped, unresponsive ample midsection— "is now in the land of the dead that he can't tell us where he hid our fortune. Well you couldn't be more wrong."

"How's that, boss?"

Clewt smiled. "I'm so glad you asked, Rufus." He turned a kindly smile on the man. "You did notice that the man had a wife, right?"

Rufus grinned and blushed, stared at his too-big boots, scuffed at the dirt as if he were complimented on the playground of the local school by a pretty marm. "Yes, sir, I reckon so."

They all knew that Rufus was keen on Mrs. Winstead.

He'd all but tripped over himself when they'd first arrived to make sure she had water from the well, firewood brought into the kitchen, the porch swept. Despite his best efforts at impressing her, Rufus couldn't raise a smile from the woman.

Clewt couldn't blame her—Rufus was a simp, good for one thing, nervous at any time but in a gunfight. The man was a decent shot at close range and he had no qualms about striding forward into the thick of a blue-smoke gun battle. Only an idiot would behave as he had in all these skirmishes since he'd found the man down in Mexico. But Clewt couldn't fault him when it came time to pull triggers.

And somehow Rufus had managed to escape with no more serious harm to his person than split buttons, holes blazed in his rough-cloth jacket sleeves, and one pucker in the thigh of his trousers—right where his leg, by all rights, should have been. A couple of the mostly Mexican men in the gang swore that Rufus was either blessed or cursed. Either way, they had decided to leave him be, just in case.

As for Clewt, he didn't much care one way or the other which way Rufus's luck ran, for that was all it had to be— and as Clewt always knew, luck ran out eventually, just like women and booze.

"Well that woman, my merry men, will know of the whereabouts of her husband's secret stores of wealth. For not only is she a handsome thing, she's also a woman of high taste and low tolerance, I'd wager. And that combination adds up to one thing—no tolerance for secrets from her man." Clewt narrowed his eyes and leaned close to Rufus, but said in a stage whisper, "You know what I'm talking about, don't you, kid?"

He looked around at the other men, pulling nervous laughs from them all, though Clewt bet not but one or two of them had any idea what he was leading up to. "Why," he said, "she'd cinch the hem of her nightgown tight, and that, as the wise man said, would be that."

Rufus's brows sparred tight above his eyes like wooly worms in a fisticuff match. He didn't follow a thing Clewt had said.

"Think on it, kid. It'll come to you. In the meantime, let's us deal with ol' waste of space here."

They all looked down at the dead man in their midst.

"Barn Cat and Paco, you take him two arroyos over, in that direction, cover him over with rocks. Mind you do it now, you hear? I don't much care for the man, but we don't want all manner of critter rummaging at his corpse, bringing an arm or a foot up to the front door of the ranch like a stray dog with a bone. And while we're on the subject." Clewt pulled his serious face. "I will not"—he punctuated his words with a pointing finger—"have anyone letting on that this man is anything but as we told Mrs. Winstead earlier, on a buying trip for cattle. Is that understood?"

Again, they all nodded, murmured their assent.

"That clear, Rufus?"

"Yeah, sure, boss. I hear ya."

"Good. Now drag him outta here before the buzzards circle." Barn Cat and Paco bent to heft the man and position him into a more comfortable pose for dragging. But Clewt stopped them. "Hold on a minute, boys," he said when they'd flipped Winstead belly up. Clewt bent and pulled the gold pocket watch from the dead man's paunch vest pocket, hefted it in his palm as if weighing it, then tugged the chain free from its fixture on a button. He stood, smiling. "Okay, now you can get his stinking hide out of here." He was smiling as he landed a last kick at the man. His boot toe barely grazed Winstead's shoulder.

As they dragged the body of his old nemesis away, Clewt had looked down at the dead man's watch now in his own hand, and wondered why killing Alton Winstead hadn't felt as good as he'd imagined it would for all those years. The one thing he'd dreamed of doing had come and gone way too soon. He straightened and looked in the direction of the Double Cross ranch house. Too far to see from that knoll, he nonetheless envisioned Winstead's freshly minted widow in her kitchen, perhaps, and vowed he'd make up for the loss of his full righteous revenge with something . . . a little more satisfying.

Chapter 11

The silence in the room threatened to topple Ty's just-waking mind. He knew why Hob was angry, couldn't blame him. Ty should have explained it all last night, but he fell asleep before he could. Hob took first watch and a goodly part of the second, much to Ty's annoyance. He hated it when others shouldered his load.

And now, even after a couple of hours of sleep, Hob wasn't talking, either. Not like the old dog to keep his peace. He was more inclined to blurt out whatever it was that rested topmost on his mind than to sit and fester. Of course, by the time Ty had sipped a half cup of Hob's syrup-thick, scalding coffee, he knew just what the old man was peeved about.

He set down the hot mug. "Uncle Hob, I—"

And then it came. . . . That knobby old spoon whipped right out of the porridge pot, flecking hot oats across the room. "You don't get the right to talk first. That's my right, by gum!" He whanged the spoon handle on the edge of the pot. "And another thing, what's the story with you? Used to be you'd come on home and tell me what you'd been up to. Case you hadn't noticed, I don't get around much no more!"

Ty sighed. "Hob, the pity gambit doesn't suit you much. You might want to try just getting to the point. Or letting me talk so I can tell you what it is you want to know."

"Oh, and what's that, mister smart?"

"That is . . . that you want to know why we were being shot at last night, right?"

The sputtering man at the stove grumbled something and turned back to stirring the pot. But Ty could tell that he was eager to hear what Ty had to offer. "I'll give you a tightened version of what happened to me yesterday."

"Oh, don't bother. It's just old me, you know, the one who got shot at." Hob ladled a dripping big spoonful of over-cooked oats into a bowl.

"Okay," said Ty, doing his best to hide a smirk. "If you feel that way about it."

"What? What?" Back came the spoon. "Don't you dare let up on what you was about to cut loose with!"

"Okay, okay. But put down that spoon and pass those biscuits, will you? A man could starve to death in here."

"Ain't happened yet."

Ty bit into a biscuit, chewed, then said, "You remember I said yesterday morning I was headed out to look for strays over in the hills north of here, right?"

"Yep. Them little rascals can't keep clear of there."

"Right. So I cut their trail, a handful of them, about mid-day. But they all had headed over onto Winstead's land. Not surprising, but what I found not long after was."

"Well, you gonna keep me guessing, or am I going to get some sort of story?"

"Keep quiet a minute, will you? I'm thinking. So anyway, I head up the leading edge of that arroyo, you remember the one? Few years back it was filled with choke weed, where that calf broke its leg? Well, it's not that way anymore."

"What's in it?"

Ty sipped his coffee. "A body."

"What?"

"Yep, and not just any body—it was Alton Winstead."

"What?"

"Yep, dead. And you might want to think about broadening your vocabulary."

"What?"

"Anyway, I found Winstead dead. He'd been savaged by someone up close; looked as though they had plugged him in the back with a small-caliber pistol. His head looked to have been battered a bit, too. It was not good, Hob. The only reason I found him was the yipping of coyotes looking to get a turn at snacking on him."

"Well, can't say that I wished the man that sort of ill will. But he was big enough to feed a passel of coyotes. So, what'd you do then?" Hob finished ladling the breakfast goop into a second bowl and slid it across the table to his own spot, then poured each of them more coffee before sitting down.

"I chased off the coyotes first thing. Then I glassed Winstead's place."

"What'd you see?" said Hob, spoon paused halfway to his mouth.

"Strangers, a small gang of them."

"And Sue Ellen? She okay?"

Ty knew the old man still held a soft spot in his heart for her, even though outwardly he spoke of her little and when he did it wasn't in the kindest light, mostly because he was so fond of Ty.

"She looked okay. But I was about to find out firsthand."

"What?"

"There you go again." Ty spooned in a few mouthfuls of oats. "Yep, they saw me up on the ridge, must have been a reflection off my spyglass. Sent two riders up to inspect me, then retrieve me."

"They didn't hurt you, did they?" Hob bristled, his bottom lip outthrust as if hearing an insult.

"No, relax. I wanted to go down there. Turns out it was a

good thing I did. And when I left I could have sworn they were convinced I knew nothing about Winstead's body. I was that far away from it when the two riders came on up. But—"

"But nothin'. They know you saw him. Or they're taking no chances and killing anyone who might have gotten close. But what would make strangers come here and kill Winstead? I know he was a pompous windbag with a lot of money—"

"I think you just answered your own question."

"What?"

Ty sighed. "Winstead. He's loaded with cash, right?"

"Was."

"And he and I never got along, right?"

"Right, but for good reason."

"Good or no, the fact remains that when the law comes snooping, they'll find a dead Winstead, shot in the back, and me as the leading suspect."

"How you figure that?" Hob's eyebrows rose and he struggled to gain his feet, ready to take on all lawmen for the sake of his nephew.

"Because everybody knows Winstead and I had more than one beef with each other. That was common knowledge in these parts. And for lots of reasons."

Hob nodded. "Yeah, any of which lesser men would kill others about. I hear ya." He rasped a bony hand across his salt-and-pepper-stubbled face. "Don't mean I have to like it."

"Thanks, Hob. Good to know we're on the same side." Ty stood and stretched. "I have to get back out there and take care of that Mexican fellow before he gets ripe. It's feeling like it's going to be a hot one today."

"What are you going to do with him?" said Hob, eyeing Ty.

"Might be I'll bring him to town. Tell the marshal what happened."

"Not a good idea, boy."

"No? Why not?"

"That old windbag was tight buddies with Winstead. You bring a body in, even one of a stranger who was trying to drill you full of holes, and you know what's going to happen?"

"Tell me," said Ty, already knowing the answer. He dropped his hat on his head.

"Nothin'. Unless you count a noose around your own neck, rope paid for by the taxpayers of Ripley Flats. You'll be swingin' for something, sure as I'm a world-class cook."

The old man stared at the young man, a resigned look on his lined face. Still he said, "You sure this is what you think you need to do?"

Ty was quiet for a time, then said, "What would you do?"

Hob sighed. "Same thing."

Ty smiled and swung the door open wide. "Well," he said as he crossed the porch, "then that leaves me just two options. Bury him here. Or something else."

"What?"

"There you go again, Uncle Hob. Saying that word. You might want to get that thing looked at."

"What? What are you going to do with the dead man? Ty, you come back here when I shout at you! When I shout at a man, I want him facing me! Ty!"

Ty didn't turn around, just offered Hob an easy wave. He knew Uncle Hob wasn't going to trail after him. But he had given him an idea of what to do with the Mexican. And it didn't involve burying him on Ty's property.

Chapter 12

"What is it you're doing, Rufus?"

The horse-faced Southern boy swung his big head up from his bent-over position, rummaging through the large wooden locker of tack, saddles, and other horse gear that had been locked in what had appeared to be an office lean-to built onto the custom horse barn.

"Oh, oh, boss, I . . . I didn't mean . . ."

Clewt's face softened. "Take it easy, Rufus. What you are up to is quite apparent to me. What you hope to gain is also quite apparent. And I can't blame you. While the rest of these idiots are off guzzling their dwindling supplies of liquor, you are rummaging about this plentiful place, seeking to feather your nest, no?"

The big Southern man squinched his eyes a moment; then as if a switch had been tripped, he smiled, enlightenment dawning on his long face. "Yeah, that's about it, yeah, boss. So . . . you're not sore about me um, you know, breaking into this locker and taking a peek at the saddles and what-nots?"

Clewt stepped up beside Rufus, eyes fixed on the goods within. "Not if you don't mind sharing your find with me, eh, Rufus? My old saddle's about wore out and from the looks of things, this haul would cover both our horses in fine shape. And leave enough for us to bridle up, and then some, eh? Oh, look at these."

Clewt reached for a shining, supple set of saddlebags, black leather with braiding along the entire outer edge, tastefully set with silver conchos. He held them up, admiring them, turning them this way, then the other, and finally pulling them close to his nose and sniffing them. "These have never ridden on a horse. Winstead must have spent a fortune on all this gear. And never used it. I wonder if he ever intended to."

Clewt looked at Rufus, but the big man's droopy eyes were fixed on the fine brand-new saddlebags. "I . . . dunno, boss." There was a hint of disappointment lingering on his horsy features.

One side of Clewt's mouth rose. "You like these, don't you, Rufus?"

The big man's eyes brightened. "I do, indeed. They're pretty as a peach pie."

"Yes, they are." Clewt regarded the sleek black bags a moment, then laid them against Rufus's chest. "Take them. You've earned them. You discovered the cache, after all. It's only right."

The big man's hands closed over them. "You mean it, boss?"

Clewt straightened, surveyed the rest of what the cupboard had to offer. "Of course I mean it. I never say a thing I don't mean." He turned a tight smile on the happy Rufus. In a low voice he said, "Which is why I tell you that everything worth anything in life comes at a price. Do you follow along with what I'm telling you?"

The big man's eyebrows drew together again. That must be a familiar pose for those bushy things, thought Clewt.

"I . . . I think so, boss."

But Clewt knew that the big drawn-faced man didn't really understand. Yet. But by the time he did, Clewt knew that Rufus would wish he had never left the warm, peachy bosom of the old Deep South. By then, of course, it would be too late. Far too late.

Chapter 13

By the time Ty saddled Stub and led him out of the barn, trailing a lead line attached to a pack pony, Hob had finished tidying the kitchen and had plopped down on the porch for a few draws on his morning pipe. The scattergun leaned within reach against the railing, and the cat No Ears lay sprawled in his lap, eyes mere slits and a contented purr rising from deep within his throat as Hob's knobby right hand none too gingerly working the cat's scarred head.

"You gonna do what I think you ought not to do?" Hob gestured at the horses with his smoking pipe.

Ty nodded. "I reckon."

"I figured." Hob resumed puffing on his old briar piece.

The younger man led the horses to the loafing shed. Since he'd wrapped the dead man in canvas last night after they ate supper, then bent the man double at the waist, all he had to do was drag him on out and heft him aboard the pack pony and lash him on.

Despite the fact that he'd chosen this animal for its calm demeanor, the sturdy pony still fidgeted and eye-rolled at the smell and feel of the dead man being lashed to its back.

"Whoa, now. Whoa, girl," clucked Ty in a low, calm tone. It eventually did the trick.

"Tell 'em I said howdy."

"I will," said Ty, climbing aboard the Morgan.

"And, boy?" said Hob, rising to his feet, displacing the annoyed tomcat.

Here we go, thought Ty. Can't let me get on with things without a few words of wisdom. Not like he really minded, though, as Hob was more of a father to him than a business partner.

"Likely those boys, bad as they seem to be, will want a piece or two of your flesh. Likely they won't give up so easy as they did last night. Likely"—he shook the pipe at Ty— "they will do their best to lay you low. You ready for that?"

"I'll do my best to avoid it, but, yeah, if it comes to that, I am ready to give as good as I get. But I don't think it will come to that. Not just yet."

"Then why are you bound and determined to force their hand? From what I saw last night, those boys are on the prod for some reason that's beyond my ability to figure out, and you are their target of choice."

"I know, Hob. But I have to figure out what's going on up there. Sue Ellen's alive, and looked to be unhurt, maybe a little overworked, but seemed okay. But after last night, I'm not inclined to let it go. No matter what she said. It's been gnawing away at me since I left there, and no matter the amount of water we have under the bridge, I can't stand by—"

"I get ya. But you don't come back by dark, I'm ridin' out, and there ain't a thing you can say or do to change that, you rawboned pup!" The pipe hit every word Hob said like a hammer hitting a nail head.

Ty grinned and touched his hat brim. "I'm counting on it, Uncle Hob. But I'll be here."

"See to it!" the old man shouted.

Ty waved a big hand and rode on out, heading northeastward.

He'd also packed a sack of lime in one of the panniers, intending to visit Alton Winstead—or what would be left of him once the critters got hold of him. But first he had to make sure he wasn't being trailed or watched from afar. Not much he could do about some of that, but he could do his best to stick to the treed trails, stay on the southerly slopes and not skyline himself.

It took him an extra half hour to make his way close to the spot; then he reined up, and scanned the graveled ground for continued sign of the man who'd accompanied the ambusher. Since leaving the ranch he'd spotted random signs here and there, especially of tracks headed away, until they veered off in a sharp northeasterly direction, which led right to the Double Cross.

One set had been deeper and followed a straighter, truer path, indicating that the horse was weighted with a rider, the strides were lengthened from those of a walk, so the rider was likely in a hurry, and direction was one the rider was sure of.

The prints left by the second horse, however, left a more erratic trail, and didn't press in as much. This told him it had to be the riderless horse that belonged to the dead man bouncing along just behind him on his packhorse. The Mexican's horse must have spooked eventually and run back toward where it came from, perhaps the Double Cross. Though if the man's horse was one he'd brought with him and not from the Double Cross, then it was possible the horse might stray, lost in the hills.

Likely its bridle would foul on a branch or brambled thicket. Weighted under a saddle, if it hadn't already slumped and swung underneath, hanging from its belly, it might well not last long. And then the critters would find it in short order. He'd not put it past wolves or lions to deal it damage sooner than later.

Again, Ty scanned the ground, eventually seeing prints off to the north upslope of him. From there he couldn't tell which horse made them. As long as it wasn't a fresh rider, he didn't much care. He'd help the riderless horse if he came upon it, but he wasn't going out of his way just now to track it. He had bigger problems to deal with.

Stub's ears perked forward, and Ty followed the horse's sightline slightly upslope toward a stand of ponderosa pine. The horse's nostrils quivered; then Ty smelled it too. The distinctive, off tang of decaying flesh.

Ty quietly patted the horse's neck, and one ear flicked at the reassurance. They were not far, just one arroyo back from where he'd found Winstead. So the rank scent was most likely the unscrupulous pudgy rancher, dragged there by the squabbling half-starved coyotes, or a lion, a wolf, a grizzly. Could as likely be a dead beef, a bear's kill—grizzly were fond of letting a kill rot and swarm with maggots before they tucked in, enjoying it good and rank.

Ty had already shucked his Colt Navy a half-mile back downslope. Now he thumbed back the hammer and quietly nudged Stub forward with his heels. The horse didn't want to advance toward that thicket, but he did as Ty bade him, as he always had, and Ty suspected he always would. Best horse he'd ever known. A whole lot of stubborn in him, and an ornery streak wider than a barn, but he was always there, willing and able, when Ty needed him. A whole lot like Uncle Hob, he mused.

They drew up within a dozen yards of the trees. Out of the corner of his left eye he saw the packhorse and its gruesome load, all still with him. Good. If anyone had been hiding in the trees, waiting to clip him, they likely would have done so by now. There was no way in there except straight ahead. And his suspicion that the smell was Winstead was far too strong to ignore. So he gambled and nudged the horse once more.

He would have to go just inside the shaded cool of the trees—the day, though in autumn, had already turned off warm and promised to unravel into a late-season scorcher. They were few and far between this time of year, but that didn't mean they were done for the season.

But once he dismounted, tied off Stub well to a stout branch, stepped inside the shade of the little stand, the stink hit him twice as hard as it had just a few feet back, out in the sun where the air kept a slow, steady flow. It took him but a moment more to notice Winstead's leg protruding from behind a gray-black boulder.

The boot, poking upright, jostled and wagged. Whatever was hidden from view, tugging on the man, was so intent on its snacking that it hadn't heard Ty's approach. He quickly stepped around the rock and came into view of the entire stinking, chewed mess, locking eyes with a lobo just raising its head. It didn't look as if the creature had been feeding, just tugging and nudging at the body, still on its back, probably in an effort to determine just what this creature was and why it happened to reside, unguarded and unguarding, way out here.

"Git!" growled Ty. The beast padded backward one, two steps, then stopped, its top lip raised almost comically, exposing long, curving white fangs that even in this shaded dark of the tree cover looked menacing and surgical in their intent.

"I said 'Git!'" Ty stepped forward again, his pistol thrust outward, pointing finger poised on the curving trigger, ready to offer one single effective slight squeeze. "If I didn't have to mind my shots for fear of drawing attention, I'd give you a couple good ones right now, you cur."

Ty hoped he sounded menacing to the beast, enough so to drive it into the woods as he had done to the coyotes the day before. In truth, he wished the wolf no ill. The wolf must have sensed something menacing about Ty's voice and demeanor, for it backed farther away, snarling and showing tooth. Ty lunged fast toward it, feinting an attack, and the lobo dashed off, tail tucked. He made sure it kept going. He tracked it with his eyes far westward, out of the trees, and away over the closest hill.

Satisfied it would not return soon, he shifted his gaze to the aromatic mess that had been his former neighbor, the man who stole his land and his girl. "Not so much to look at now, are you, Winstead, you poor bastard? I'll admit I was never fond of you, but I'd not wish your fate on any man." Ty's thoughts turned to the men at the Double Cross holding Sue Ellen hostage. "Well, maybe on a few. Might be I can make that happen."

He shook his head and walked back to the packhorse. He approached easy, knowing the animals would still be skittish from the scent of the dead man and the wolf. He unpacked the sack of powdered lime and brought it back into the copse.

It clouded and swirled around his feet as he dumped it from the cotton sack, liberally dosing the chewed parts of Winstead's anatomy and covering the rest as best as he was able. When the sack emptied, Ty stuffed a corner in his back pocket and began gathering rocks, feeling a sense of urgency now, knowing his horses—and his troublesome load—were potentially exposed to the prying eyes of anyone riding by. Most likely that would be someone from the gang of ruffians at the Double Cross.

Piling the rocks atop Winstead took longer minutes than he intended, but Ty knew, even with such precautions, curious critters would still, despite the stink-quelling lime and the rocks, find a way to dislodge and work on the body. He'd done this mostly for Sue Ellen's sake. And for his own, if he had to be honest with himself. So he wouldn't feel guilt over it. So he could look at his own reflection in a stream as he drank, or splashed his face of a cold mountain morning, when he camped alone up in the high places, his favored spots. Alone is what he'd be with his thoughts and a cold bedroll. But at least he'd be able to tell her, and himself, that he'd done what he could for any man all his days. Including that skunk Winstead.

Ty mounted up and switchbacked up the slippery, scree-riddled slope until they topped out near the spot where he'd found Winstead the day before. Another short piece and they made it to the overlook where he'd waited for the two rascals from the Double Cross. He'd not bother glassing the place today. Today he'd ride in alone. At least the only living man in his party. Whether he rode out of there in the same shape remained to be seen.

Something was very wrong down at the Double Cross, and he needed to find out what it was. And how to save Sue Ellen. Trouble was, he didn't have a single decent idea how to go about it.

Ty set his jaw and let out a long, slow breath as they descended the long ridge in much the same fashion as he'd gained the top from the other side.

Chapter 14

It wasn't until Ty passed beneath the arch that an alarm was raised by a loafing hard case leaning in much the same spot he'd been the day before. Ty paid little attention to the man's shouts. Good, at least they weren't waiting for him. All the long, straight lane up to the place, he'd kept a keen eye on the terrain to his left and right.

Clewt Duggins walked out on the porch, that curious stiff-legged gait making him look uncomfortable. He shaded his eyes and squinted toward the arch. Then he shouted, plenty loud enough for Ty to hear: "Well, well, what have we here? As I live and breathe, it's . . ." He shook his hand as if trying to call up a name from long ago. He continued his theatrics and rubbed his chin, rolled his eyes at the timbers of the porch above his head. Then he snapped his fingers and said, "I've got it—Ty Farraday. That's your name, isn't it?" His shouts covered the hundred or so yards separating them. "To what do we owe the pleasure?"

The words barely echoed, carried off on a stiff northerly breeze that had kicked up as Ty descended to the valley floor. Dust eddied and dry debris skittered across the late-season hardpan.

Ty dismounted, kept his hat tilted low so he could let his eyes rove, and with a few quick slashes from his Bowie knife, freed the lashed down, tarpaulin-covered corpse of the Mexican. He glanced once more across the packhorse's back, over the dead man, did his best to take in the entirety of the place.

Of Sue Ellen there was no sign—she wasn't hauling water, wasn't off to either end of the house, hanging the washing. Maybe she was out back, maybe in the kitchen. If he could only see that she was there, alive and, if not well, at least not being abused. He cursed himself for not making a play for her sooner, no matter her obstinate demeanor. She must have been coerced into acting that way. Daylight glinted off the house's many windows, two floors full, but in none of them could he see her staring out.

Ty shoved the dead Mexican by the boots and the bound carcass pitched forward, landed hard. Dust rose, swirled off on the breeze.

Clewt watched the man with a steady gaze. From the looks of him the day before, and again today, he appeared seedy, frayed around the edges like a saddle bum. No, that was not quite right. He had a stately edge about him, as if he were somehow better than the rest of them all. But it was not an attitude that he had pulled on like an old coat.

It was something that was part of him, something Ty himself *was*, not something he chose to be. And that's what bothered Clewt the most. This man, this Ty Farraday, he was dangerous. Someone who maybe had designs on the ranch himself. Someone who maybe had designs on Mrs. Winstead too. He'd bet money on it.

There was something that passed between them yesterday when he'd ridden up, larger than life, and sat his horse, staring down at the rest of them, how he seemed casual but held a steady gaze, even on the woman. Yes, thought Clewt, there was something there all right. He'd bet good money on it.

*   *   *

By the time the men on the ranch house's porch recognized Ty's dropped bundle for what it was, several seconds of silence had passed. Then, as one, they jerked to action, shouting and waving arms. Only Clewt Duggins remained immobile. But Ty fancied he saw the man's theatrical smile disappear. Several of the loafing men had bolted toward the barn, but in a voice as loud as his mocking tones of moments before, Clewt shouted, "Hold! Hold, I say!" His arms were poised as if he were conducting an orchestra.

Ty, mounted on Stub, had turned the horse sideways to the house and buildings, and squinting against the dust-pocked breeze, once again took in the surrounding landscape, his eyes roving quickly back to the ranch house and the man holding court there. Duggins's annoyed minions fidgeted and waved their own arms in anger.

They must know exactly who he'd dropped there in the dirt. Up until then, had they expected the Mexican to ride up with news of Ty's own death? What of the second man? For there had been a second man, of that Ty was certain. Maybe he never returned? Unlikely, for if the Mexican's death was a surprise to them all, it was more likely that the second man played it poorly and lied when he returned alone from Ty's place. Or hightailed and didn't return.

All these thoughts and more raced through Ty's mind even as he paralleled the ranch and buildings, under the pointed glare of Clewt Duggins and his seething men. What was that man's game? Ty had his rifle laid across his lap, barrel pointed at the ranch, his Colt Navy ready to be slicked free, and still Clewt watched him depart, this time in a southerly fashion, along the flat, primarily so that Ty would not leave with his back to the nest of vipers.

And for as far as he rode, he took care to ensure, if they followed him, he was well out of range or else ready to return fire as good as he got. But as he passed over the long ridge, many miles to the southwest, roughly in the direction of home, he saw no riders departing from the Double Cross.

That meant only that they were biding their time, likely waiting to strike him at home, once again, right where he hung his hat. Well, Ty knew one thing for certain—he and Uncle Hob would be ready.

Chapter 15

"I'll return when I can. Just as soon as I've taken care of the business I told you of."

The woman stared at her husband, Henry Atwood, former marshal of Dane Creek. He knew by the sadness in her eyes that he had not lied to her well enough. She knew the reason he was leaving, knew as well that he might not return. Nonetheless, he decided to keep up the pretense. It would be easier this way, also for the boy. When it came time to explain to him just what had become of his father, she would be able to tell him, knowing at least that she was telling him what her husband had told her. She would not be lying to him, not really.

"This business, will it return you to me whole and alive?" She asked him this, but turned away as soon as she said it.

Henry knew she was crying. Knew, too, that it had taken much for her to muster the courage to say this. He felt sure he had never made her cry. Certainly he was not a man to strike a woman. He had seen too much of that himself as a boy, and had found such men to be weak, cowardly things, prone to crying and simpering when they should have been working and making the most of their days. To her silent tears, he could only stay strong and answer with more lies, lies that he hoped would be proved true.

"I will return to you, of course, my sweet girl. As soon as I am able." He turned her gently by the shoulders and smiled, a forced effort that surely must have looked as hollow as it felt. "I will bring you back finery. Perhaps some embroidered cloth, fancy thread. And a good little pocketknife for the boy, yes?"

He knew she wanted to answer, to tell him once again that she only wanted him to return. But this, they both knew, this they both wanted. None more so than him, in fact, but though he was many things, he was not particularly handy with a gun. Oh, he had done, time and time again, what needed doing. But only when forced to, and usually only against adversaries with more gun than skill and sense.

As marshal of Dane Creek, Henry Atwood had seen his share of bad things and bad people doing those bad things. Now he had retired from the position, had taken his wife and son to stay with her sister and her husband and children, good people. But he still had an obligation to right wrongs, the ragged results of a situation gone awry during his time as marshal.

Every day that passed he blamed himself for the lives lost to bad men doing bad things. Lives that he knew he could have saved, should have saved. But he had tried, too many times as it turned out, to save lives by talking, by trying to calm the killers. Sometimes it had worked. Most of the time, in fact. Not all of those hard-edged people had been killers, of course, but enough of them that his efforts at winning the upper hand through peace sometimes failed.

For a long time he had believed that being an officer of the law and a keeper of the peace meant that it was his duty to steer the killers to solid ground, take their weapons from them not by force but because they offered them. And because killings had been rare in the early days, this had led him to believe that his methods were right and good, just and successful.

And he was so wrong, as it had turned out. For as time wore on and the town's coffers filled with money from mining, and then cattle drives, the town filled businesses that catered to easy-money people. Bordellos and bars and gambling dens and places where, no matter how many times he and his short-lived deputies rousted them, broke them up, and sent them packing off to other holes in town, drunken men would find ways to savage one another. In alleyways between these tall new buildings from which fake women moaned and drunk men raged. In those alleys men died lonely, bloody deaths, found in the mornings by him, gutted with knives that once again rode somewhere in town safely in the wielder's belt sheaths.

And then when he thought that he might have begun to develop a harder edge, despite his efforts to avoid such things, the town burst wide open with too many people, too much money, too much promise . . . and not nearly enough law. And just when Henry knew that at least, as bad as it had become, it could not get any worse, that was when Clewt Duggins and his gang rode in and stayed, long enough to rip open the oozing wound of a town and leave a trail of dead behind, among them his deputy.

Henry Atwood bent low, kissed the shiny black hair of his beautiful young son, Henry, a mere stripling, at six years of age slight and delicate like his mother. He let his thick-fingered hand rest atop the quiet boy's head while he looked once again at his wife, Maria, nearly twenty years his junior, and a tender butterfly of a woman, as mysterious and open and beautiful as the Mexican countryside in which she had been raised.

Beyond, gathered in a humble cluster, tearful as well, stood her sister and her own family. Henry owed them much and had entrusted his fortune, such as it was, to his brother-in-law, to help with the eventuality of his not returning. All this went unsaid in the days leading up to this. But his plans were plain enough. They all considered him foolish and wrong to pursue the notorious Clewt Duggins and his gang of killers, so Henry had merely given up explaining why it was so important.

One look at the dusty graves in the little cottonwood grove beyond the southern end of town, with their wooden markers leaning, curved and split from sun and wind—those were all the reminders he needed.

If Henry could but stop Duggins, he had convinced himself that act might erase the terrible burden of guilt he carried daily from the job to now. He owed the dead at least that much. No matter what his family thought.

With uncharacteristic haste, Henry Atwood kissed his wife tenderly, thumbed away two tears, rubbed his boy's promising young head hard, nodded once to the silent family beyond, and mounted his horse. He looked once more on his family, nodded, did not even bother with a forced smile, and rode away leading his packhorse, northward toward California.

Henry had been told by someone who had met someone who had sworn they heard that Duggins and his gang were headed that way. Henry had nothing more to go on, but it was enough. It would have to be.

Chapter 16

"Is dinner prepared, my dear?" Clewt fingered the fresh gash on his face, a smile betraying the cold glint of anger in his eyes.

From across the kitchen, Sue Ellen returned the look of hatred from the chair in which she was lashed. Much as she had been the night before—wrists and ankles securely lashed, a stout length of torn sacking wrapped tight around her face, wedged in her open mouth so that any sound more intelligible than a growling howl she might make would be squelched. It worked. But it didn't keep her from glowering.

"Really, my dear, is this the way it's going to be? I treat you well. Then you lash out and hurt me? I don't think I can take much more of that. So, until you tell me what I need to hear—and you know exactly what that is—I have no choice but to keep you trussed up like a prize holiday bird. Is that clear?"

Sue Ellen stopped struggling, and she looked at Clewt with what he took to be her attempt at genuine confusion. This was becoming ridiculous. He sighed a genuine long sigh. "Woman, look, ask any of those dolts out there," he gestured toward the front of the house and the porch beyond where his men lazed. "They will tell you that I have a reputation as a man who does not suffer fools gladly. I would much rather shoot them. As it happens, I am inclined to shoot you just as easily as I would a man. And given how shabbily I have been treated by women in my life, perhaps I am inclined to shoot you down even more so."

He watched Sue Ellen's face for any sign of reaction. "Do you understand me? And just because you have information I need does not mean that you are the only person with that information. Or that I will never find out the information on my own. For I will. What it does mean is that if you do not tell me where it is located, I will kill you."

He said it so conversationally that Sue Ellen wasn't sure she heard him correctly.

"Oh, yes, my dear. Do not think I will put up with any more of this." He grazed the back of his fingertips along his tender cheek and shook his head. "It will not happen." He saw the alarm on her face then. And he liked it. "Good, you look sufficiently worried. I'll leave you to your thoughts. And when I come back in . . ." He pulled out her husband's pocket watch, flicked open the cover, and looked at it. "In three hours, you will tell me what I want to know."

Clewt gingerly closed the pocket watch and slipped it back into his pocket. Then he lifted free his sidearm, checked the cylinder slowly, rolling it along his arm and eyeing along the barrel. "Or I will send you away, to the same place I sent your husband. Is that understood?"

He looked at her as if in sympathy, head cocked to the side, mouth pulled down at the corners in a frown. "I see by the shock in your eyes that it is. But I still need you to tell me that you understand what I have told you. Wouldn't want there to be any question down the road. So, do you understand what I have asked? A simple head nod will do, my dear."

He watched as Sue Ellen nodded, though it appeared she still had to uphold the pretense of appearing confused by his request. No matter, she would soon comply. Or he would make certain she never again threw another china cup, never again pleased a man in the way only a woman can, never again enjoyed a sunset or sunrise, or whatever it was that such refined women took pleasure from.

Clewt turned from her and left the room, gently closing the door behind him. He ventured out onto the porch and beckoned to his men, all there less one—Paco, the Mexican. "First things first. Rufus, I want you to go fetch Paco. Drag his sorry hide to that last latrine off yonder behind the cook shed."

"Then what, boss?" said the dim Southern man.

Clewt sighed again. "Do I have to tell you when to breathe and how much, Rufus? You walk around to the back, lift that low, wide doorway. There will be a pit back under there where all the . . . ah, worked-over food goes. Yes?"

The men all laughed, though nervously, Clewt was pleased to note, and Rufus's face colored a deep crimson. "Sure."

"Good. Now when you have that door lifted, you give ol' Paco a kick and push him in there. Okay?"

"But, boss, that's . . ."

"Yes, Rufus? It's what?"

The tall Southerner looked at Clewt, then at the other boys. "Nothing. It's nothing. I'll do it."

"Good." Clewt turned to the other men, but Rufus continued to stand there with them. Clewt arched an eyebrow. "Well? Get to it."

"Yes, sir."

More snickers from the others trailed the ungainly Southerner as he walked toward the front gate. He stopped, hitched up his pants, and changed his direction toward the horse barn. More laughter reddened his face again. He didn't look over at them, but Clewt knew the man was in a fluster, and not a little bothered by the request. Good, keep them all guessing and keep them worried that they might be treated that way next. He didn't want any of them thinking they were special or would be treated any way but poorly by the boss.

"The rest of you, I'll give you ten minutes to saddle up, load every weapon you have—including the ones you've stolen from Winstead's collection. Don't think I haven't noticed everything you've laid hands on. Just make sure they're loaded, sharpened, and ready for use. Then meet back here. Ten minutes. Now . . . go!" He clapped his hands and shooed them away as if they were troublesome children. All but Paddy skedaddled.

As Clewt watched them hustle toward the barn, shooting him nervous backward glances, he half wished he was saddling up and going with them. But he had more important matters to attend to.

"Say, boss?"

Paddy, the Irishman, walked over to where Clewt stood on the long low porch of the ranch house, enjoying one of his dang dog-turd smokes. They looked just like something a sick coyote would leave behind and smelled twice as bad. But the boss laid into them as if they were going out of style.

"What can I do for you, Paddy?"

The boss seemed in a slow, jovial mood. Paddy hoped it lasted long enough for him to get out what he had to say. "This little run you're sending us on."

"Yeah? I expect you see why it needs to be done."

"Sure, sure, the man's a snooper and needs to be taught one of our famous lessons, right?" He smiled, but the boss's smile drooped. I'm losing him, thought Paddy.

"What are you getting at, Paddy?"

Out came the smoke, down came the boss's lizardlike eyelids. "I've been with you the longest of all the current crop of fools, right?"

"Tell me something I'm not sure of, Paddy."

He smiled, but again, the Irishman received little else but the cold-eyed stare. But he knew he had to plow on through, get said what he needed to, then ride on out and . . . nothing would have changed, he knew. But at least he would get it off his chest. At least the boss would know where Paddy stood, that he refused to be played for a fool.

"So that means I should be in on a . . . a good haul, eh?"

"Yeah, Paddy. But I'm confused. We've been over this. So why bring this up now?" Clewt sighed and tossed the smoldering nub of cigar to the porch floor. He stamped it with a boot toe. "Look, you have work to do, right? And so do I. It's your job to deal with that rawhider who keeps on showing up, killing my men, and making me angry—and slowing us down from getting rich. And while you're up to that, it's my job to find out from Mrs. Winstead just where the treasure is. I expect, given the modest, though not all that bad, condition of the place here, that Alton Winstead must have quite a bit left of that fortune. A heck of a lot of it, in fact."

Clewt smiled and clapped Paddy on the shoulder, gave it a shake in a friendly manner. "Look, Paddy, we're in this together." He leaned forward, narrowed his eyes, and looked right then left. "It's me and you. Okay? That's the way it always has been, that's the way it always will be. Why in the heck do you think we've each lasted this long?"

Paddy shrugged, not taking his eyes from the gang's leader.

Clewt backed up, extended his arms wide. "Because we're a team, man! Those other fools are just that. Fools. I'm not afraid to say it. Neither of us would be where we are today if it weren't for the other. And I hope, if you're the one to find the treasure, that you'll remember old Clewt. And likewise, if I happen to be the lucky one, then you can be certain I'll hold off counting it up until you show your homely face, eh, Paddy?"

Paddy stared at Clewt, finally forced a smile, knowing that what the man just said to him was nothing he hadn't heard the likes of before. The man was notorious for telling people just what they wanted to hear, then doing whatever he needed to do to make off with whatever it was that happened to be at stake, be it a woman or a fortune or a horse or a bottle of snake oil to make the night pass quicker.

"Okay, then, boss. I'll make sure the boys do what needs doin'; then we'll be back and we can help you find what it is we all came here for."

Smiles had all passed, and the two men, old friends, of a sort, eyed each other for a long moment, each understanding the other's rough intentions and not daring to admit it, maybe not wanting to. Paddy broke, finally turned toward the barn to saddle up his Appaloosa. "Okay, then, we'll be back . . . boss." He nodded once in a curt manner and went to catch up with the boys.

Paddy cursed himself silently, for he hadn't done what he had intended, which was to make certain somehow that the boss wouldn't kill her and leave him with nothing more than a handful of dead people and a tired horse.

As Clewt watched Paddy head off to the barn, he shook his head and spoke to himself in a low voice. "Ain't no way you're going anywhere but in the outhouse. Maybe join Paco down there, rooting for treasure." His husky laugh bookended the visit that had just happened between two old acquaintances.

He sat down in the chair he had begun to favor, a fancy rocker that he guessed, from its size and thicker spindles, was the one of the two rockers on the porch that Alton Winstead had used. It made him feel good to be able to take advantage of every little thing that vile demon had left behind. A smile crept onto his rough face. Once he had the last bit of information he needed—the location of the rest of the treasure—

then and only then would he allow himself to savor the very last thing of any worth that Alton had left behind. That thing was in the house behind him, struggling in her chair and wondering, he just bet, how she was going to escape.

Clewt laughed as he watched Rufus ride his horse out to the gate, tie it, then struggle with Paco's dead body. He lifted it, got the corpse's head slapped against the saddle; then the horse fidgeted. The body pitched forward, landed with a thud that Clewt heard even from a distance. Then big gangly Rufus lost his footing and fell forward onto poor dead Paco.

"Oh, you dang fool boy," said Clewt, snickering into his hand.

Rufus offered up a strangled cry like a young girl might make on being offered a box full of snakes. He tried twice more, and on his third attempt managed to drape the dead man over the saddle. He clamped a long arm over the canvas-wrapped body while he cursed at the horse and finally got the reins untied.

It was a long time before he made his way back to within shouting distance. Clewt couldn't resist. "You know, you could have just dragged him—I daresay Paco wouldn't have minded at all. Especially not where he's headed."

As he trudged by, Rufus, red-faced from his exertions, nodded but didn't look up. "Yes, boss."

"Oh, Rufus?"

The tall man stopped, swung his long face toward Clewt. "Yeah, boss?"

"When you've finished with Paco, stick around. Don't go with the other men. I have need for you here. The other boys are already saddled and headed out—loaded for bear."

"Bear, boss?"

"In a manner of speaking, Rufus. They all are going on a hunting trip." Clewt leaned back and dug a cigarillo out of his vest pocket. He giggled as he scratched a match to life and lit the little black cigar. I have no real reason to be so blamed happy, he thought. But I can't help it. That unexpected and very annoying Ty Farraday will soon be got rid of, the woman of the house will come to her senses and see that I will not be bested, no matter the person, no matter the weather, no matter a single thing.

And when I get what I came after, I will take care of the rest of these fools, maybe keep one along for good measure. The very man I cannot let the others think I am making too much of a pet out of. Keep him from whining or warping just yet.

Chapter 17

Stub carried Ty into the yard of the Rocking T at a hard gallop, lather worked up on the Morgan's gleaming hide, the pack pony keeping up behind, its own body covered in sweat. Ty's hat, pulled down low, shielded the rancher's tight, grim face.

Uncle Hob peg-legged out of the barn, a pail half filled with oats in one hand, and a three-tine hay fork in the other. Ty was pleased to see the man wore his old service revolver strapped high on his left side, just the right height for his drawing arm.

"What's this all about? You fixing to ride that fine Morgan to an early grave, boy?"

Ty rode over to Hob and dismounted. "I don't think we have much time, Uncle Hob."

"You stirred up a hornet's nest, boy, didn't you. . . ? Heh-heh. Couldn't have taught you better if'n you were my own."

As he led Stub to the corral rail and began stripping off the saddle, Ty said, "Yes, I do believe I stirred up a nest, all right. And what's worse, I saw no sign of Sue Ellen. I have to go back, but judging from their reaction to my dumping off that dead man at the gate to the Double Cross, I'd say they're not going to welcome me in through the front door."

"I'd say you're right about that, boy. But what's the hurry?"

Ty stopped uncinching the saddle for the moment and looked over the horse's back at Hob. "I hope I'm wrong, but my hunch is they're going to ride this way, looking for me. If we thought last night was a shooting party, I think we're in for a real corker. I hope I'm wrong."

As he expected, he saw not fear and shock on the old man's lined face, but a spreading grim smile and gritted teeth. And a glint in his eyes that he'd not seen on Hob in a long, long time.

"Oh, I hope so, too, boy. But hope never got anybody nowhere. Work and planning's the only things that pay off in life. Now tell me, boy. How many are there and how ruthless do they seem?" Hob rubbed his hands together as if he were kindling flame between his horned old palms.

Despite the possible dire situation, Ty couldn't help but chuckle at the old lawman. He was genuinely excited at the prospect of trading shots with that foul pack of gunhounds.

"Near as I can tell there are six left, plus their obvious ringleader, fella goes by the name of Clewt Duggins."

Hob's smile slid like fat off a tipped griddle. "You . . . you sure about that name, are you?"

"Yeah, why?" Now he had Ty's attention.

"Well," Hob's bony old Adam's apple bobbed as he swallowed, "if'n that's the case, we're going to need all the guns we can lay hands on. Plus a whole lot of luck."

Ty finished tugging the saddle of Stub's back. "Hob, just out with it, will you? You know of this Clewt fella? You sure it's the same hombre?"

"I guess it must be. Who else would go by that name? No, has to be him. Describe him to me."

"Well, he's about my height, dark hair he keeps combed back, dresses like he wishes he was a dandy, but he doesn't quite have the manners for it. There's a long scar down his left cheek, but both his cheeks are pocked anyway, probably from childhood, I'd guess. Oh, and he's got a wooden leg!" Ty smiled and nodded. "But he's got you beat, Uncle Hob."

"How's that, you insolent boy?"

"His tree's full length." Ty winked and lugged the saddle to the barn, shouting over his shoulder. "Walk with me, tell me what you know about this Duggins fella."

"Oh, he's a snake in the grass. Lower than one, in fact. If he is the man I recall, and I'd guess he is, then we best take care. Murderous snake, he is. Last I heard tell, he was in a Mexican jail for all manner of thievery. Why they didn't do us all a favor and kill him while they had the chance, I'll never know. I'll tell you more later. Right now, I'm off to the house to get out everything we have that shoots."

Within half an hour, the two men raced through the little cluster of buildings. With help from a well-rested pack pony, annoyed, Hob told him, as soon as its pasture mate was hauled off for the day by Ty, the rancher was able to form a barrier of sorts with their two wagons, one broke-down old buggy that Ty had intended to repair for Hob for years but never seemed to get around to. All the while he worked arranging the wagons and other props he felt might be of a size usable to hide behind, Ty ruminated on what he might do to stem the tide of blood sure to flow before long.

He didn't have proof that Clewt and his little armed mob were going to pay them a visit; it was more of a feeling. But it was feeling enough, bolstered by Hob's curious reaction, that he felt justified in taking these precautions. And if the expected did not come to pass, if the gunmen failed to show, all the better. He'd have been out only the time and labor he'd expended in setting up these bulwarks.

"You about done out there?" Hob shouted from the porch. "I got biscuits and beans on. Might as well eat now; there sure as shootin' won't be time for a bite later on. Come and get it whilst you can, boy!"

As if in response, Ty's gut growled like a two-week-old bear cub under a berry-laden branch just out of reach. "Okay, pony," he said, turning the beast back into the corral. He wanted all the horses in the corral just in case the expected raiders put torch to the buildings. He could release the animals a whole lot easier from the old corral than from stalls in a burning barn.

Then with a last glance at the long, darkening hills to the north, he headed to the house for a quick meal with Uncle Hob. He prayed it wasn't their last together.

In between bites of their meal that each wished they could have lingered longer over, the two men worked out a rough plan of action. Hob would stay put and hold forth from the front of the house, using the three windows facing the yard. He could unbar the others as need required, with the house windows barred and blocked from the inside and the back kitchen door dead-bolted, blocked, and barred.

It was decided without words that since he was older, slowed by his obvious infirmity, and less than able to cat-foot about the place, he'd be the draw, the one the attackers might think was the primary target.

The younger, spryer rancher would be the wild card. It was agreed that he'd range about the place, roving from spot to spot, hopefully getting the drop on the suspected intruders.

"I figure," said Ty, sopping up the last of his bean juice, "that I can get at them before they make it down here to the ranch. Trick is, I don't want to be the first one to shoot."

He washed down the bite with piping hot coffee.

"Boy, you'd best revisit that thought, because you know what's going to happen. Soon as they find one of us, they're going to throw a lead party. Ain't nothin' in their minds about the good or bad of shooting first. The real trick is to be the one to shoot best."

"Yep, I know that. But I do not know just yet how I'm

going to avoid shooting first. I might not have a choice, after all. And if I don't get out there, I'll never know." He stood, wiping his mouth again on the napkin, then folded it and set it back down at his place. He hated that every little action seemed to carry with it a sense of finality, as if foretelling their failure. For all he knew, their efforts would gain him nothing more than an overturned ranch and a nerved-up old man ready to shoot at something—anything, in fact.

But what if he was right? What if those men were already on their way? Now that was something he could understand and hopefully prepare for.

Hob's voice, bold and filled with conviction, cracked the tense quiet of the room. "I know why we can't get the law in here, nor the townies neither. But it don't mean I don't wanna have someone here, sort of like witnesses. 'Cause if there is killing and it's done by us, just like the Mexican, well, you know what I'm driving at."

"Yeah, yeah, I do, Hob. Someone's got to pay. It's simple, really. But that's what we're stuck with. I can't risk bringing anyone from town out here, least of all the law. They all loved Winstead like he was Father Christmas and a generous banker all rolled into one."

Hob nodded. "It's because he spent money, lots of money, in the town. And he wasn't shy about spreading his wealth around."

"As it is, we're operating on borrowed time," said Ty. "Someone's bound to come out to the Double Cross soon and find that gang of squatters instead of Alton."

"How would that be a bad thing?" Hob's eyes were wide, as if the notion had just occurred to him.

"I thought originally that it might be helpful, and it still might be, but there's something more going on there, something I need to figure out. And I'd bet the farm that if a bunch of those well-meaning but foolish townsfolk wandered on in there, bad things could happen. You know the sort of men we're dealing with."

"But what bothers me," said Hob, "is how a smart girl like Sue Ellen got herself so turned around by him. I never would have thought—"

"Can we just let that ghost lie, Uncle Hob? At least for the rest of the day. We have a big enough challenge facing us in the next few hours."

"You're right, boy. 'Bout time I get them other shotgun shells from the stable, then see to barricading that back door. I might even bring in the last of the smoked shanks we got in the root cellar. Never can tell when a man'll get peckish."

The remark was humorous because for as long as Ty could remember, Hob hadn't ever finished a full meal. The man was all stringy muscle and bone, always had been, always would be. "Why don't you let me get those shells from the stable? You tend to the back door. I have to get a few things from the barn anyway."

With that the men nodded at each other, left the kitchen for their respective tasks. On the way to the barn, Ty felt a prickling in his neck, as if he were being watched. He looked up toward the northern hills and just as he did so, in the gray, overcast early-afternoon light, a rider emerged on the ridge top. Then another, and another.

So, they were already closer than he expected. And judging from a quick flash, they'd glassed him and maybe knew that he'd seen them. What he was unsure of was whether they were aware of Hob yet. Could be the second man from last night had heard Ty yelling to Hob. Or maybe he'd seen him hobbling from the house.

Ty fought down the urge to dash back to the house. He had to keep calm, pretend as if nothing was out of the ordinary.

He'd go to the stable, fetch the two boxes of shells, then calmly walk back to the house, make sure Hob was set and ready. Ready as he'd ever be.

By that time, the attackers should be down into the thickest part of the ponderosa-covered slopes. The trees should obstruct their views enough to allow him to skedaddle onto Stub and still give him enough time to foul their attempts. Somehow. At least he had an edge over them in that he knew the terrain. It would almost be better if it were nighttime. But beggars can't be choosers, he told himself as he snatched down the shells and walked as fast as he dared back to the house.

Just then he saw Hob emerge onto the porch. Ty kept his arms down but said, "Stay inside, Hob. Get back in there. We have company already and I don't want them to see you— might be you'll be a surprise to them yet."

"Oh, I'll surprise 'em all right, boy," he said, chuckling and clunking back into the kitchen.

Chapter 18

"Paddy, you rode with the boss back in the Chihuahua days, right?" The man speaking held a sleeve to the side of his long nose and sprayed a trail of snot, just missing his own leg. He rasped the sleeve under his red nostrils and coughed. None of the men wanted to get close to him. The man was forever sick with some sort of dripping-nose affliction that looked foul and sounded worse. They called him "Barn Cat" to his face because farm felines frequently suffered from such snot-faced symptoms.

Paddy held his course at the point of the small group of riders, elbows of his ratty frock coat wagging with his mount's jouncing gait through the winding trail south. He didn't reply, since Barn Cat and everyone else in the gang knew full well that, in fact, Paddy O'Donnell was the only one of the current gang to have been with the boss back in Chihuahua.

"So what I am wondering is . . ." Barn Cat coughed again, sent a gob of phlegm groundward. "Why ain't you his right-hand man? You know what I'm saying to you?" When he got no response, he kept on, working to rephrase the question. "I mean, don't he confide in you? Must be he knows where this so-called treasure is, right?"

Finally, Paddy spoke. "What makes you think I don't? In fact, what makes you think at all?"

"Hey now," said Barn Cat. "Ain't no call to get all uppity on me. I am just trying to pass the time and get a few things straight in my own head afore we go in there delivering our deadly beans, you know?"

Not receiving anything more than a glimpse of the side of Paddy's face, jaw muscles bunching, Barn Cat dropped back, shaking his head and trying to catch the eye of any of the other men with whom he might commiserate. But no one wanted to talk with him, especially not about Paddy, who was riding right there in front of them.

Just because Barn Cat was dumb enough to not be afraid of the Irishman, especially when Paddy wasn't in his cups, didn't mean the rest of them weren't. They'd heard stories, seen a few light episodes of his brutality—the purpled eyes of a barman who served him warm beer, the welts on the face and neck of a fidgety horse.

But Barn Cat was a different breed altogether—he was dumb like a fox. As one of the newer recruits to the gang, he seemed to the other men initially as if he were too stupid to ride with them. Always asking obvious questions, forever annoying them with his various ailments. But they realized that he was asking questions, pushing the boss and Paddy, and to a lesser extent, the other men, in ways that resulted not a few times in fistfights.

And when it came time for Barn Cat to defend himself, they saw just what a scrapper Barn Cat was, especially with close-in fighting. And when the scraps finished, which he usually lost, he always smiled as if he had won anyway. He was an odd one, no doubt. But they all paid him careful attention lest they end up a victim of his, somehow.

The men rode along in silence, brooding on the fight soon to come. Then Barn Cat's voice piped up again. "Hey, Paddy?" He waited for an answer.

Eventually the Irishman sighed and said, "Yeah?"

"Why ain't we just going to burn this Farraday fella's place to the ground? That'd be a whole lot easier than goin' in there and wasting a lot of bullets, putting our lives at risk."

"Like you and that foolish Mexican did last night?"

Barn Cat hung his head. "Aww, look, Paddy, Paco and me, we didn't mean nothing by that. But truth be told, Paco and me thought we was going to pull an easy one. Make the boss happy. Maybe impress him."

Paddy snorted. "Yeah, that worked well, didn't it? You got your partner killed and your future in the gang ain't looking too good, I'm here to tell you."

Barn Cat continued his long-face, hangdog look, slumping in the saddle, his shoulders sagging as if weighted by sacks of rocks. "Aww, don't say that, Paddy. I done my best to get him to see the light, to just do what the boss wanted, which was just to follow the man, see where he holes up. I for one did not want to tangle with him."

"And yet you did. Forget about it now. The only thing you can do to redeem yourself in the eyes of the boss is to make sure we do just what he wants today. We have to make sure the man who shot Paco dies himself today. You got that?"

"Yeah, yeah, Paddy. I do. But, Paddy?"

The Irishman sighed. "What now?"

"Why ain't we burning him out?"

"Is everyone in your family born stupid or do you all have to work at it?" Paddy shook his head. "I'll say this once, loud enough for you all to hear me: We'll not be burning the man out. Not yet, anyway. We're just going to go in there, kill him with knives. And if that doesn't work, then we'll shoot him. No burning because the boss doesn't want to attract anyone from that little pimple of a town, Ripley Flats, back a few miles from here. Or from any other neighboring spread.

"And why, you might well ask me, would that be a bad thing? Fine, I'll tell you. Because the boss says we're very close to finding the treasure. And the last thing we need is to attract notice of the local folks, especially the law. That's why he's so steamed about Barn Cat and Paco riding in there on their own. They left him alive. Now that gave him the chance to go to town. But he didn't. Not yet anyway. So we have to drop him in his tracks. Else he really will bring attention to us and then we might as well give up ever becoming rich men. You hear me now?"

The men nodded, offered sharp answers of "Yeah, we hear you." They all had visions of the enormity of the treasure cache. And they all wanted their share.

Chapter 19

Henry Atwood knew it had been fifteen days since he left his wife and son back in Dane Creek. But try as he might, he could not figure out what day of the week it was. He could have sworn he had left on a Tuesday, so that would mean this day should be a Wednesday. But that did not feel right to him. Sweet Maria had never hesitated to tell him what day it was should he ask. Her week revolved around attending Mass on Wednesday evenings and again on Sunday mornings.

Eventually she had worn him down and he had begun attending Mass with her. But he drew the line at twice weekly. Sundays would be just fine. He recalled as a boy going to big, daylong prayer meetings with his family far to the northeast, somewhere on the great grassy sea of the prairie.

It was so long ago he had no notion of what state or territory it might have been. Nor could he remember what particular brand of religion they had been. Just that no one smiled very much, and not just at church, but anytime. Nor had they worn particularly festive colors—black dresses and shawls, even in the high blazing heat of the summer. Not like the Mexicans.

Those people knew how to live with heat, to celebrate it with their clothing and their smiles and the colors they wore. Even their food was so much happier-seeming, filled with spices, flavors, and colors that he rarely saw on the tables of the people from which he himself descended. They were dour, thick-faced, bearded men and squat, scowling women in drab clothes muttering about the vileness of nature and cursing their lots in life, praising the old country, never taking time to enjoy themselves. Not like the Mexicans. . . .

Finally, Henry sighed at the folly of spending so much time thinking of such things. He had to concentrate on the job facing him. Had to stop thinking of his wife and son. Had to become the lawman he wished he could have left behind. If he didn't, he knew he was all but pulling the trigger on his own death.

What he had in mind would require all his concentration, all the abilities he had ever learned about defending himself, about protecting other lives, about taking a man's life. If he didn't, Henry knew he would not return home to his family. And a man such as himself, older and all but spent, surely owed it to them and to himself to not fritter away this last chance he would ever have at a life of happiness.

Clewt Duggins. That was the name of the man for whom he risked all. And what's more, if the vermin didn't use that name, Henry would recognize the beast anywhere. That limp, that demeaning way of talking, the constant haze of cigar smoke. Henry had no firsthand knowledge of how Duggins came to lose his leg, but he assumed it had been in the war. Hadn't all men, from young to old, somehow been affected by the terrible, long war?

Henry certainly had, nearly lost his life—his left hand went up to gingerly touch, as if to reassure himself they were still there, the poorly healed knobs of scar tissue that were his daily reminders of the terrors of war. He had been convinced he was going to die right there on the battlefield. But then he had been trodden on by two medics stumbling under the weight of a pair of bodies on one stretcher. Henry recalled seeing the canvas, ragged and filthy with the churned guck of the battlefield, and dripping blood as steadily as a leaking bucket wells out its cargo.

They stepped on his hip and wrist. He felt a thumb snap and it was the best thing that could have happened to him, because the pain of the thumb breaking forced a strangled sob from him. Had it not been for those men thinking he was beyond dead, merely one more battlefield corpse that wouldn't mind them taking the direct route to the hospital tent, he would have sunk deeper into death. He never would have known when his shredded guts had ebbed the last of him into the mud or death's clammy embrace had begun.

But they had pulled from him, inadvertently, a howl of agony, and it was enough to make them stop that day. They bent to him, muttered something, and weak as he was, he figured they would rob him, steal his teeth, sell his hair, take his clothes, his few personal things from his pockets. But he had been wrong.

The men checked the two bodies they carried on the bloody stretcher, dumped off the top one, just then realizing he was dead. Henry still remembered the sound as the man hit the ground and other bodies, a squelching, final-sounding slap. Then they lifted him none too gingerly by his armpits and legs and dumped him atop the other man, then continued on their way. The pain from his various wounds was so intense he hoped he'd die. If he didn't, he hoped that at least he'd pass out. That didn't happen either.

That had been so long ago, though every time he ventured northward, as he was now doing, the rheumatics that deviled those wounded spots—his scar-knobbed side and his busted fingers—ached all over, as if he had stones in his boots and sores in his teeth.

Henry soldiered on, alternately riding or sliding stiffly down from the saddle and walking slowly alongside his dog-tired horses, the primary saddle horse and the packhorse, which also served as a mount, though less reliable on the trail. She was prone to skittering at unexpected rock sounds, shadows, wavering jags of branches. Still, she was a decent beast, too. And he was grateful for the two of them as company.

He talked and talked in a low near-mumble. He knew that in the sun, and with water an unreliable necessity, he should keep his mouth shut and save his breath, but he was lonely. And so he walked and talked, or rode and talked. It helped pass the time. He also told himself it would help him plan what he was going to do once he caught up to Clewt Duggins and his gang.

He told himself that, but really it was just another way of avoiding thinking about what he faced. Since the war he'd worked hard to live forcefully, to make things happen in life, to bend as much of what surrounded him at any given time to his own will. Sometimes he was shocked to find it actually worked. He'd wanted the job as lawman in a town somewhere warm and dry, and he had secured that job. He had wanted to remain a single man, to enjoy the small, slight benefits of being one. And that too, at least for a time, had worked.

Henry had run his town with a gentle hand, firm but kind. And that also had worked. For a time. At least until the rich ore was struck and the cattle drives became more frequent. And then everything changed. Everything. The only good and constant thing in his life was sweet Maria, then the boy, named Henry after himself, but with a middle family name from his mother's people—Joaquin—and lastly, his own family name of Atwood.

Henry mused on his boy, on the strong, fine man he would one day become, on the fact that he might never see him reach his next birthday, seven months away yet. But he hoped someday the boy would understand just why it was his father had had to do this, to go on this trek for revenge. And so it was while in the midst of gnawing that oft-chewed bone that Henry felt a sting like a bee punch into his shoulder.

It didn't occur to him until he was flat on the hardpan earth, staring up at the dancing hooves of his horses, that maybe he'd been shot. Because he was quite sure there was no bee on earth that could knock him from a saddle.

Henry groped along the wounded shoulder until he felt wetness, pulled away the fingers and saw the tips had reddened. He scrunched his eyes shut tight, shook his head, and bellowed a wordless cry, pure anger like steam venting up from his parched throat. His voice cracked and trembled and pinched out and the horses danced more than ever, then trotted off out of sight.

Mustn't let them get away. He worked to raise his head, managed to get his left elbow underneath him, propping up his torso. The right shoulder stung and throbbed something fierce now. His hat had tumbled off somewhere. He'd worry about that later.

Henry squinted ahead, but what direction was that? Where was the sun? He looked up briefly, trying to locate it in the high, bright blue above, and the world spun as if he were riding a giant roulette wheel. That left elbow gave out and his head slammed against rock. It didn't rob him of consciousness, but he felt as though it might any second.

Presently he heard what sounded like far-off hoofbeats drawing closer. His mount and packhorse coming back?

"Hey, hey, what'd I tell you? That ain't him!"

"Naw, gotta be. I am a sure shot, I tell you."

"Ain't nobody debating your shooting abilities, Mort. But you shot the wrong man."

More hoofbeats drew closer; then Henry heard the voices resume.

"Oh, I have shot the wrong man."

"That's what I told you."

Henry tried to speak, but no words came. He licked his lips, ridged and chapped, tried again. "You . . . you help me up."

He heard boots slam down to earth, heard spurs chink, one man, then a second. Sweet shade and relief from the sun in his eyes. He forced them open just as a fresh slice of pain lanced from the new wound. Why would anyone shoot him? Unless somehow it was Clewt. Maybe he had heard of his intentions to track him? No, that would be impossible, only his wife knew the full story. Impossible, but . . . His wife! Panic pinched his throat, lodged there like a tiny fist. His eyes shot wide.

Leaning over him were two cowboys, youngish men with concerned looks. No, it was more than that, it was fear pulling at their faces. "Mister, I am so sorry." One of them said, "I . . . I shot you." He leaned back out of Henry's sightline, said, "Oh Lord, no. This can't be."

"Help me up." Henry struggled to get his left elbow underneath himself again, but dizziness came at him again like a sudden gust in a sandstorm, knocked him down once more.

"Look, Mort. He's going to make it. He's talking and everything. Hey, mister . . ."

Something slapped at Henry's face. He fluttered his eyes open again.

"Mister." It was the other cowboy, tapping his fingers on Henry's face.

"Who are you, mister?"

The young man's voice sounded shaky, nervous to Henry.

The other man returned, his spurs clinking fast, like tiny bells on a sleigh. The man dropped once again to his knees beside Henry, and soon he felt cool water drizzling on his mouth, his cheeks, around his face, along his neck.

"What are you doing on this range?"

"I . . . am bound northward. On the trail of . . . bad men."

"Oh Lordy, it's even worse than I thought," said the one named Mort in a low voice. "I have shot a lawman."

Henry knew, even through the veil of pain, that these men had no idea who he was, but at least they believed him to be a lawman. In a way he was. Retired, but still, he believed in the darkest corner of his heart that he was serving the law by riding to eliminate Clewt Duggins from the world.

Chapter 20

Ty slammed the two boxes of shells on the table. "Uncle Hob." He fixed the old man with a hard look. "They're here."

"Hang fire, that's all we need. I ain't half ready. Still got dirty plates on the table."

"I don't think they're coming for a social call."

"If they got burning us out in mind, I've laid in a few buckets of water, have 'em settin' about the rooms. Beyond that, I can't do much. Hope you know that, boy."

"I do. If they torch the house, get the heck out and head for the root cellar. Don't let them see you. I'll find you. Whatever you do, don't get out in the open—you can't out-run them. I'll do my best to head them off, take as many out as I can before they get here. By my count there are five headed this way. That means, with the Mexican dead, Clewt Duggins and one other aren't with them. Unless he is and left someone else in his place, watching over Sue Ellen."

The men looked at each other.

"You reckon he's up to something he didn't want his men to know about? Something with your girl?"

"She's not my girl," said Ty.

But Hob heard the worry in the man's voice.

"Get on out there, Ty. Take out as many as you can, leave the rest to me. You ride and after you've done what you can, you keep riding. Go get her. You'll never have a better chance, if'n he ain't guarded, as you say."

Ty shook his head. "No, Hob. I can't do that to you. I won't run out on you."

"You don't think not helping Sue Ellen right off wasn't running out on her? You got an obligation to that woman, boy. You best do what you can while you can. Me, don't worry about Hob. I got enough firepower here to start a war." He racked in a shell. "And that's just what I aim to do. Now git gone, boy. Clewt ain't about to wait on you, nor any man. Grab it while you can."

Ty paused a moment, and then his eyes widened. "No, Hob. That's not what I was getting at. I won't leave you here to deal with those jackals yourself!"

In two strides, Ty was back at the front door. He knew time was wasting, but he didn't have a clear idea of just what he should do. He didn't want to abandon Hob, but if there was any man capable of handling himself in a rough situation, it was Hob. Ty walked back across the room, stuck out a big meaty hand. "See you soon, Uncle Hob."

The old man leaned his sawed-off against the warm stove and grasped Ty's big hand in his own, covering it like bread on a sandwich. "This here's the perfect opportunity, don't you see? Don't waste this chance. Clewt'll never be more wide open. Makes it more of a fair fight. But keep in mind he don't fight fair. You do what you need to to make sure that girl don't get hurt. 'Cause you mark my words, he'll do whatever it takes to make sure he gets whatever it is he's after. His type always does. I'll be here taking care of things when you get back." Though his voice was firm, his eyelids quaked with emotion. He nodded. "Now git, Ty, afore I shoot you myself."

He shoved Ty's hand away and snatched up the shotgun, half turning from Ty and dragging his old flannel shirtsleeve under his running nose.

Ty paused at the door. "Recall the waterfall, Uncle Hob? I reckon it's as good a place as any to meet up. It's closer to the Double Cross than it is to here, and our camp is likely still there. So if I can't make it back here by tomorrow morning, that means I'm likely in trouble. I'll head there and hole up if I can."

Hob nodded, still didn't look at Ty. "I'll be there. Count on it."

Ty headed back across the ranch yard, hoping a rendezvous wouldn't be necessary. Within minutes he had saddled Stub. The horse was less rested than he would have liked, but Ty wanted the sure-footed horse under him for this tricky bit of riding. The Morgan was nearly tireless, and that was the mount he needed for the coming fight.

Trails cut by years of herding young stock west, then northward, curved around the nexus of the Rocking T's home base, laid out in widening arcs and spiderwebbing off to the various holding grounds and pastures used by Ty and his seasonal help.

He reasoned that they wouldn't split up until just before cresting the last ridge overlooking his place. Then they'd probably range right and left. He doubted any of them would take the direct route down the middle, on the lane that led to his buildings. If one did, well, he'd just have to figure out a way to deal with him later.

First things first. He had no time to devise much more of a plan than to ambush them somehow before they did the same. He might not be able to get them all, but he'd do what he could before he headed to the Double Cross. He urged Stub into a lope, and crouched low in the saddle. The powerful horse seemed to know what was coming and dug in hard, sending scree spinning down the craggy slope dotted with sparse pines. If he could just make it to the top, there was a rocky knob that wouldn't be seen by the invaders until they were close by.

If they continued to ride where he expected they would, they could easily pass just under the rock. And after two more twists in the rough trail, he spied the natural hoodoo, jutting high over the immediate surrounding landscape, There was a spot at its base that provided an ideal overlook onto the trail. He hoped he had enough time to get settled there, hunkered low and poised with his rifle aimed.

Just below the last curve up to the spot he'd just been thinking of, Ty slowed Stub, found a spot where the horse would be relatively concealed from view from below. He slipped from the saddle, paused, heard nothing . . . yet. He cinched the reins around the base of a wind-stripped, petrified old tree trunk, still firmly rooted into the rock from which it had grown. He stuffed extra shells into his pockets, left the rest in his saddlebag, and low-walked up the rocky grade.

Halfway up, his right boot slipped on loose rock chips, sending a short rain of gravel down the sheer forty-foot rock face atop which he would soon be perched. He reached the top with the spot looking much as he recalled it when he'd first ventured up there three, maybe four seasons before. He couldn't recall. He'd long been intrigued by the strange rock formation surmounting the rocky knob and finally one day, after moving young stock from one small range to another, he decided to take a quirly break. But when he'd looked up as he built the smoke, he found himself sitting on his horse at the very base of the knob.

Since he had had no pressing work requirements for a few hours—one of the many advantages of being his own boss—Ty had decided to skip the quirly and make the climb. It had been a slippery slope at times, but well worth it once he gained the top.

As he gazed, he had taken in much of the surrounding landscape that he'd not seen from anywhere near that spot. A

series of three ripple ridges to the northeast obscured the
Double Cross buildings from sight, but that hadn't stopped
him sitting there long after he'd gotten his wind back, staring
off in the distance toward just where he knew those buildings
sat, tended by the woman he should have married. The thought
dug at him from the inside out, like a boring worm with a heck
of a set of teeth.

In the few years that had passed since then, Ty visited the
site occasionally, as the views were unmatched. And yet, as
he was counting on, anyone sitting where he was would not
be seen by riders following the narrowing trails that wound
through the rocky cleft. With his rifle and two pistols at the
ready, he vowed with a renewed determination to deal with
as many of these men as he could right away, then head
straight to the Double Cross.

Ty held no illusions about how he'd have to treat these
men. They needed killing, if only because they had already
killed and now were hell-bent on killing him and Hob. Despite that, the idea of shooting a fellow, no matter the vermin
he might have become, didn't sit well with Ty. He'd never
ambushed a lone man before. But five of them, now that was
an even taller order.

Ty wished for an alternate way out of the situation. Some
way to scare them badly enough that they bolted from the
valley for good. But he knew that was the basest form of
wishful thinking.

And then he heard it, the faint, irregular sound of hooves
striking rock, stepping steadily, ridden by men who sounded
as if they had more confidence than they ought to. Ty eased
back the hammer on the rifle. A set of fresh shells sat in a
small pile beside his propped left elbow. The sound grew
louder, the murmur of voices increasing, one of them sharper,
reedier than the others. These men still felt they had the upper hand. But he knew they would soon split up—unless they

already had, and then his one and only chance to incapacitate as many as he could was past.

The voices drifted up to him, and the closer they drew, the more distinct the sounds they made became. From the hoof-beats and the voices, Ty could tell there were but three of them. That meant the others were lagging behind, or more likely had already split off. He hadn't seen them wind around him on the western trail, so they must have taken the eastern edge, and would come up on Hob from that direction, prob-ably separating further once they got close to the buildings. Then Hob would have his hands full. But Ty knew never to underestimate the old war dog.

Ty was still too high up to hear what they were saying, but it sounded in tone at least to be nothing more than dull con-versation, as if they were on a slow ride to town to pick up supplies and not headed to a nearby ranch to kill its occu-pants. Maybe he had it all wrong. Maybe they were sent by Clewt to make a truce of some sort.

And then, just as he saw the tip of a horse's muzzle, it stopped, and he heard one of the voices, the reedy one, say, "Hold up—my horse just perked. I bet you a whole shiny dollar there's another horse nearby."

As if on cue, Ty heard Stub offer up a short whinny. Curse that horse, he thought, gritting his teeth and holding still. One of their horses whickered, but was cut short, had to be by one of the men pinching his fingers into the mount's nostrils. An old but effective trick.

He didn't dare poke his head over the edge. The men had fallen silent, but he heard the gritty grinding sound of boots placed cautiously, the flutter of men's whispers, short and clipped commands as one told the others where to head.

If they were worth their salt at all, they would have looked up at the sheer stony walls to see if there was a spot a man with ambushing on his mind might await their arrival. The thought that they might get away from him, all because of his blasted nosy horse, forced Ty to push himself, belly down, along the rock slope paralleling the trail below.

The overhanging rock shelf drooped lower, grew tighter to angle forward into. Ty lifted off his hat and set it farther back into the shelf. As he inched his head out toward the edge ever so slowly, he kept his eyes trained downward toward the trail.

Just after he heard someone whisper-bark the word, "There!" he felt a buzzing breeze close to his forehead. Too close. An eyeblink later, something *spang*ed and zoomed off the rock face behind. Ty had already whipped his head backward, gritting his teeth and not breathing. It wouldn't do to be killed, and especially not this early in the game when Hob and Sue Ellen depended on him.

He let his breath leak out slowly. They knew he was up here, but they didn't know if he was alone, didn't even know if it was him, he'd bet. He scooted backward, wishing they would at least make some sort of noise. Now that they knew someone was up here, they'd have the advantage of being able to come up on him from at least two directions. They'd probably try to keep him pinned down by firing from below, keep him occupied while one of them moved in on him from the back side of the knob.

He laid the rifle down to his left, within easy reach. He wouldn't be able to lean out enough to use it, so he pulled out his Colt Navy. If they did send a man up behind him, it would take a few minutes for him to make it up here. And unless the man was light-footed as a goat, Ty would hear him long before. That left him just enough time to see if he could do some damage from above.

He had to draw their fire somehow. Preferably without sticking his head out there again. Next best thing, he thought as he looked around and his gaze fell on his hat. He snatched it up and, holding one edge of the brim in his right hand, he nudged it close to the edge, all the while angling himself farther downslope from the edge. When he'd reached his spot, he nudged the hat outward over dead air.

Immediately the hat jittered in his hand as it took a bullet that once again zipped by his waiting head. But this bullet hadn't been aimed at his head, because they were still expecting his face to appear somewhere near the same spot on the rim.

And he was going to show them.

Just as soon as the bullet hit the rock and kept on going, Ty pulled in as far and as low as he could, then peeked, and finally thrust the serious end out over the edge.

He hoped to land a solid punch. Once more he indulged his childlike side, albeit it was far less risky than sticking his head out. Another bullet *whang*ed off a rock, but Ty barely pulled back. Instead he took his time, dipped the revolver over the edge, squinted an eye shut, sighted down where a slight cloud of gun smoke was just drifting skyward, and squeezed the trigger. A second later he heard a scream and a man's voice saying, "Gaaah! Oooooooh, my eyes! I'm blind! I'm blind. . . ."

The bullet had ricocheted off the smooth rock wall and spattered rock chips straight into the man's eyes. The stricken man lurched into sight, stumbling and screaming, his hands clutched to his face. Streams of blood welled out from between his fingers as he ran, shaking his head as if in disagreement with someone. His shouts had dwindled to a steady moaning scream.

"Shut up yer cryin'!"

The voice came from someone still hidden, and there was a lilt to the words. The Irishman who'd been lounging on the steps the day before. He had borne a look of some import among the other members of the little band of outlaws. Perhaps a second-in-charge.

The wounded man kept right on running in circles. At one point he pumped his legs faster and ran smack into the rock wall, only to bounce backward, still clutching his face, still screeching that awful, garbled, crowlike sound before struggling no-handed to his feet again to whip his head slower now, but no quieter.

"Shut up, man, I tell ya. You'll be heard clear to Ripley Flats!"

Still the man howled. Pangs of guilt nibbled at the edges of Ty's mind, slight, like twinges of hunger a working man feels an hour before dinner. The crack and rolling echo, quickly diminished, of a gunshot accompanied the blinded man's last lurch and spin. He stiffened, his legs twisting together as if his boots were held together while some unseen giant hand twisted his body in a circle. Then he dropped to the ground, his shoulders spasming even as his head bounded off the unforgiving stony ground.

Ty shouldn't have felt as shocked as he did, but he didn't want to believe that these men were as ruthless as that, brutal enough to kill their fellow bandit for squealing too loud in his agony. And yet there was the pooling of the bloody truth. From the looks of it, if there was an upside to any of it, the shot had been clean, in the back, straight through the man's heart.

All of this happened in mere seconds, but before Ty could draw back fully from the edge, he heard a slight sliding and scuffling sound close behind him. He spun, thinking of the man who he suspected would be circling around behind him, cursing himself for not paying more attention. And then there he was, one of the Mexican-looking men from the porch. The middle-height fellow carried a revolver straight out in front of him as if it were a barely held dancing snake in his fingers. The way he advanced and the half-nervous look twitching his swarthy features told Ty that here was one fellow afraid of heights. But before Ty could use that in his own behalf, he had to bring his own pistol into play.

Not as easily done as said, since it was still clutched in his hand, and that was propped back close to his side. He had no leverage to squeeze a shot, since he'd have to thumb back the hammer first. And the nervous man before him was fully cocked and advancing. And Ty realized at the same time the back of his head, perhaps also his shoulders, had to be visible from below. That Irishman could surely place a killing shot from down there.

Time to move, he told himself, and rolled hard to his right, raising the pistol at the same time, thumbing the hammer back to the deadly position even as the Irishman sent a volley of shots skyward. Too late, thought Ty, as he rolled toward the inside wall of the precipice, close to his rifle, cocked and waiting.

Another shot, this time from the nervous man, seared a trail along Ty's outstretched arm, plowing a slight furrow up his arm from the outer elbow, barely ridging the meat of the arm almost to his shoulder. It stung immediately, and his Colt toppled to the rock face as his arm jerked.

"Got you now, jackass," said the nervous man. And though he was still half smiling, his gun-hand shook uncontrollably. He glanced at it as if he were seeing a terrible dream come to life. His red-eyed gaze skittered from the shaking hand to the open-air view beyond. It seemed as if he had forgotten Ty, who took full advantage of the moment to snatch up his pistol and crank his hammer back once more.

"Don't do it, mister," Ty said to the shaking man, whose face had lost its color, as if drained somehow. That caught the man's attention, and he jerked his gaze back to Ty.

"Get up!" he hissed, his gun hand shaking less. "Get up." Still nervous, he forced the words through his teeth.

"No," said Ty. "Come and get me."

"I don't need to. I only have to shoot you now."

"And yet you haven't. Why is that?" Ty held his gun firmly on the man's torso. He didn't trust himself to aim any higher. A shot to the head would be too good for this man, but from his awkward position he might well miss. Better to wound than miss.

"I . . . I could take you to the boss myself. Skip Paddy and get more of the treasure for me. Then the boss would see I was the man did the job."

Treasure? thought Ty. What treasure? That's what this is all about? "Oh, I'm not so sure your boss cares if I'm alive, so long as you can prove to him that I'm dead, right?" Ty hoped this would confuse the fool enough that he could rise up to squeeze the trigger with accuracy.

Then the man surprised him by taking a step forward, almost as if he were being ruled by the thought of the glory he could attain by getting in the boss's good graces. In doing so, he ignored the dangers before him.

Another half step and . . . there it was, the man's curious half smile became capped by raised eyebrows. His mouth formed into an O and his gun fired even as he pitched forward, glancing down briefly to see that Ty's boots had snaked around his own, tripping him and sending him falling forward.

The pistol dropped before he did. There was no stopping him, even if Ty had wanted to. The man's momentum was too great, the edge of the rock, forty or more feet from the little canyon's unforgiving floor, came up fast to meet him, and his face drove right into the edge, bounced up high, sending blood and fragments of his rotted teeth and pulpy matter from his smashed nose outward in a time-slowed spray, clouding and raining down on the screaming man as he fell.

Ty looked over his left shoulder, saw him drop like a sack of stones. He heard a slapping sound as the man hit the rocky floor hard, sitting up; a quick snap as the man's spine broke, whipping his torso, weighted by his big greasy head, forward to slam on the rock between his legs, before it collapsed back in a bloody mess.

Silence was broken only by the soughing of a slow breeze. Ty felt it on his face, stinging in the wound grazed along his upper arm; then he heard boots on stone from down below.

"You might as well give up, Mr. Farraday!" The shout echoed down the small canyon's rock walls. "The boss man, he's surely disposed of the woman by now. That's right."

Ty could hear the smile in the man's voice. The bum was enjoying this.

"She's told him all he came here for and that makes her useless to him. Or nearly so, anyway!" A cackle of a laugh capped off the gruesome sentence. Ty knew the Irishman was trying to goad him into poking his head out of hiding, yet he sorely wanted to rush down there, sure he'd find the fiend lurking around the corner. He'd give anything to drill the devil in the forehead with one quick shot.

He closed his eyes a moment, pulled in a deep draft of air, then rolled to his left, snatching up his hat and jamming his Colt back into its holster.

His arm throbbed, but he was pleased to note it had already stopped bleeding—sure to leave nothing more than a painful scar as a reminder. He hoped so, for then it would mean he'd lived through this mess.

He heard a sharp crack, as if someone were slapping something open-palmed. This was immediately followed by the churning clatter of hooves on stone. He rolled back onto his chest and peered over the stony edge—just in time to see a man in a ratty black wool coat and a bowler hat tucked low thundering south down the narrow declivity, straight toward the ranch. Had to be the murdering Irishman.

Ty jerked his rifle before him, levered a round, thumbed

the hammer, and didn't bother aiming, just squeezed the trigger—chasing the devil a finger snap too late. He rounded a far bend that marked the end of the small canyon and opened up to the trail leading to the ranch. Ty knew he'd missed, but maybe the shot had put some bit of fear into the Irishman, though he doubted it.

By the time Ty made it back down to Stub—relieved to see the bold horse still stood where he'd tethered him—he was more determined than ever to get to the Double Cross. He hoped he wouldn't be too late. Hob was right; he had to face it alone. And he had to do it now.

Chapter 21

Meanwhile, back at the Double Cross . . . After he watched the men depart, Clewt headed back into the ranch house. A grin spread wide on his craggy features, like a slick of spilled lamp oil.

"Oh, woman! Woman?" he shouted, standing in the open doorway. He spread his arms wide and laughed, a rasping, coughing sound, the result of years of smoking cheroots down to the nub, pulling the dark thick smoke deep into his lungs, holding it there, savoring the burn, then expelling it.

It always made him feel a little like a dragon pluming smoke and flame into the sky. He recalled, now and again, his grandmama reading a story to him about a man who slew a great winged beast that flew all over the countryside, making life miserable for everyone he came across. Then a strange man had slain her, with young Clewt hiding under the bed, gnawing his own knuckles to keep from crying out at the sounds of his grandmama's pain.

The thrashing the man had given her, the almost crushing feeling of the bed pressing down on him, again and again, his grandmama's cries growing fainter all the while. Then her hand had dropped over the side of the bed, blood trailing from it, dripping before him on the wood floor of the safest place he had ever known.

Clewt remembered wanting to hold her hand as the fingers trembled their last, but he was too afraid to touch it, all the blood, the man still there. Then he saw the boots slam to the floor, and the sagging weight of the bed suddenly lifted off Clewt. The man opened the wardrobe, slammed around in the chest of drawers, tossing about grandmama's precious things. Clewt had brought his hands tight to his face, only his other senses taking in what was happening.

But then he smelled smoke, something that was not fire but a cigar. He had seen men sucking on them in the streets, in the fancy parlor where grandmama went to work. And the smoke made him think that the man must be a dragon, a dragon in boots, making life miserable for everyone, and somehow it had been their turn.

Clewt could not utter a peep. Dared not. . . . Even for hours after the big leather boots slammed out of the room, after the smell of smoke faded away, after the boots stomped down the steps, the sound of crunching gravel becoming less and less.

The thought that the man must have been a dragon gave Clewt much comfort, and he recalled always wanting to be that dragon, wanting for years as he grew up to be that great and mighty beast, spraying trouble all over the countryside, making people hurt and scream and shout and sometimes even fight back.

Sometimes they even said, "No! You shall not do this thing! I and I alone will stand up to you!" And yet every single time, Clewt and his lesser dragons, the ones who trailed behind, mewling for scraps and squabbling among themselves, always came out on top, leaving great, vast stretches of countryside a smoking wreckage behind.

Wasn't that the case with that wretched little lawman down in that tiny border town that had the silver strike? What was the name of that place? Dane Creek? Yes, he was almost sure of it. Not positive, though, because he'd been drunk much of the time they were there. And the opium! Oh, that was something to remember—too bad he couldn't recall much.

But he remembered that lawman, all right. Remembered how he came to them, the entire gang lined up there at the bar in that glitzy place with the brass cuspidors, fancy mirrors, and girls in colorful dresses. They had even had a full mariachi band. But that lawman had visited them, hat in hand, practically begging them to reconsider their evil ways, to give thought to the children of the town. The children! Ha. He had asked them to leave the town alone, to ride on out and to not bother his people.

Yes, that was right, Clewt now recalled. The man had called them "his people." What a fool. He remembered asking if the man was married. The lawman had taken his time in replying, considering, no doubt, whether to tell Clewt and the boys about his personal life. Finally the man had said yes, indeed, he was a married man. With a child.

"How," Clewt had said, "does your wife put up with your simpering?"

That brought a hearty round of laughter from the boys, sure, but also from the entire bar full of miners, women, and gamblers—his sort of people. Workers who would drink and become careless with their pokes so that before the end of the night arrived, he and the boys had seen nearly every poke, knew every person they would waylay outside. One of his men at a time following one or two stumble-down-drunk gambling miners on out the door, knocking them in the heads, slicing throats wide open if need be.

The lawman had become angry then, had turned on his heels, tugged his hat low on his head, and headed back through the batwings. Then he stopped, turned red-faced, and said, "You will regret that, sir. You will regret it." Then he'd turned and walked on out. They didn't hear a peep from him for the rest of the night. And they had a long, good laugh at his expense.

But even through all the fun, Clewt remembered that threat the lawdog had made. It hung around his neck all night, festering like the rotting carcass of a small animal. By the wee hours, he had begun to grin, and Paddy had nudged him. "What's doin', boss? We on for something? That look . . . I've seen that look, boss." But Paddy was smiling, too.

And by the time the sun's first rays touched the Sunday-morning town of Dane Creek, Clewt Duggins and his boys were long gone, struggling at first to stay in their saddles from the drink and debauchery they so prized. But after a time, they rode hard and well, laden with silver, gold dust, cash, anything of value. And those who refused to give it up—why, they did anyway. It just took more convincing. The sharp-edged sort. Of course they had to bring along a number of fresh horses as pack beasts in order to divvy the load and not tire out any beasts before their time was due.

And as the first puffy-eyed inhabitants stepped out onto the boardwalks, shielding their eyes from the day's first rays . . . they saw the poor, unfortunate dead of the town, how many Clewt could no longer remember, among them a few waifish looking creatures who may well have been children, women and men, too. Even a few old ones. And now that he thought back on it, one had been a lawman of sorts, a deputy, if he recalled correctly.

It had been a necessary rampage that the dragon had got up to. One that he relished for many days to come. That tingle that had trailed along his spine like a cold fingernail dragged upward into his hair, that had made it all worthwhile.

How long ago had that been? Months? A year past? Hmm, not that it mattered much, but he did occasionally wonder what that foul little lawdog had thought of it. Clewt hadn't had to leave any sort of note, no calling card other than the line of neatly laid out bodies in the street. Still, it would have been extra delicious to see the lawman's face that sunny Sunday morning, as the weight of realization dragged his features downward, from rage to grief to guilt, the lowest form of feeling a man could indulge in.

Clewt breathed deep, coughed at the hitch in his lungs—small price to pay for being a dragon, he thought—and smiled as he stuffed the end of a cheroot between his lips and thumb-nailed a lucifer alight. Ahhh, that first long pull of fresh smoke was still a treat. Made him feel positively impressive. And knowing he was about to become wealthy beyond his wildest dreams put a little extra spring in his step.

"Oh, woman." He peeked around the doorframe leading into the kitchen. "Clewt the Dragon's here. . . ." He blew out a thick plume of smoke that just reached her face. She jerked her head to the side but couldn't avoid the blue-gray cloud. Though her mouth was bound and gagged, she still sneezed and blinked her eyes to dispel the foul stink.

Clewt smiled and waggled his eyebrows. "And he's come to tell you"—he stepped close and looked down at her—"it's now, or it's never."

He shucked the long, gleaming blade from his belt sheath and flipped it end for end in the air. The staghorn handle landed smack in his hand with a satisfying thunking sound. He grinned and waved the blade tantalizingly, like the mesmerizing tail of a scorpion, before her pulled-back face. "I expect all this playacting over the past couple of days has left you feeling as though you just might figure a way out of this. Why, it must be a nightmare to you." He canted his head to one side and adopted what he guessed was a look of pity. Not having much experience with such things as offering pity, Clewt only guessed at the expression. "I'm here to tell you that you will never, ever escape me. You understand, woman?"

Sue Ellen squinched her eyes shut tight, and thin tears squeezed out. But the rest of her face was resolute. And when she opened her eyes she stared right back at the smiling face of the killer, the man who had killed her husband.

He reached forward and she felt the edge of the blade, cool against her cheek. Their eyes met once again, briefly; then he turned his wrist and the blade slit through the length of torn curtain binding her, gagging her. She spat out the spit-sodden, balled-up rag in her mouth, worked her tongue behind and around her teeth, stretched her neck and her mouth.

"What happens if I don't give in to your demands? If I don't answer your questions?"

"Why, then, my dear," he said, "you will be given, as they say in the old-time pirate tales, a long walk off a short plank." He leaned forward. "You will be . . . no longer necessary. In fact the only reason you're still here is because I have found you rather amusing. But my appetite for humor has just about been fulfilled. I expect I'll need to do something completely different now, if only to support myself in my dotage."

He winked at her, but she had already turned her face away.

"What is that? A smirk? What are you doing?" Clewt turned on her, pointed an accusing finger in her face.

"I . . . I don't know what you mean." She shook her head, a look that was a mix of exhaustion and defeat on her drawn features. "I just can't help you. . . ."

For what felt to her like the hundredth time, the foul killer bent low before her, his tobacco-and-boozy breath gouting into her face. She saw the oily skin of his pocked face, the dried blood from the cut her thrown cup had given him, and it felt good to her. He looked uncomfortable, unhappy, and angry. And she couldn't care less.

Up until a few moments before, she'd had no idea where Alton could have hidden away a treasure of such vast proportions as Clewt had so elaborately described. The more he spoke of the treasure, of the fact that Alton had been a conniving, sneaking man capable of running out on his friends, the more holes she found in Clewt's claims. She refused to believe all of it, at least until she could prove or disprove it for herself. First, though, she had to convince Clewt she had no idea where Alton could have hid such a treasure.

"How could I possibly know such a thing—especially if I didn't have a clue that he was the sort of man you say he was?" She had tried this argument on him a number of times, but Clewt refused to believe her.

"You are a liar," he had told her time and time again. And this last time he stood in the middle of the kitchen, running his long, nicotine-stained fingers, with their curving yellowed nails like the claws of some half man, half animal, through his oily pepper-dust hair.

Finally he sighed long and low. "I will ask you once more to tell me where the rest of his hidden gold is. Once you tell me, I will retrieve it, and if everything is to my satisfaction, I will ride on out of here, slick as you please, and other than a few . . . ah, alterations me and my boys made, why, you'd never know we were here at all. You follow me?"

And that's when it hit her, just like that. Sue Ellen was pretty sure she knew where Alton would hide a treasure if he had one to hide. It was so obvious and so simple she was surprised she hadn't thought of it before then. It also occurred to her that she might be dealing with Clewt in the wrong way. If he became convinced that she really didn't know where Alton had hidden the fortune, then he would see her as having no use to him, and that would mean only one thing to such a man. He would no doubt kill her.

She fought down the urge to turn her head away, to gasp for fresher air. His breath was so rancid. This close she couldn't help but see the blackening of his teeth. At least he wouldn't be long for this world. And neither will you, Sue Ellen, she told herself. If you don't figure out a way to convince him you might know where his precious treasure is.

"If I did know, what makes you think I'd tell you?" Sue Ellen hoped this different approach would work. But she wasn't so sure. He kept staring at her.

Finally he straightened. "Nothing I have tried has worked. I am beginning to think that you aren't lying at all to me. I am beginning to think that you really don't know a blasted thing about the gold, or for that matter, about your husband. What on earth did you two discuss for all those years of your marriage?"

He stood and rubbed his forehead viciously, then stopped as if he'd come to an important decision. "Aha, yes, yes, that's it. But I don't believe you, my dear. You are still lying, only now you're lying to save your pretty neck. Which means that you probably don't know where anything other than your own collection of pretty dresses is. Am I correct, my dear?"

Could this be a trap? Could he be trying to trip her up and get her to admit to something? It seemed unlikely. But then again, anticipating such a large fortune could make a person do strange things.

He walked quickly behind her and grasped the high-back dining room chair. When he tilted it back she let out a shriek, but he kept yanking, dragging her backward out of the house.

"Where are you taking me?"

"Oh, I think you'll recognize it once we get there."

The mysterious location turned out to be the root cellar, built into a rise off the kitchen end of the house. He fumbled with the sliding wooden dead bolt, flung the bar out of his way, then dragged her deep into the dank space—the dead smell of musty earth, spiderwebs dragging over her face, the grit from the unknown scuffing underfoot. She'd not been in the root cellar for a very long time.

"No," she said, eager to move on through this mess. "I . . . I don't want to be here. Don't want to know what all this means, what sort of foolishness you have cooked up in your own sick mind, but I can assure you, Mr. Duggins, there is nothing I can offer you that you would find of use. I gather you are angling for information about this supposed fortune my husband has buried about the place, like a secret pirate treasure."

For a brief moment, Clewt froze, his eyes reflecting a rare instance of terror, before realizing that she was lying. She and she alone had to know of its location. He'd not come all this way to be hoodwinked by a woman!

He let go of the chair, which sat at an awkward angle on the rough, uneven dirt floor. It had broken since he dragged it, clunking down the back stairs of the house toward the root cellar. He came around in front of Sue Ellen, bent at the waist, and snatched up a burlap sack that held something weighty in the bottom. She saw it in the swinging light of the oil lantern, which still squeaked on its nail from when he'd clunked it into place moments before. The something in the sack moved when he tugged and swung it.

"What's that?" she said to him, though she hated the guess her mind had formed.

He shook the sack and rattling and hissing sounds filled the small dark dirt room.

Sue Ellen shrieked and tried to back away, succeeded only in recoiling a few inches. "No! No, not snakes, oh no, no, no. . . ."

"Well, my dear, for all that fear and terror you are now exhibiting, I'm afraid there's little you can do about it. . . ." He leaned in close, giving the bag another shake. "The only thing you can do at this point to save your hide from a long, slow, drawn-out, painful-beyond-all-belief death, all alone, a death in which when you get bitten—and you will be bitten many times—is tell me where, oh, where is my money? That's it, that's all I want to know."

Sue Ellen, a taut, rigid body strapped to a broken chair, quivered uncontrollably. "I . . . I . . ."

"I? I?" Clewt laughed long and loud, swung the top-tied sack close to her face, held it there.

"Give me time! Give me time, I tell you!"

"No, no, I don't think so, Mrs. Winstead. Time has all but run out."

"Oh, please, please. I . . . I . . ."

"There you go again, with the 'I . . . I' business. Seems to me at this point you'd just give me what I wanted to know. As if anything you have to hide could be worth your life."

"What . . . what exactly do you want to know?" she said, and knew as soon as she said it that it sounded exactly like what it was, a desperate bid to buy herself time. This would not end well. She could see no way out of this.

But then the miraculous seemed like it might happen. Clewt's face became serious again, and he bent low over her again. "One more time, Mrs. Winstead, I'll tell you what I want: I want to know where your husband buried all the treasure. The loot he didn't spend buying this place. You don't understand what it's like to go without anything, mostly without food, for days and weeks and months. You have no idea how it is to live without finery."

He drove his sweaty face close in to hers again. "Can you tell me what I want to know? Can you guarantee me all these things that you have?" His smile widened but the madness lingered in his eyes. He coughed once, twice, then shook his head when she didn't respond soon enough.

He stood upright, all business again, and began untying the rawhide thongs wrapping the sack's top. From within, a dry, slapping, rattling sound arose.

Chapter 22

The first feeling he had was of a mouth packed tight with spoke shavings. Or river sand. When he had finally decided he was alive, that maybe he was just a little under the weather, Henry tried to force an eye open. It was a more difficult task than he imagined it would be. He tried again. Nothing. One more time, and he heard a voice.

"You're awake."

It sounded as if it reached him underwater. A man's voice? A woman's? Hard to tell. Husky, low. Somehow he got his tongue, thick though it felt, so that it rubbed against the backs of his teeth. The action made him want to swallow, but it hurt to do so.

"Take it easy. You need water."

He tried to speak, but could not, then felt a coolness on his lips and was able to force his thick tongue between them, felt the cool liquid on his tongue, and let some of it drizzle down his throat. It was long minutes before he was able to open his mouth further. Then one eye popped open and revealed a fuzzy, dimly lit world. He worked to get the second open, tried to reach up with a hand, but it hurt like the devil.

What had happened to him? Last he remembered he'd been . . . on the trail, yes, on his way northward in search of the very devil who laid low so many good people. Yes, now it was coming back to him, and the more Henry remembered, the more he tensed, felt a knotting sense of urgency deep in his bowels.

"Easy, no need getting worked up just now. There's nothing you can do about anything. I should know."

He saw her then, for the first time, as she straightened and turned away from him. She looked to be a tall woman, thin, with long dark hair. Hard to tell in the room. The room itself, now that he noticed, was darkened, but there was light coming in through gauzy curtains.

"Where . . ." he said, then coughed. The cough hurt, like gravel scraping up through his throat.

She turned back to him. "You're at my home. At my horse ranch. Only ain't much of a ranch anymore. Used to be called the Lazy D. For my husband's family, the Dundersons. Only thing is, there ain't no more Dundersons in the line. Leastwise not that I know of. And there ain't no more horses at the Lazy D, neither. Except for my one, Lilly. She was out to pasture when they rode 'em off."

All this information made little sense to Henry. He tried to take it all in, but she seemed to have forgotten him. He tried to speak again. "What happened to me?" His voice came out as a whisper, raw-feeling, but she heard, and looked at him. He saw her face for the first time as she bent close.

"Why, you've been shot. By my men. My last two hands."

A few moments passed while Henry worked to make sense of all this. In his mind, a bucketful of mixed pictures, smells, and sounds all jumbled together like a stew. It felt as if none of it would ever get sorted. Then he remembered a man's face bent low over him, just a flash of a memory, but it was enough to help. It was the man who'd shot him. But there were two, and they'd said something about shooting a lawman. Then he remembered no more. Until now.

"I'm . . . they thought I was a . . ."

"I know," she said, almost smiling. "Those two fools are long gone by now. Afraid you'd wake up and have them hung. I led them to believe that might be the case. Truth is I didn't want them around no more. They only stayed out of a guilty feeling. But with the killin', there weren't nothin' they could have done. They been frettin' like old hens since, riding out, keeping an eye. Useless effort, though. Even the posse was a short-lived thing and of no use. Ain't their fault—we're out in the midst of nothing. Too far from a town of any consequence. Took 'em days to learn of it all. Besides, them outlaws they've been scouting for ain't likely to come back this way. I got nothing left to give."

"But I'm not a—"

"Not a lawdog anymore, right?"

He looked at her. "How did you know?" Coughed again. She drizzled more water into his mouth. She smelled like some sort of soap, her hair was loose, brushed against his arm. He was so confused. Why had he left home? He'd been a fool; that much was certain. Then he remembered Clewt Duggins again and the final pieces of the hazy puzzle fit into place.

"You spoke in your sleep. Tossed something fretful. I had to tie you down for fear of you opening up that wound."

"My shoulder," he said, trying to raise his arm.

"You see? Men can't take a woman's word for it, have to find out for themselves. Crazy, that's what it is." She untied a loosely wrapped kerchief from his wrist. "You best take it easy, though. No thrashing or I'll tie you down again. I didn't dig out that bullet and sew you up only to have you pop open all my work. I have better things to do than tend to you."

"I appreciate it. Why did they shoot me?"

"My two hired fools thought they'd finally found one of them bad men. But it was only you. Not really their fault, though. They said you was crazy looking. Talking to yourself and waving your arms, shoutin' at nothin'. Made 'em nervous." She laughed then, a short, cackling burst.

She crossed the room, past his line of sight, but he saw more light, felt a bit of the sun's warmth on his face. She'd slid open a curtain.

"How long have I been here?"

"Oh, not long, a few days. I took the liberty of doping you up a little since you were thrashing so hard. That bullet was in there pretty good. I expect you'll have problems with that arm working right, but then again who knows? My Jay, now he took a handful of lead in his day and seemed to work his way through it. No offense, but you don't much remind me of my Jay."

"Who is he?"

"My husband, of course." She acted as though he'd said something most foolish.

"Where is he? I'd like to thank him as well. All this trouble over me. I should get going."

"Going? You ain't goin' anywhere, lawman. You're barely healed. So get used to that. Besides, Jay's dead."

"Dead? Your husband? But I thought . . ."

"Thought what? That I'm a woman and I'm here alone? Is that what you were thinking Mr. High-and-mighty Lawdog?"

Henry needed to think. He didn't much understand this situation. He felt as though he needed some sort of touchstone, something he could call his own, even a memory. He called Clewt to mind, gritted his teeth again. If it weren't for his own stubbornness, or his foolishness back in Dane Creek at having goaded Duggins into his foul play . . .

"Take 'er easy, lawman. I didn't mean nothing by it. Truth be told I've been alone for a month now, maybe longer. I don't recall what day it really is." She sat down with a sigh on the edge of the bed, and stared off toward the window once again, seeming to have forgotten him.

Henry's thirst had come on in a big way, and he longed for a proper drink. But he didn't dare interrupt this woman. Somehow she seemed on the very edge of screaming or crying or turning on him. He didn't dare risk it. He'd seen such behavior before, as a town marshal, and knew it was as unpredictable as playing with a snake, though the outcome was usually more easily predicted. Then she spoke.

"They were killed by him, lawman."

"I'm Henry. Who was killed?"

"They were killed by him, Henry Lawdog."

"My Jay and my Billy and my Little Tully too." Her face collapsed then, as he guessed it would. Just worked inward into a mass of sad wrinkles, making her look much older than her thirty-five or so years. Henry wanted to say something more, was half afraid of what it might do to her, but something told him she wanted to, needed to, talk.

"Who did it, ma'am? Who killed them?"

She looked at him, eyes glistening, snot running from her nose. She made no motion to wipe it. "They was my boys. My husband and my sons, but I called them all my boys. We ran the Lazy D as a family. Raised some of the finest quarter horses you are likely to ever find, I'll warrant."

"Isn't there anyone else here to help you now?"

"What would I need help with? Hmm? Ain't a horse on the place but my dear Lilly. And your horses."

"My horses? They ran off."

"Of course," she said, dragging a shirt cuff halfheartedly across her top lip. "But my boys brought 'em back. And your gear is stacked in the corner over yonder. All but your tack. That's in the barn." She looked at him. "But I am taking right good care of them horses. Only the best, or at least the best of what's left. When that killer and his gang rode in I knew all was lost. Soon as they crested the southern rise. I remember it well. It was late afternoon, and the sun lights that hill real nice along that time of day. I always make a point to look out there, see if any of them stock are standing skylined there. It's a sight to behold when that happens, I tell you what." She smiled, but it faded as quickly as a moth that flits too close to a campfire flame.

Henry's heart quickened. "This killer, did he give you a name?"

She nodded, not looking at him, just staring at what he guessed was the southern wall, as if she could see the very hill through the planking.

"His name was not something I'm likely to forget anytime soon. He robbed me of everything but the Lazy D. And now that my boys and my stock ain't here to share in it, I got nothing but a hard, black heart to sit here and stew over."

"The man, did he have a name?"

"Yeah, it's Duggins. Clewt Duggins." She turned her wet-eyed gaze on Henry. "And I aim to track him down and kill him five times over." She held out a work-hardened hand, didn't notice she'd dropped a handkerchief from it, and counted off on her fingers: "Once for my Jay, once for my Billy, once for my Tully, once for my sweet horses."

"That's only four."

"Huh? Oh yeah." She looked at Henry again. "And lastly for me, for my poor, broken black heart. I reckon it won't make any of it better, but I tell you what, it'll make me feel just fine when I stick something dull and rusted into him and twist and twist until he knots up inside. And all the while I will smile and stare right into his evil eyes. I will." She nodded, standing again with a sigh. "I surely will."

Henry decided right then and there he had to get out of this woman's house as soon as he was able to stand. And by his reckoning, that should be very, very soon.

The haggard woman crossed the room then paused by a door, her hand on the knob. "And you, Henry Lawdog, are going to help me do it. 'Cause I know that you are tracking him, too."

Before he could reply, she left the room. He heard the dull scratch and click of a key turning in a lock, her heavy footsteps receding down a hall, then down a flight of stairs, treads squeaking all the way.

Chapter 23

Hob closed his eyes a brief moment, held his old head to the outside wall of the kitchen. He was hunkered low, his gimpy pin stretched out before him. He nodded and smiled. That was the noise he'd thought he heard. A horse, coming hell-bent, straight in. But it wasn't Stub the Morgan. No, it was someone angry and not giving a lick for his own safety. Or spooked. But it was a man on horseback, the horse sounded heavy that way. Good. Had to be one of the rascals.

He dragged himself on his belly along to the front of the house, toward where he guessed the rider was headed, and eased his head up into the corner of the one window he'd left unshuttered. Soon, he figured, he'd not just hear the rascal, but see him. And that's when he'd open the ball. As he waited, taking shallow breaths, he thought briefly of Ty—he hoped the boy hadn't been waylaid by any of these vultures.

Hob didn't have any more time to wonder. Just as the rider he'd heard thundered into view—a bowler-hatted man crouched low on an Appaloosa—hoofbeats sounded from the back of the house as well. Good, then he at least knew of two attackers. They were flanking him, guessing, no doubt, that there was someone else other than Ty, living at the ranch. Hob figured Ty's surmise had been right—the man who'd escaped the night before must have told the others there was a second man at the ranch.

From his crouched vantage point on the kitchen floor, Hob examined the situation, watching with one eye the fool circling the courtyard on his Appaloosa with gun drawn and a daring, devil-may-care look in his eye. Hob wanted nothing more than to send that bowler-topped jackanape straight to his eternal sleep.

The one Hob envisioned for all of the attackers was a particularly roasty place with tall, licking flames, a howling demon lurking in the shadows, and an eternity of pain that never abated and sores that never healed. The thought made his finger twitch and a grim grin pull at his mouth corners. But he daren't. . . . Not yet, anyway. He'd let them make the first hostile move; that's what Ty would want. Hob would rather blast the weasel right out of his saddle.

The man on the Appaloosa turned and faced the house. "Curse you, mister! We know you're in there. I done for the other one of you. He'll be a burr under our saddle blanket no longer. And now it's your turn!"

"Aw, heck." Hob chewed the inside of his mouth, and finally said it again. "Aww, heck. . . ." Then thumbed back the hammer on the rifle—he'd save the shotgun for close-in work. The throaty clicking sound seemed to echo and fill the house and drift on out the window opening. As if invited to do so, the man on horseback leveled his gaze at the house, directly at the spot where Hob hid. The man sneered wider and clawed for a second sidearm, but Hob feathered the trigger on his rifle and did what seconds before he'd merely dreamt of.

The bowler man's shot caromed off the roof of the house even as he jerked to his right. The horse whipped in the opposite direction, spooking into a violent run.

The rider howled something that to Hob sounded like,

"Saints preserve us!" as the man fought to regain control of his mount. It thundered off toward the gap between the barn and the corral. He hadn't quite regained his upright posture on the saddle when they came up fast to the barn. His wounded right side slammed into the hard plank corner of the barn, pinwheeling him backward out of the saddle. The bowler hat spun into the air as if tossed in a stiff gale, and the rider arced wide over the horse's rump, clawing at the cantle to regain his seat.

But it was too late—he slipped from atop the bucking beast, down its left side, his boot still caught in the stirrup as they bounded around the corner of the barn and thundered out of sight, the man's shouts becoming fainter.

Hob wanted to cackle in glee, but since he'd heard at least one other rapscallion lurking nearby, he settled for a low, "Heh heh heh. . . ." and gave it a full grin. "One down, old man," he whispered to himself and eased away from the window, keeping his back to the thick log wall to wait out the next attack.

They can't all be this easy, he thought, rechecking and re-cocking his weapons. And he didn't have to wait long. Hoof-beats thundered closer, one, two horses. And from different directions. One rounded the south end of the house, headed toward the loafing shed. He guessed that was the second man. The other one was approaching from straight on, as Bowler had done.

Much as Hob wanted to cut loose at them, perched on the porch or at least peering through the window, he knew he had to use caution. He was older than he'd ever been—every day piled on another shovelful of dirt in that direction. And he was also gaining distance daily on his old gun-fighting days.

And then he heard a clunking, thumping sound coming from the back wall, but rising, as if someone were . . . climbing the wall? Hmm. He thought he'd dragged away every-

thing that could be used to scamper on up there. And then he
remembered the rain barrel. It'd been mostly full and too
heavy to move without dumping. That was not even a consideration in these dry times.

Yep, someone was cat-footing along, down at the far end
of the house, above the bedrooms. Hob dragged himself on
down there, hoping his commotion didn't attract too much
attention from outside. The sounds from above stopped. He
couldn't be sure where the man was. He was too far from the
chimney—all the way on the other end of the roof—to drop
something down there. What could he be up to?

Hob looked up at the ceiling, trying to gauge just where
the man had stopped. Hard to tell, but if he had a half guess,
he'd let fly with a couple of hot rounds, make the man dance.
Or drop.

But there was no more movement. And then it occurred to
him—this was nothing more than a distraction! He spun on
the floor, levering himself into a sitting position as he did so.

At the same time the front door rattled hard in its frame,
giving Hob a flash of a second to roll onto one knobby-boned
left shoulder—he heard something crack, felt a popping deep
in his old upper wing—and come up onto his good knee just
inside the second bedroom's doorway. He was still half-in,
half-out, his rifle snout poking like a long, accusing finger
down the hall at the front door, when the thing burst inward.
It banged off the wall behind, spasming, the frame hanging
loose in a jag of long, splintered planking.

A howling war whoop accompanied a tall drink of water
as he ducked low, fanning his six-gun for all he was worth.
His shots crashed into the log walls beside and behind Hob,
plowed furrows in the plank floor, and missed him altogether.

Hob cut loose with a few choice sounds of his own, none
of which he was ashamed to use in such company, and gave
as good as he got, thumbing the rifle's hammer hard and fast.

He heard no moans of pain, saw no blood on the floor, but he knew the skinny invader was somewhere in the kitchen. Silence overcame the crashing, roaring sounds of dueling guns that had held sway over the space seldom accustomed to much more noise than Hob's constant yammering. The air in the cabin hung heavy with smoke, as if a downy blanket had been shaken and the contents left to slowly fall.

Hob let the silence reign a moment more, then, tiring of inactivity, said, "I ain't dead, you idiot. Not even close! Come on if you're comin', and let's get to it."

Another silence. Hob gritted his teeth, his cheek muscles bunching. If there was one thing he hated, it was waiting. For anything. If he was to die in a gun battle, then by gum, he wanted to get on with it. If he was to win, then he wanted that to happen right quick, too.

"Hey, old man . . . I believe I'm shot. I don't rightly know how, but I believe your aim was true."

"Truer than yours, at least. But I ain't buyin' what you're sellin', stick man! Get on outta my house if you're really dying. I don't want blood all over my kitchen. Take me forever and a day to scrub it off the floor!"

A voice, close behind him, said, "I wouldn't worry too much about that, old man."

Hob jerked around and through the dissipating haze of smoke he saw a man hanging half in the end window. It was hard to tell just what sort of man he was, but Hob could make out dark features and with a face full of rangy hair.

"Your scrubbing days are over," said the intruder.

So there had been two. And here he was, pinned between a skinny liar skulking slowlike down the hall from his kitchen, and this mangy beast poking in from the window. Must have kicked it in when all the shooting was going on. It was normally fairly dark in this end of the house, and as the daylight waned outside, light came in around the man, through the busted-in window. Hob hoped the man was having as much of a hard time seeing him as he was seeing the villain.

"You have me at a disadvantage, stranger. Seems like you are trying to get in. Why don't you use the front door, like your compadre? Least he had the sense to knock."

While Hob spoke, grabbing any words that came to mind, he shifted his hands slightly, trying to angle the rifle not into a position of play but away from his body enough that he could snake out his pistol. He managed to wrap his fingers around the handle as the man said, "Not so fast, old man. I need to know one thing before I kill you."

From behind, Hob heard the skinny man's slow steps coming down the short hallway. He wouldn't have much time to make his play.

"Oh, and what might I help you with? A cup of sugar? I'm afraid I am all out of such delights." He ripped free the pistol, already hammered back, and drove a bullet in the man's general direction, all the while shouting, "But how about a couple of lead pills for your ills?"

The shots had the effect he'd hoped for—the man in the window, caught unaware, shimmied back out the hole, and the lurker in the hallway hotfooted it back to the kitchen.

Hob worked to control his breathing, all the while stuffing in fresh rounds to replace those he'd fired. He wouldn't have much time before they reconnoitered and came at him again, in some new fiendish way. Just enough time, though, for him to kick farther back into the shadow. He hated to hole up like this, but with his bum leg and being outnumbered, he'd take what cover he could get.

Chapter 24

By the time Ty made it back within sight of the Double Cross, he could tell the long day's grueling rides had taken a toll on his horse. He needed to rest up for a long while. They both did.

"Not much longer, fella," said Ty, rubbing Stub's neck. "I don't know how all this is going to play out down there, but I can tell you that I'll do my best to make it final. One way or another, you won't have to ride back at a hard pace. Now let's go see what trouble we can stir up." He nudged the horse into a trot downhill, making certain to stick close to the tree line. It wouldn't do at this stage in the game to get picked off by an unaccounted-for sentry, or by Clewt himself. He hoped there weren't any of Clewt's men left behind, but he couldn't be sure just how many had trekked to his own place. He only knew of three for certain, five possible, so there could well be someone left behind.

It took Ty half an hour to circle wide around the place to the south, sticking to the scattered trailing tree line of ponderosas, risking exposure as little as possible. In some spots it was impossible to do so, as he intended to come in on the ranch house from the southeast.

He reached the last of the woods closest to the house and slid from the saddle, making sure, deliberate moves, nothing hurried that might attract the attention of scanning eyes. Stub immediately adopted a hipshot pose of rest. Ty had watered him at the creek to the south of the trees, and now he stripped off the horse's gear, everything but a halter—that would make it simpler to catch Stub later. The horse, though free, didn't rove. He stayed put, uninterested in what Ty was up to.

"Once you figure out that you're free to do as you wish, my friend, I hope you'll take it into your head to head back to the Rocking T. If Hob's still firing, he'll take care of you. If not, then at least you'll be on my range. I can't risk leaving you saddled, as tired as you are feeling right now." He realized he was whispering not so much to the horse, but to keep himself from second-guessing his hasty plan.

"You wander off and get snagged on a branch, and the worst happens to me, might be you'll end up like I suspect that Mexican's horse did. I'd sure hate to see you starve to death, fetched up and withering, chewed by coyotes and buzzards. Best you're free to roam. If you're nearby here, I'll be back to this spot."

He faced the house, visible through the trees. "I hope we meet again soon, my friend." He ran a big hand under the horse's jaw. Stub nodded, as if in agreement with the sentiment.

"Wish me luck, boy." He slid his rifle from the saddle boot and headed to the edge of the sparse tree line. Still half concealed behind the largest tree close by the rear southeast corner of the Double Cross ranch house, Ty chewed his bottom lip, regarding the quiet place through squinted eyes. He put all thoughts of Uncle Hob and his own place out of his mind. He had to focus on saving Sue Ellen. Even if she no longer cared for him, she didn't deserve to be with these men one moment more. He only regretted he hadn't done something sooner to help her.

He shrugged off the useless thought. "I'm here now," he

said, and advanced from the woods. "Time to pay a visit to Clewt Duggins, see what that snake really wants."

Ty wished he was making his move later in the day, when the sun had at least begun its descent. Unfortunately he didn't have a choice in the matter. Clewt had forced his hand, had forced the entire issue by arriving at the Double Cross and carving a path of murder through the heart of it. Ty only hoped the killing hadn't continued.

He cat-footed low from a jutting boulder to a thicket of bramble to the beginnings of the immaculate and unused outbuildings arranged as any rancher might in laying out a picture-perfect ranch. He had to hand it to Alton: The man might not have been much of a rancher, but he had high-brow taste and a coin purse to match.

One last outbuilding separated Ty from the main house when he heard muffled shouts from somewhere on the far side of the place. He believed that was the ell that contained the kitchen, judging from the arrangement of the chimneys and the fact that the day before he'd seen Sue Ellen come out of the ell carrying the galvanized pail.

But the sound hadn't come from the house, it had come from somewhere behind the house, or so it sounded. And it sounded like a combination of voices, maybe even a man's and a woman's. Sue Ellen? Ty's heart pounded harder; he looked left and right, saw no one fore or aft, then bolted and broke from under cover of the shed. He passed the last little outbuilding without pausing, and made the last dash to the near corner of the house.

He pressed his face close to the white-painted clapboards, rifle cocked and upright, folded tight but ready for action with one quick, clean move. A little closer, and then he peered in the window he'd nudged up to. Through glass panes that gave the effect of looking through water, a film of gauzy, lacy curtain obscured the details of what appeared to be a finely appointed room within.

He saw the shapes of thin, fancy chairs surrounding a long, polished table, the wood of which glowed a rich honey color in the afternoon light slanting in from the front of the house as the day aged and mellowed. He saw no one in there, but ducked low and continued on toward the far end of the house, crouching low to avoid detection, stopping before each window for a peek inside. The result each time was the same.

He did all this as quickly as he could, knowing that the muffled shouts he'd heard but moments before no doubt signified something sinister occurring. One more set of windows lay ahead when he heard another round of shouts, louder this time, from ahead. As he'd suspected, it arose from a place beyond the house, but it didn't sound like it came from outside, rather indoors somehow. Maybe there was another of Alton's infernal sheds off the far end of the ell.

As soon as he heard it, Ty broke into a run, rifle held facing forward, stock gripped tight to his gut. He didn't bother ducking under the last two windows, but headed straight for the end of the building. It was all he could do to jerk to a stop at the end of the building. Prudent as it was, he paused but a sliver of a moment before spotting the source of the sounds— sounds that increased in tenor and urgency. He dashed straight to a door built into a tidy log-and-sod facade. It led back into what looked like a large rising mound—a root cellar, had to be.

His boots gouged the dusty earth, carving a trail from the kitchen to the root cellar door. There they ended. The door wasn't closed tight, but hung ajar a few inches. A bunched burlap feed sack wedged it open enough for Ty to pull up short and listen in.

There came a fresh round of muffled sounds, sobs from a woman. He wrenched the door open wide and peered into the gloom before him, the sunlight providing the only light.

There sat Sue Ellen, the top and bottom of her mouth separated by a tightly wrapped length of dirty rag. She squinted at him and he realized she could only see the outline of someone, could not tell it was him. She could barely keep still in the chair, kept thrashing and bucking. The closer he drew to her, striding down the dozen or so feet of low, packed-earth tunnel to get to her, the more she thrashed and howled.

"Sue Ellen, it's okay! Stop—it's me! It's Ty!"

But she didn't seem to hear him. She gave a final heave and shout and the chair pitched sideways. As she slammed to the dirt floor, he saw them—half a dozen wide-girthed diamondbacks, each as thick around the middle as his wrist.

Her screaming, and her wriggling feet and hands had annoyed the serpents, stirring them into a defensive, writhing frenzy of buzzing rattle, flicking tongue, and dripping fang.

For once Ty wished he had Uncle Hob's sawed-off scattergun instead of the rifle. The Winchester would have to do. "Pull back," he growled at Sue Ellen, knowing, even as he said it, that she was tied to the chair, hands and feet, and couldn't do much more than stop thrashing and pull her hands and feet in as tight as she could. Every second he delayed, the snakes drew closer to her.

Ty leaned the rifle against the close wall with his right hand as he clawed free his Colt Navy with his left. In the same motion he slicked back the hammer and stepped into the midst of the pulsing mass of angry snakes. He stepped once more, positioning himself in the few inches available between Sue Ellen's upended form and the oncoming snakes. Ty cranked off round after round with his left hand and shucked his Bowie knife with his right, beginning with the venomous demons closest to Sue Ellen's trembling legs. He hacked with precision with the gleaming well-stropped blade, severing snake heads, the jaws of which continued to snap and pop in reflexive anger.

Ty held his ground firmly, not daring to step right or left, knowing that he might well tread on an undamaged snake, poised to strike at the nearest thing—and he didn't want that to be his legs.

The sound of gunfire in the dank hole of a room deafened them both, as he knew it would, but there was no alternative. The poor woman would have been bitten too many times to prevent anything but a nasty, drawn-out death. He'd seen in others the excruciating spasms of pain that would leave her puffed and agonized.

When he ran out of bullets, he kept Sue Ellen, by feel against his own legs, well behind him, and using the butt of his Colt and continuing to wield the knife, he did his best to ensure each of the vile snakes was well and truly dead. Or fast approaching its final moment.

The thunderous echoes rendered him all but deaf. It was long moments before he heard anything but the staccato hammering of gunfire that seemed to have seeped into his very brain. He turned, bent low over Sue Ellen, and waved an arm to help clear the smoke. She was there before him, her eyes wide with fear. He couldn't hear himself but as he worked to untie the filthy rag from around her face, he hoped she hadn't been bitten. If she had, he had to get her out of there fast—and hope Stub could be found, and then had the stamina to carry them to safety.

"It's okay, honey." He said that last word before he could stop himself. He didn't care. She probably couldn't hear him anyway. As he freed the rag from around her mouth, he cupped her face in his big hands and she stared up at him. Then her eyes widened and she screamed something. She was frantic again with a new wave of fear. In the second that followed Ty wondered if he'd missed a snake. He bent low to her, trying to soothe her, shouting, "It's okay now! It's okay!"

But then he saw she wasn't looking into his eyes anymore. She was looking beyond him, over his shoulder.

As Ty turned his head to see what it was she was looking at, through the clearing haze of smoke, he caught a quick glimpse of blue and red—where had he seen that pattern? As a hard, sharp pain flowered up the side of his head, he felt himself spinning, or maybe it was the world that was spinning and he was the only thing in it standing still.

And then he felt himself dropping, hitting hard on something, the floor? None of this made any sense. A blackness crept in fast, pulling at him, and joined the pulsing roar left behind by the gunfire. The second-to-last thought he had was of Sue Ellen—what had happened to her?

The last thought that came to him was of where he had seen those colors—blue and red—on a fancy shirt worn by Clewt Duggins. Oh no, what have I done to Uncle Hob? Sue Ellen? All lost, all because of me. . . .

Chapter 25

"I tell you I am going and you can't do a thing to stop me. Now you untie me this minute!" Henry's chest rose and fell with the effort of the shouting, and he knew even as he raged that the crazy ranch woman was right. There was no way he was going to be able to fend for himself on the trail, let alone when and if he met up with Clewt Duggins. But that didn't stop him from being angry.

He sank back to the pillow, sweat popping out on his forehead.

"I told you."

"And I told you I need to get out of here. I can't stay, blast it! Every day I spend here is a day more that he gets away."

She said nothing, so he continued. He could not help himself, he was that riled. "Furthermore, ma'am, I believe you are keeping me here, lashed like this . . ." He raised a tethered hand and let it flop to the bedspread. The action prodded a lance of pain to shoot up his arm. He grimaced and continued. "I believe you have something in mind. What it is, I truly don't know. But it can't be a good thing. No, no." He shook his head, his face heating up and feeling the glow of high, righteous dudgeon overtake him. "I fear for myself, I do."

She placed the empty lunch tray aside on the chest of drawers and cocked a hip, set her work-hardened hand on it.

In the few days that Henry had been there, he had come to recognize that as her way of slipping into rumination, as if she were disappearing into her own mind for a time. And she did it this time, too. She was silent for a few long moments, staring at a spot somewhere on the tall, carved mahogany headboard above him. He knew better than to try to shake her from the reverie—it never worked.

Finally, her gaze seemed to clear and she looked at him. "I have a solution that will solve both our problems." She looked right into his eyes and for the first time in the short time he had known her, she smiled.

"I don't think I am going to like what you have to propose."

"And I don't think you have much of a say in the matter. You've a strange flair for the dramatic, mister. It's odd."

Henry closed his eyes and concentrated on what she'd said. He suspected she would want to go along with him, but that was not even a consideration, nosiree. "Never mind my flair or whatever you called it, what I want to know is what you have in mind."

"All in good time, Mr. Henry Lawdog. All in good time. I am not the fiend you think I am. In fact, I have only been trying to help you by doctoring your wound. I felt a responsibility, being as it was my cowboys who shot you and all." She backed toward the door.

"And I appreciate it. But look, I have a long, hard trail ahead of me and if you are thinking of fogging it, or worse, joining me, it will only slow me down."

"You don't understand, do you?" She paused with her hand on the doorknob. "What you want is of little matter to me. What I want—what I need—is plain old revenge. That's it, that's all." She exited and slammed the door and Henry waited to hear her slow, measured steps retreat down the hall, then down the stairs.

He struggled and stretched until his arm flexed and bulged with the effort. The length of hemp rope had been worked by him for many hours, and it finally gave out with a snap. The force slammed his fist straight into his forehead, dazing him even as he fought to suppress a giggle. How funny that would be—coldcocking himself just when he had the chance to get out of this crazy woman's house.

It was the work of but a few moments to free his other hand. She'd left each arm's rope long enough that he could somewhat feed himself, but had little possibility to do anything else. He appreciated that she was concerned for his health, but now that he knew the whole truth, he wanted out. And he could think of no better time than that very night.

From listening, he knew her routine was habit and didn't vary much. He also knew that he was on the second floor and that his clothes and gear were still in the room. It took him long minutes to climb out of bed and stand for the first time in days. He felt weak, but determined. She'd been feeding him well, and other than having to empty his bladder—it had been hours—he was ready to fight her every step of the way down the stairs and out the front door to the barn. It was plain wrong to think she could keep him here.

As they had nearly every hour since he'd been shot, waking and sleeping, Henry's thoughts alternated between visions of Maria and his boy, Henry, and exacting revenge on Clewt Duggins.

But as he'd spent long hours incapacitated, healing in the dark upstairs bedroom, it had eventually occurred to him that maybe his motives for chasing down Clewt Duggins and running him aground weren't as pure as those of the crazy rancher woman. Her entire life had been gutted because of Duggins. Lord only knew what the snake and his boys had done to her after they'd killed her husband, sons, and ranch hands, and stolen whatever they could—including her beloved horses.

What had Henry lost? His reputation before the people of his town? The life of his deputy? The lives of a number of innocents in his town? Surely his suffering was secondary to those loved ones left behind to live with the pain of such loss. Just as this woman had been.

These thoughts dogged him as he tugged on his clothes, reacquainting himself with his various garments. He found that they had been laundered and folded, and the shirt he'd been wearing when he was shot had been cleaned of most of the brown bloodstains left behind. The hole had been neatly sewn together with tiny, intricate stitches. He thought of how she would have no men to tend to any longer.

He knew that many wives and mothers defined themselves by what they could do for their families. The thought made him sigh. He bent to retrieve his boots at the bottom of the stack and found his revolver, holstered with the belt coiled around it, at the bottom of the stack. It appeared to have been tended by her, with the leather oiled, as had his boots.

He regarded himself, felt much better now that he was once again upright and dressed in his own gear, and almost tiptoed to the door. Then a thought of the woman downstairs stopped him. She would hear his boots, no doubt, probably already had heard him clunking about up here. What of it? He was no mouse. He was a man who had been tended by a kindly widow and who now needed to move on. Simple as that. He pulled in a deep breath and strode to the door, lifted his fawn hat off the hook, and plunked it on his head.

He didn't normally wear a hat indoors, but he felt he needed to, somehow, to help him prepare for the coming confrontation he was sure to have with the woman.

One last look around the spartan room. There was the bed with the rumpled blankets and sheets, and the pillows, where his head had lain for too many days. And beyond, the window, half-curtained and letting in late-afternoon light. Perfect for setting off. With any luck she would be in one of her reveries.

He could leave what money he could spare on the table, tip his hat to her, and perhaps check in on her, should he be lucky enough to find himself alive and riding back southward to Dane Creek to see his wife and boy. Yes, he thought. That is what I will do. I will check in on her when I can—a promise that came too easy at a time such as this.

Still holding his wounded but healing wing bent against his chest, he stuck the hand up to the wrist in the top of his vest. It was a decent spot for it, as each step jostled and sent needles of pain from the wound downward into his arm and chest.

The door was not locked, and it occurred to him that this was the case only after he closed it behind him. Had she merely forgotten to lock it? Not likely. The galley-style upstairs hallway was not what he expected. It bore a short railing that overlooked a great room downstairs, dominated by a large fireplace. Immediately he knew that the place was a top ranch—or had been.

Few folks of his acquaintance could afford to have such a home built. And she had told him that's what her husband had done for her. Built her a fine home because she was willing to live there with him, in the middle of nowhere at all, in order to raise and breed horses. And that's what they had done, raise sons and horses. They also became known for the quality of their stock far and wide.

Henry made no effort to conceal the slow *clunk clunk clunk* of his boots as he descended the wide wooden staircase. The wood glowed with a rich, polished look, the banister rail felt slick beneath his hand, as if it had just been shined. Indeed, the entire home seemed to have been freshly cleaned. The wooden floors gleamed, the cobbled inlaid stone floor by the double-doored front entry looked swept and mopped. The furniture, heavy, fancy pieces made of thick wood and leather, all glowed.

He cleared his throat. "Ma'am?" No sounds came to him. "Ma'am?" he said louder. Still nothing.

He rummaged in his pocket, but found that his coin purse was light. He could have sworn he had at least twenty dollars left in there. Maybe he'd lost it? Surely she wouldn't have taken it. He checked his other pockets, but turned up nothing. Finally he just shrugged and headed for the door. He wasn't about to roam the vast house and search for her. Know when to get out, Henry.

Soon he found himself standing in the middle of a long covered porch pulling in fresh evening air. How long since he'd truly appreciated the wonders of breathing in pure, clean air? Before him he saw a long, winding walk that branched off in a few directions, but the one he was most interested in was toward one of several barns.

He knew which he was headed for because his horse was saddled and his pack animal stood beside it, loaded with his meager load of gear. Both animals looked healthy and ready for the trail, standing bored and hipshot, flicking ears and swishing tails.

She must have heard him slowly getting ready upstairs. Then his wary smile slipped—only trouble was that must mean she was also somewhere close by, ready to ride, too. But he reasoned that there was little he could do about it and ambled toward his waiting horses. As he approached, they turned to watch him, showing no alarm. They looked to have been very well tended, their coats shining, his saddle and gear all spiffed and tied up properly. And his rifle jutted from its boot.

"How are you two doing, eh? Look to have been well cared for. Might be I should get shot more often. Then you could rest up, enjoy the good life." He ran a hand along their necks, patting and talking in a quiet voice.

"Their shoes are done, too."

Henry turned to see Crazy Horse Ranch Woman, as he'd come to think of her, standing in the barn doorway. She held reins in her gloved hands.

"But what about your house? Your ranch?"

"No matter," she said, mounting up. "I expect I'll not return here. And if I do, I'll find what I find. Squatters or the remains of a fire, or looters. I don't know and I don't care anymore. Me and Lilly are all that's left."

Henry didn't quite know what to say, just stood there with one hand on his saddle, his brows furrowed.

"You are too much in your own head, Mr. Henry Lawdog." She said this as one might state a bald fact such as, "The sky is dark and rain will come by evening."

He shook his head and tried to ignore her. A thought occurred to him as he raised a stiff left leg and managed to jam his boot into the stirrup on the first go. He bounced on his right leg once, twice, held tight to the saddle horn with his right hand, then raised himself upward and astride the horse. Relief flooded him, not quite as powerful as the fresh, throbbing pain that pulsed anew from his shoulder wound. When it subsided he said, "Their graves, would you like to visit them, before we leave?"

"Already have, Mr. Henry Lawdog. And I'll thank you for not working to come up with more excuses to keep me here and you gone from here as though we weren't going to be traveling together. This is the way it has to be and you know it. You need me, and I need you."

"I need you?" said Henry, adjusting the reins and trying not to draw attention to the obvious—his sore, wounded arm.

"Yes, you do, but not for that bullet wound."

"Oh? Then what for, may I ask?"

"There you go with that theatrical speechifying again. It's

because I happen to know where we can find Clewt Duggins and his gang."

Henry's pulse jumped "Where is he?"

"I'm not so easy or daft as that."

For once, Henry had nothing to say. He looked at her lined, wind-burned face, the graying hair wisping about her eyes, the worn gear that fit her as only gear worn for long hours in the saddle can, the way she sat her fine horse, the packed saddlebags, the stained, patched duster. He knew there was no way he could make it without her and no way he could deny her the one thing she needed—deserved—left in this life. Her revenge.

"Fine then. Lead on."

She nodded and nudged Lilly into a walk before him. Henry sat his horse a moment, then said, "Just a minute, you said you needed me. What exactly for?"

She didn't even turn around, just said over her shoulder, "Strength in numbers. You're a former lawman, aren't you? I expect you know how to use that iron of yours. If not, maybe you'd better stay here." And for the first time that he could recall, she laughed. But kept riding north.

Henry followed her, working his left arm slowly up and down, side to side, occasionally reaching down to brush his fingertips across the butt of his holstered Smith & Wesson revolver.

Chapter 26

He knew the attack was coming; he just didn't know when. But Hob couldn't think of a better spot for an old gimp like himself to hole up and wait for it. He had shadows, guns, and a big knife to keep him company. And solid log walls around him. The cursed raiders could only come at him from inside the house or through that window hole—and that rascal wasn't likely to try that again anytime soon. The only thing he wished he had was a few quick pulls on the medicinal jug. His leg stump was paining him something awful. All this crawling around on the floor. You'd think he was an alligator and not a man the way he'd been forced to carry on all day.

Just when he thought that, all things considered, he could be worse off, a peculiar tangy smell tickled his old hair-filled nostrils. He tipped his head back, sniffed, narrowed his eyes and sniffed once more. Then he opened them wide in the near-dark. "Blast it!" he said through gritted teeth. They had set fire to the place.

Both he and Ty had been sure they wouldn't do that. Wouldn't dare risk attracting attention, since a house or barn ablaze would be seen for miles around and be sure to set folks acoming, partly, he knew, to help, partly to gawk. He couldn't blame them; he'd done it too. Something oddly entertaining about other folks' misfortune.

Maybe they were only going to smoke him out. Think, man. Have to think of a plan. . . . Then he smiled, because he knew what to do. He only hoped there weren't any slimy critters down where he planned on going. Talk about behaving like a crawling thing—this day had better end well, because he aimed to give ol' Ty Farraday one big heaping helping of Uncle Hob's wrath. . . .

And with that, he set to work feeling along the floor under the bed for the loose boards they'd left unnailed when they built the place. It had been a good hidey-hole for valuables should marauders come about. That had been the plan, anyway. But they'd never had much in the way of valuables, and things with Sue Ellen hadn't worked out for the boy, so the hide had been forgotten.

As he groped in the dark, Hob tried to recall just what he'd find under there. The smoke grew thicker, seeping in from somewhere. Maybe crawling under the house wasn't such a keen idea, given that they'd probably started the fire around the outside of the house, at the base.

Then he heard shouts outside. Could Ty have ridden back? Not likely. He hoped not. This was his one chance to save Sue Ellen—if she was still alive for the saving. No, the voices were muffled but just outside. One was shouting, sounded hysterical. They were men's voices, at least two, maybe three. The crazy-sounding voice kept rolling right over the others. The smoke increased enough so that Hob yanked his kerchief from his back pocket and hastily tied it up over his face, the hanging point tucked into his high-buttoned work shirt.

He would have to come up with a plan and fast. Much more of this and he'd just plain ol' expire right there, sitting pretty on the floor with an arsenal in his lap and a dumb look on his face. Nah, can't let that happen, he thought. He heard the first crackles and snaps of flame finding purchase in dry wood. Blast them, this had been a good home, more cabin than either of the two bachelors deserved, and it had served them well.

He'd have to force his way out, no time to rummage under the floorboards and hope to find a channel large enough to burrow his way to one end or the other under the house, then dig under the logs. Foolish plan, anyway. . . .

The crack of gunfire paused him a moment. Who'd be shooting at whom out there? Surely it wasn't Ty? Townies? Nah, no reason for that. No one ever came out this way. Maybe the heathens were fighting among themselves. He clung to that notion as he ducked low and, keeping his shotgun poised before him like the prow of a ship, he cut his way through the fog, inching along the hallway, sure he'd come face-to-face with that gangly bandit. But he didn't. He made it to the front door, hanging in long, cracked-board tatters, and peered first into his smoke-filled kitchen, saw no one, then peered outside through a gap in the broken boards. He saw no one, but heard ragged breaths from one man, to the north, alongside the house.

Hob bent low, scooted to the far side of the doorframe, and jerked the rifle stock to his cheek. Here came the tall man, stumbling along, droop-headed and weak-kneed, only he wasn't holding a gun, but clutching his own gut. Even though the thickening smoke filled Hob's nose and mouth as if he were being dunked in it, he saw the front of the man's shirt was a spreading mass of blood; runnels seeped from between the man's long fingers. Gut shot and dying.

Hob considered giving the man one in the eye, in part for the trouble he'd helped to cause and in part because it would be a kinder way to go than to bleed out for hours beside a burning building. He opted to leave him be, and decided that though it was too bad for the tall man, it was at least one less rascal he'd have to deal with. By his count there was but one man left—that rogue who'd tried to slink in through the window. And Hob believed he'd dealt him a rough blow earlier. But time would tell. And quick, if he knew his raiders. . . .

Must have been the dark-skinned window man who did for his compadre—not a friend Hob wanted any part of. But he'd be glad to dispatch him as any decent man might a rogue dog. Then he froze, squinting toward the still slowly stumbling tall man. What was that he was hearing? Yes, he was sure of it now—two more voices. He'd been all but sure that there was only one left. Must have been another that rode in after. No matter, he still had two men to face down.

The tall man headed toward Hob but didn't appear to see him, given the filmy look of his eyes, the twitching lids, and gaping mouth. Then he dropped to one knee, colliding with the slowly smoking log wall of the cabin. The force of it pitched him onto his right side. He coughed and groaned. His hands fell away from holding his gut, but he didn't make much effort to grab at himself again. Even though the man was a no-good killer, Hob felt a twinge of sympathy for him. No man should have to endure that sort of pain.

The shouts came to him again, drifting from the back of the house, louder now, as if to be heard over the increasing roar of the flames. Hob pulled back inside the doorframe and made the quick decision to try the back door off the kitchen. If he couldn't snipe them from there, at least he could keep low and hide behind the back gate. Maybe with all the smoke they wouldn't notice him. Fat chance, but the only one available to him. That or risk a run straight out the front. If they caught sight of him, he'd be out in the open with no protection, no cover at all. No, he'd take his chances with the back. And shoot first, if he could get a clear angle on them.

His eyes ran a steady stream of tears now due to the stinging smoke. He heard the licking of flames, grown louder out back. So that's where they'd started the fire. The smoke was thicker there too. You'd never know that the day had come off as a cool one, for all the heat the fire had thrown. He didn't think the house, as solid as she was, would stand for too long once the blaze got a good toehold. She was a wood structure, dry as she could be. Beside the back door, he placed a palm against the log wall, and it was warm to the touch.

Hob sighed and readjusted his kerchief. It was a shame, for this house had been well built. If they lived through it, he knew they'd build another. Maybe even bigger and better. In the meantime, he had to worry about surviving this attack. He stretched his wooden stumpy leg straight out in front of him, angled down the steps. He could barely see his own hands before him. They looked wavery and distant, as if he were seeing them through water.

More shouts came to his ears, and he instinctively pulled lower, shotgun jutting toward the end of the house. All he saw was thickening smoke, now more black than gray, underpinned by a hedge of dancing flame straight down the length of the house. Whoever had set it didn't do anything by half measures.

"You don't get outta my way—"

"Boss said not to fire it!"

A couple of seconds passed. Then another gunshot sliced through the smoke and flame. Hob pulled his head down again, afraid he'd been seen. He looked down at himself, but could barely see his own chest or shirt or boot. He felt okay, no new holes that he was aware of. What was going on? Man was shooting his own kind. "Won't leave me any work at all," said Hob, in a low grumble.

He made it down the last couple of steps, kept low along the ground, his gimpy leg preventing him from crouching even lower, and edged as close as he could to the house.

Hob nearly made it to the south end of the house when he heard a voice from behind shout, "I see you, old man! Don't think I'm so blind as all that now!"

The man had barely shouted the words when he sent a

shot plowing into the log to the right of Hob's cheek. Splinters burst outward, stabbing him. He instinctively flinched, dropped even lower, and rolled around the corner. At least from there, provided no one was crouched in wait at the far end of the house, he could maybe get a drop on the shouting man who'd been killing his fellows.

From behind, the voice called out again—"Old man! Give it up, why don'tcha?"—and rang a bell. Hob knew who it was—the Irishman who'd ridden into the dooryard earlier, bold as brass. Hob thought for certain he'd killed the man! He'd shot him, then watched as his horse had slammed the man's flopping form right into the corner of the barn. And then the man had snagged in the stirrup and been dragged, screaming, off around the barn.

He'd advance, and if he was alone could come in around either end. If there were two of them, Hob was a dead man—he'd be pinned between them. Best he could hope for in that case would be for them to shoot each other if he ducked low enough. Ha! The thought of it, despite his grim situation, brought a smile to his sooty face.

"Old man!"

The voice was closer, probably by the kitchen door now. Hob tried to listen for him, but the sound of the flames had increased. He pulled air in to shout, but smoke filled his windpipe, doubling him over in a coughing spasm. He tried again, got a leg up over the smoke. "How's your horse, Irishman?"

"Dead—I shot him before he dragged me to death!"

Hob squinted toward the corner, expecting to see a dark form emerge from the smoke. So far, nothing appeared. "You appear to be on a shooting spree!"

"And I ain't done yet, old man!"

Closer than ever. Hob dropped to his good knee, left the bum leg sticking out to the side as a support. As long as no one crept up behind him from the other direction, he'd have a clear view of the Irishman when he came around the corner. And he wouldn't expect Hob to be so bold as to pose right there in front of him, waiting in plain, though somewhat smoky, sight.

But the cursed Irishman did not show himself. Hob hunkered lower, squeezing his eyes shut tight quickly, then opening them. It made little difference. The smoke was just smoke, no man came lurching or barreling out of it. "Blast him, anyway."

Hob kept staring at the corner of the house, where he had last heard the man calling from, and inched back toward the relative safety of the burning building. Each second that passed convinced Hob more that the man had circled back around the house and would come at him from the front.

He figured his only options were to meet the man head-on—which put him at the same risk he'd just run, leaving him open from behind should the Irishman double back on him—or he could try a mad, peg-legged dash for the wood yard and chopping block, some thirty feet off the end of the house. It was where he and Ty would go to work up a sweat or an appetite, or both. Or just to get away from the other.

There was never any shortage of firewood that needed crosscut sawing or splitting, stacking, drying, hauling, restacking in the house. And for once Hob was thankful that the various stacks that usually represented countless hours of work were all large enough for him to use as a barricade.

One last glance back at the front corner of the house, less obscured by smoke than the rear, and he bolted for the woodpiles, bum leg arcing wide as he used it as a pivot. He hoped that he'd beat the Irishman to the punch—he also hoped that the wooden leg wouldn't slip out from under him. Always a danger, since he couldn't be sure it was well placed with each lurching step he took. Since he had no feeling in it, he never knew if it was on solid footing or canted enough to topple him to the ground.

Still two man-lengths from the nearest woodpile, he heard a gunshot and felt himself going down hard. Hob pitched face-forward in the dirt as if he he'd been punched by a mammoth hand from behind. His shotgun flew from his grasp. The smoke-filled air whooshed out of him, and his chin bounced off the hard ground and left him gasping for a breath. He wondered if he'd been shot, though he didn't feel any of the familiar searing pains that accompanied a bullet wound.

Maybe this is how it feels when you get the final shot, the one that finally does you in? He gritted his teeth, tried to suck in air, had no success. Then he felt something kick him hard in his ribs. And it hurt worse than whatever had knocked him down.

"Now that I have your attention, old man, you'll see I am in no mood to play more of these games."

Hob looked up into the hazy air and saw a man standing over him. Or rather leaning over him. He was obviously in pain, and he was obviously the Irishman. Minus the silly bowler hat. His left arm swung at a painful angle, and even through the smoke Hob saw the staining where his own bullet had pierced the foul killer's shoulder. The Irishman was also holding a revolver in an unsteady grip, though at the range of three feet, Hob knew the wounded man didn't need much of a grip, or aim, to do the deed.

He wanted to say, "What are you waiting for?" Wanted to shout and spit at the man, swing a mighty blow at the leering, battered, puffy apple-doll face, wanted to break his already snapped, bleeding nose, wanted to . . .

"You listening to me, old man? Said I'm going to kill you now, but nice and slow."

The Irishman spoke loudly, wanting to be heard, forcing

the words through his puffed, split lips. He was trying to smile, but Hob was only partly paying attention. The shaking gun bothered him not a little, but he was snaking his right hand down to his waistband, where his skinning knife lay sheathed.

He had no way to make a grab for his own revolver, holstered as it was on his left side, nearest the Irishman, and where the rifle landed was anyone's guess. But maybe he could slip the knife free while looking up at the Irishman as if he were trying to raise himself up with his left hand. That and the drifting smoke might shield his actions enough that he could tug the knife free.

"Now, hold on, fella. I . . ."

The Irishman's boot lashed out once more, the toe catching Hob's rib cage in the same spot. He felt something crack, lost his wind again. He clawed at the kicking man's boot, felt the dusty leather beneath his fingers, but couldn't gain purchase as the boot pulled from his grasp. All the while he scrabbled for the knife with his right hand, then felt the reassuring bronze-and-wood hilt and handle as his fingers curled around it.

The Irishman stomped down hard on Hob's left hand, ground down with his heel, and howled with laughter.

Hob felt as if he'd been holding a handful of nitroglycerin and razor blades, and his snapped fingers clawed in the dirt. As the pain intensified, he slipped the knife free and, using his pinned hand as leverage he swung his right arm, knife handle clutched in a jabbing grip, in a wide, fast arc angled low over his head.

Too late, the cackling Irishman saw the dark steel blade driving at him, clutched in the sinewy arm of a desperate man. The Irishman jerked, instinct hindering his futile move. Hob yanked his smashed left hand backward, tripping the man. At the same time, his blade drove deep into the meat of his attacker's leg. He pushed against the knife's hilt, ramming and twisting the blade, carving a ragged cave in the jerking limb.

Hob guessed that rolling away from the Irishman might make it easier for him to be shot, even in the Irishman's weakened state, so as he clung to the knife, working to keep it lodged in the muscle of the man's calf, Hob rolled, pushing with his good leg, toward the screaming, falling man.

Too confounded by his sudden agony, the Irishman forgot for the moment that after he had freed himself from that nasty dragging horse, he had limped back to the ranch house wanting nothing more than to kill the very man who was now savaging him. Despite his pain, it didn't take him but a few moments of dazed struggle to realize he still possessed his revolver. Where was the old man? The pain from his leg, washing upward like a pummeling reverse waterfall, soaked his body from the wound in glowing, smoking pain.

He came out of this bitter fog enough to swing the pistol weakly at the old man just rising up onto his one good knee. The old man was saying something. Paddy saw his lips moving, but couldn't make out a word. The old man's eyes were blazing, angry. He had to shoot him, had to get away from him, kick him to the ground like a sick kitten. The old man was responsible for everything that had gone wrong to him today. This should have been an easy job, should have been so simple to just kill that Farraday man and this old dog. But they were tough, tougher than anyone they'd come up against in a long time.

Reminded him of that woman on the horse ranch somewhere south of here, far south, that ranch in the middle of nowhere. She had been tough, too. Tough like an old boot. She'd taken so much from them, and still she lived. Why he'd let her live he'd never know. Maybe it was just to spite Clewt.

Yes, that was it. Clewt was really the one to blame, wasn't

he? None of this had to happen. All he'd had to do was work Winstead a little harder. The man had been a soft man a decade ago. Now he was a fat and rich soft man. He would have buckled if Clewt hadn't lost his temper. How did he get to be the boss, anyway? Wasn't Paddy an Irishman, after all? And from a long line of connivers from Connemara? He'd been on the trail with Clewt longer than any of them.

All these thoughts collided in Paddy's jouncing mind as he fought to regain his pain-blurred vision. The old man's face leered in and out of focus, and Paddy felt something tugging at his gun hand—No! Mustn't let go of the gun. Hold on to it at all costs. You give up your gun, you give up your life. That's what he always told himself.

Paddy bit the inside of his mouth, bit down hard on the soft flesh of his cheek. It helped to sharpen his thinking, and he saw the old man struggling with his one good arm to jerk free the knife from where Paddy had fallen on it, pinning it beneath him. Good, at least he'd done something to slow down the nasty old demon.

He gripped the pistol harder, felt the old walnut grip, its smooth, worn contours as comforting as the lap of that night girl back in Taos, the one he'd known for a long, long time. The one who never asked questions, just seemed to like him for who he was, not what he was. Then, come morning, never asked him to stay. As good as that was, sometimes he wished she would ask. He squeezed that grip tight, tighter, and something exploded, bucked, kicked back at him, slammed hard into his already aching head.

What had happened? He didn't know, maybe death. Maybe that's all there was to it.

Chapter 27

A ringing sound like dozens of large brass bells heard up close jolted Ty awake. Or back to consciousness—he didn't know or care either way. But he did come to feeling confused. He jerked his eyes wide, but the bell sounds kept right on clanging, softened somewhat by daylight, harsh and cold. And judging from its angle, it was morning light. The events of what he hoped was the day before came back to him in a flood of memory. He struggled to rise, found that he was in a seated position, on a floor, perhaps.

The light stabbed at him, made his head ache. The back of it felt as if someone could lift free the entire section of skull and that might somehow make it feel better. But he also knew with a sudden clarity where he was, who he was there to save, who to kill, and nothing that had happened the day before had changed that at all.

He also realized he was bound fast, hands behind his back, and lashed at the ankles. His fingers rested in a sticky, thick paste—his seat felt wet with it. What was it? Too thick for water. A shadow passed before his light-filled eyes and then something smacked him in the back of the head—the sorest part. A hot rush of pain flowed over him, setting his teeth tight together and his eyes clamped shut.

"Wakey, wakey!"

Another clout landed on the same sore spot.

"That's just for starters, Mr. Farraday."

The voice came to him close and loud, and though it startled him, the fact that he could hear it also made him realize that he hadn't been permanently deafened in the barely remembered close-quarters gunfire. What had that been for? Sue Ellen, yes, now he remembered. And the snakes, the awful snakes. He stiffened, gritted his teeth against the urge to gag—he was sitting in the bloody mire of dead snakes. A gruesome mess he had made. He only hoped Sue Ellen hadn't been bitten.

In a rasping tone, Ty called her name, barely heard his own voice, tried again. All he heard was laughter, not his own. A man's laughter—the voice of whoever had just spoken in his ear.

And then he knew who that was, too—Clewt Duggins. And the whole awful mess of the past couple of days flooded back to him. Ty forced his eyes open, squinted against the harsh light. "What have you done with her, Duggins?"

"Why . . . nothing she doesn't deserve . . . Farraday."

A shadow shifted, Ty flinched, moved his head to the left.

"You're a quick learner, boy. But not quick enough." Clewt rained a series of hard, fast slaps to Ty's face, whipping his head back and forth.

"Stop it!"

A woman's voice.

"Sue Ellen?" said Ty.

"Yes, it's me. You're going to be okay, Ty. Don't worry."

Ty managed a weak smile. "That's what I was supposed to say to you."

"You both are rather optimistic, really. But I have to tell you that none of it's going to matter. Chatter all you want. I won't stop you. Why should I deny short timers the chance to fritter away what little is left to them?"

Ty shook his head slowly, trying to clear away the cob-webs. "What is it you want, Clewt? Why did you come here in the first place?"

Duggins walked around to stand in front of Ty. "What I want is none of your business. What I got is more to the point. Nothing and nada. Thanks to her." He jerked his chin away from Ty.

The battered rancher stretched his neck in that direction, but could see nothing beyond a dirty, ripped length of fabric. Sue Ellen's dress. "Are you hurt, Sue Ellen?"

"Yes, yes, she's hurt. She's hurt my feelings by not telling me what I needed to know. And now I find she truly doesn't know it after all." He laughed, then said, "I guess Delbert, or whatever he called himself, wasn't what you'd call a husband who shared much with his wife, eh, woman?"

Ty heard a chair scrape, heard Sue Ellen grunt, stifle a groan.

"Pick on someone your own size, Duggins. Leave her alone."

He heard footsteps; then Clewt leaned back into view. "Don't you dare tell me what it is I need to be doing. I'm still angry with you for killing all my snakes." He stood and set fire to a small black cigar stuffed into one corner of his lips, shook out the match, and tossed it on Ty's lap. "Took one of my boys a whole day to gather those nasty things. And now he'll have to do it all over again." He blew smoke in Ty's face.

"I reckon I'll leave you both here in this dank hole with all this bloody mess you made. Maybe one of these dead vipers will slither to life and give you a few bites, save me the trouble of doing the deed. But I ain't quite ready for that yet, anyway."

"What is it you are ready for?"

Duggins laughed and walked up the narrow passageway, stopped halfway up. "Clean yourself up, will you, Farraday?

You're a mess." His laughter continued long after he slammed shut the heavy wooden door and slid home the heavy bar securing it. Bare slivers of light angled in between the thick planks.

"Sue Ellen?"

"I'm here, Ty."

"I'm sorry about all this." He felt so tired, fought to keep his eyes open. "I—"

"No, no, Ty. It's me. It's my fault. None of this would have happened . . ."

"What is it he wants, Sue Ellen? I heard one of them mention a treasure." Ty perked up, tried to turn himself toward her, but managed only to send a fresh surge of throbbing pain from his neck up into his head.

She sighed. "It's . . . I barely understand it myself, Ty. But he killed Alton, Ty. I just know he did." Her voice cracked, he heard her take a deep breath.

"You mean you don't know for certain if Alton's dead?"

"Oh, I know. Deep down, I know. He never came back from town the day they arrived. And then Duggins had his pocket watch. Alton treasured that, said it was given to him by his grandfather a long time ago. Hadn't worked for the longest time, but he said that when he finally made his fortune, it was the first thing he spent money on. He got it repaired."

Ty remembered seeing Winstead glancing at the watch a time or two in town over the years. He always thought the man did so as a sort of affectation. "I have some bad news for you, Sue Ellen."

"Oh, Ty," she said in a weary voice. "How much worse could it all get?"

"It's just that . . . I know Alton's dead."

For a few seconds he heard nothing; then in a firm voice Sue Ellen said, "How?"

"I found him. In the hills between our places." He didn't think he needed to tell her that coyotes and other critters had begun their work on him. When she didn't speak, he continued. "I covered him pretty well with rocks. It was a hasty job, but we can redo it."

"Thank you. I know none of this has been easy."

"Sue Ellen, you need to tell me what's going on. Why are these men here? Why kill Alton? What about this treasure business?"

Again she sighed.

Ty inched himself slowly over, sliding on the dead snakes. Finally he could make out her form in the gloom.

"It seems Alton wasn't what he told me. I know what you're thinking. And I guess you were right all those years ago."

He didn't say anything, just waited for her to go on. But he wanted her to hurry up—there might not be much time before Duggins returned, and at that point it was anyone's guess what that crazy man would do to them.

"Let's just say that Alton did something to these men a long time ago, before he ever came here. From what I could make out in Duggins's rambling, Alton was a . . . a thief, maybe even a killer. Oh, but I have a hard time believing that. I knew him, or at least I thought I did, pretty well. We were married for ten years, after all."

"Yeah, I'm well aware of that." Ty regretted what he said as soon as it tripped out of his mouth.

"I can't keep apologizing, Ty. It won't change anything."

"I know, I know. So what did Alton do that he deserved to die over?"

"They stole a big treasure, or something very valuable. Then Alton left them all to take the blame. Duggins and at least one of the others spent time in prison for it."

Ty nodded. "And vowed to get their revenge once they got

out. Same old story, older than the hills." They sat in silence for a few moments; then Ty said, "So did he?"

"Did he what?"

"Have a treasure? I know he spent money like it was going out of fashion, especially those early years." Boy did he know it—bought Ty's land right out from under him.

"He was wealthy. But in recent years he didn't spend as much. In the past year or so he acted more cautious with his purchases, began spending lots of time watching the roadway in, using his fancy glass to scan the surrounding hills. He always made sure I had whatever I wanted, though in truth I didn't really want much. But what he offered I didn't . . . Never mind."

Ty let that last thought pass. Too much time and much too late to think about anything but living through all this. "Duggins is looking for the treasure, then? Not just revenge?"

"That's what he said. He thought I knew where it was."

Ty looked at her. "And do you?"

She didn't respond right away. Then she breathed deeply. He saw her face turn toward him. "At first, no, I didn't. Then . . ."

"Then? You think you know where it is?" This information could save their lives—or at least get them out of this hole, and then maybe he could make a play somehow.

"Ty, do you remember . . . where you first said you loved me?"

Love? She was bringing that up at a time like this? How long ago had he told her that, anyway? Eleven years and more. Of course he knew the spot—the waterfall. It was a place he and she had vowed their undying devotion to each other. It was the spot where he spoke things he'd never said before, and he knew now that he'd never utter again to anyone else. How dare she bring up that place?

"Sue Ellen," his voice was harsh, snappy, and he didn't

care. "I will never forget that place. And you well know it. But this is no time to bring up the past. Now if you know where this so-called treasure is, you'd better tell me so we can use it to get out of this mess, you understand?" By the time he finished speaking, his voice was quavering on the edge of anger.

"Ty," she said, her voice barely a whisper. "I'm telling you where it is, if you'd only listen. And I'm not saying it out loud because he's more devious than you can imagine. I wouldn't put it past him to be out there listening, somehow."

The tension in his jaw lessened; the truth dawned on him. Yes, now he knew. The waterfall. But how did Alton know about it? Unless . . . "You took him there?"

"Who, Duggins?"

"No, Alton!" Ty felt his anger rise again.

"Ty." She sighed. "Never mind. It's not important how he found out about it."

"It is to me," he said, feeling a little like an angry child.

"Okay, okay. He followed me there. It was back in the early days of our marriage. I suppose I was unhappy. I told myself I had done the right thing, but knew in my heart that I hadn't. Without even knowing it, I'd take long walks all the time. Sometimes for hours and hours. Eventually Alton grew suspicious."

"Of what?"

"He thought I was meeting up with you, Ty."

He didn't say anything, just snorted.

"He followed me and one day caught up with me there. He accused me of going to meet up with you, Ty. Said I was a harlot and a whore and I suppose I was. . . ."

He could hear that she was sobbing. "No, you're not, Sue Ellen."

"But I went there hoping to bump into you. I thought that somehow, I could explain it."

"There was nothing to explain. You chose him over me. That's all there was to it. Look, Sue Ellen. This is all water under the bridge. We have to think of a way to get out of here or none of it will matter, anyway. So do you have any ideas? Any at all?" As he said it he remembered his boot knife, the one thing he almost forgot to tuck in when he'd left the Rocking T for the day. Maybe it was still there.

"Sue Ellen, are your fingers free?"

"I guess so. They're so numb from being tied I'm afraid I'll never be able to move them again."

"We have to try something. I'm hoping my knife is still in my boot. But I have to get over to you first." As she spoke he pushed backward with his heels against the floor, but it was still slick with snake gore and they just slipped out from under what pressure he exerted. He tried again and again, finally shoving away enough dead snake mess to gain purchase on the floor. He pushed hard, his backside sliding, until his back connected with the rocky wall. It took him longer than he would have liked to stand, but he was as tired as he could ever remember feeling, his brain had been clunked a few times too many, and his tongue felt like a dry, wooden plug—he'd give a healthy beef for a cool drink of water.

As he worked to force himself to stand, inch by inch, he thought of Uncle Hob, hoped the old man was able to fend off the attackers. Despite Hob's ornery demeanor and never-give-up attitude, Ty thought that maybe this time the bad eggs could have gotten the best of the old man. He felt guilty about making a hash of this entire affair. He should have stayed away from the ranch, ridden for the law, anything but what he'd ended up doing.

Now look at him, look at Sue Ellen, at Uncle Hob. Heck, even his favorite horse, Stub the Morgan, was now loose, wandering another man's range.

Sue Ellen's whispered voice cut in on his thoughts. "Ty, I think I hear someone coming."

He was almost to his feet, inching with his fingertips up the packed dirt-and-log walls, when a shadow outside cut across the light slanting in through the gaps in the door's planking. The wooden dead bolt slid backward, caught. Whoever it was grunted and cursed in a soft voice and rammed it harder. The bolt slid the rest of the way. The door swung outward, and bright light filled the doorway.

A tall, wide-shouldered figure filled the space, appearing only as a blackened form, skylined as he was against the light. Ty squinted. It didn't seem like Clewt. But who?

The man walked down the short hall, bending low, his features becoming more visible with each step. Ty guessed it had to be one of Clewt's men. And judging from Sue Ellen's sneering look, Ty guessed correctly.

"What do you want?" she said.

Ty had to hand it to her, she was still a spitfire, even in a dicey situation like this.

The man had a long, horselike face, and when he spoke, it was in a decidedly Southern drawl. "What in the name of all that is holy happened in here?" He swung his face toward each of them, concern and curiosity writ large on the long features. "Either one of you bleedin' bad? Dyin'?"

"No," said Ty. "But those rattlers have seen better days."

The man looked down, his mouth pulling wide in disgust as he realized what it was he was standing in the midst of. He lifted his big boots one at a time as if that might help.

"I ain't got much time," he said, glancing back up toward the door. "Boss might come back and I . . . I can't get caught doing this. He's a devil, he is. Kill a man as soon as look at him. You ought to see what he made me do with Paco."

While he spoke the man slipped a sheath knife from his belt and slashed the wraps that held one of Sue Ellen's legs tied to the chair. He pulled a revolver free and cranked it back. "No trying anything now. Either of you. I'm here to help, but I will shoot you, just so you know."

"Shoot us and your precious boss will come running. That makes you doomed, I'd say." Sue Ellen sneered a grim smile at him, her eyes hard and glinting in the bright light.

Ty had never seen that look on her before, nor heard the hard, mean edge to her voice. Then again he'd not really known her for a decade, far long enough for someone to change. And considering what she'd been through these past couple of days, he could hardly blame her for being flinty.

The tall man swallowed, appeared to be thinking over his options, and began to look rabbity to Ty. "Hey, fella," said Ty, giving Sue Ellen a quick wide-eyed stare. "You cut us loose and neither of us will try to trip you up, you have my word. Clewt will never hear of this. Right, Sue Ellen?"

"Ty—"

"Right?" said Ty, louder than Sue Ellen's protestations.

It seemed to help, because the man nodded, bent back to his task, though he kept a watchful eye on the captives. His knife was sharp and he made quick work of the hemp ropes.

Ty rubbed his chafed wrists, then offered a hand to the cramped Sue Ellen. "Why are you doing this, fella?"

"What? Oh, uh, my name's Rufus."

"Didn't ask you your name, Rufus. I asked why you're freeing us," Ty said as he glanced about the dim chamber without result, looking for a dropped weapon, maybe his skinning knife, something more they might use. But to no avail.

But the man was backing up the short tunnel, still pointing his revolver their way. "I got to go. Boss is somewheres around. . . ." Then he bolted from sight. Ty grabbed Sue Ellen's wrist and pulled her, stiff-legged, up the passage. "C'mon. We can't waste any more time."

"Ty, where can we go? It's broad daylight and Duggins has to be around somewhere."

"Who cares where we go, as long as it's not locked up in there anymore. We have to get out of here." They stopped at the doorway, blinking into the bright, midday light, looking left and right. "I don't see anyone," said Ty. "Let's make for the trees up back of this hill. We'll circle around to the other side of the house—I'm hoping Stub will still be there. If not, we'll hoof it overland."

"To your place?"

"Yep. If Hob's okay."

"What do you mean?"

"I'll tell you later."

They switchbacked up the scree-laden slope above the root cellar, breathing hard and angling as fast as Ty could urge them toward the too-spaced stand of ponderosas. They'd have to get deep into the trees before risking their wide arc toward the southwest. They made it to the trees, ducked low to avoid sparse, long, drooping branches. Ty felt fully visible from the sprawling ranch house not far below them. Not far at all.

"Ty, you're hurting me. I have to stop." Sue Ellen's voice came out in a gasping whisper.

He looked back at her. He hadn't been aware that he'd been all but dragging her along, her rope-raw wrist clamped tight in one of his gore-spattered hands. He let go of her. "We have to keep going, Sue Ellen. No time, no weapons." They were both breathing hard, and Ty was aware that at any moment Duggins might see them from below. Or maybe he already had and was tracking their progress, drawing a sight on them.

She was bent double, with her hands on her knees, her work dress a begrimed, ripped mess, her hair hanging in her face, dirt and blood smeared on her high cheeks and her bold chin. Ty thought she'd never looked lovelier and he knew, more so than he had at any time in the previous ten years, that he had never gotten over her.

"Ty?" She was looking at him. "Don't you think that was—I don't know—too easy?"

"What do you mean?"

"I mean it was too convenient. Think about it—Duggins just leaves; then a while later one of his fools comes in, without much of an excuse at all, and just lets us go?"

She was right, of course. In his haste to make sure she was okay, he'd overlooked the fact that it had all been too easy. "That man, Rufus." Ty nodded. "His answers were odd. I just thought he was nervous . . . and stupid."

"I think he was both. But he was also told to free us. I'd bet this so-called treasure on it."

"So what do you think we should do?" Ty asked as he tugged off his right boot.

"I know we don't have time to kick off our shoes and relax."

He held up his boot knife, a folding cutter that had served him well for a number of years.

"Hey . . ." Recognition bloomed on Sue Ellen's face. "Didn't I give you . . . ?"

"Yep."

"You kept it all these years."

"When something's reliable you stick with it." He turned from her, aware that his remark had barbs, and led the way northward, still crouching low, hurrying deeper into the sparse tree cover.

After a few dozen yards she said, "I don't think we should try to get back to your place."

"Where do you suggest we go?"

"Head west, toward . . ."

"The treasure," he said. Sue Ellen nodded.

"And lead Duggins to it?"

"Why not? I don't care about it. I just want him to leave and never come back."

Ty stopped again and looked at her. "You really think he's going to just let us go? Even if he has the treasure—whatever it may be? And besides, you're not even sure it's there. Or if it even exists."

She didn't reply.

"By that logic," said Ty, "he'll be tracking us, following along like a starving wolf after a sickly elk calf, waiting for us to lead him to it." He smiled at her. "Okay then, let's be that calf. And lead that wolf to something he won't ever forget."

Chapter 28

Henry and Crazy Horse Ranch Woman—though he'd never address her as such to her face—headed north on the Piker Road. The direction was as much she would tell him, which he already knew. They rode for hours while the near-full waning moon lit the roadway, a well-traveled track, as evidenced by dung and deep wagon ruts. Near as he could tell it was pushing midnight, and she showed no signs of stopping for a rest.

Henry hated to admit it, but he felt rotten all over, as if he had come down with the ague. He hoped it was just tiredness and some sort of rank feeling left over from the bullet wound. He also didn't care much anymore what she thought. He slowed his mount and packhorse to a stop. "I am loath to admit it, ma'am, but I have to climb down. Maybe grab a few minutes of sleep."

"Fine," she said over her shoulder. "When you get enough of your precious beauty sleep, then you can hurry on up the trail and catch up to me."

He sat his horse, watching her slowly disappear into the night ahead, not seeming to care one whit. Finally he sighed, tapped his heels, and the little packhorse made a disappointed sound from low in its throat, but kept on trudging. "I know how you feel, horse. But I can do nothing about it. She claims to know where we are going and I do not."

Over the next hour he tried to engage her in conversation, but she refused to answer him. Finally she said, "Why do you talk so much? No wonder my two men shot you. They told me they thought you were one of the men who had attacked us. But that you had gone insane. Now I see what they mean."

"I am not crazy. I am, however, tired and sore and annoyed. With you, if you must know. I demand to know where we are headed. Those men are fugitives and I am the law, and it is my job to uphold the law by bringing them back to Dane Creek."

"You ain't the law. You said yourself that you are a former lawman. Now, in my book that doesn't make you law anymore." She turned in the saddle and looked at him. The moonlight shadows made her look a little spooky to him, as if she had no eyes.

"Fine, then I am no different than you. I want revenge on those men. Plain and simple."

She halted her horse and waited until he rode up beside her. The moonlight still made her look spooky to him, but a little less so this close up. "It's about time you were truthful with me, Mister Henry Lawdog. That's all I was waiting for."

He regarded her with suspicion a moment longer, then said, "So you're going to tell me where we are headed?"

"Yeah, but first we need to make camp. A few hours of sleep will be good for your sore arm."

Henry sat there atop his horse, shaking his head in disbelief while Crazy Horse Ranch Woman climbed down from Lilly and led her into a clear patch just off the road. He followed suit, stripping off saddles and tending the horses. She kindled a small fire and made hot soup in a tin pot she'd tied to his packhorse's saddle back at the ranch. She also produced biscuits and jerky.

While they sipped at the thin soup, she said, "I heard tell they were headed to find a man who had done them all kinds of wrong."

Henry paused, holding his tin cup in both hands. "Please tell me you have more information than that."

"I do." She sipped, chewed a bite of biscuit as slowly as a cow might its cud wad.

"And?"

She sighed. "My word, Mr. Henry, you are a nervy thing. Duggins himself said the man they were looking for goes by the name of Winstead now. Something like that. And that he has a ranch near some town called Ripley something-or-other."

Henry could hardly believe it. After all this time, the first real bit of information he had. The first bit—and she had known it the entire time. "All this time and I could have been on the road toward Duggins? And you let me just lie in bed?"

"No you couldn't, and no I didn't. My men hadn't mistaken you for a crazy bad man and shot you, you wouldn't have come under my care. You'd have kept right on babbling and raving and wandering and the good Lord only knows where you would have ended up. Likely bear bait somewhere. And as for you lying around in bed, I had to let you rest up for a few days. Elsewise you'd be of no use to me."

Henry ate the rest of his meal in silence, stewing but elated, too, because he finally knew where they were headed. Even if he didn't know exactly how to get there. Finally he said, "I still don't know why you didn't just go on your own."

"Truth is I was preparing to when my boys shot you. I had to tend you before I could go. It wasn't an easy choice, Mr. Henry. I wanted to leave you be. But your wound would likely have putrefied. I figured that Duggins was in a longish sort of way guilty of you being shot too. So I didn't see any reason why another innocent man should die for his sins." She began cleaning the few utensils they'd used. "Not yet anyway."

"What's that mean?"

"Means I need you whole and alive and able to pull a trigger when we get there. Strength in numbers, Mr. Henry." She smiled, then unrolled her blankets, lay down with a knee-popping groan, and said, "Night."

Henry sat there for long minutes, watching the flames of the small fire dwindle, thinking of his wife and son and wondering if he'd ever be able to pull a trigger again, even on a man like Clewt Duggins.

Chapter 29

"You did good, Rufus. Very good." From the shadows on the east side of the Double Cross ranch house, Clewt stared up at the top of the ponderosa-topped slope. He ran the tip of his tongue across his teeth, played with the gap where the canine tooth had split right up the middle when that nasty woman on the horse ranch had rammed her head into his face. Good that he'd left Paddy behind to take care of her. Otherwise the dragon would have had to leave more of a mess behind.

"Okay, boss. I'm not sure what I did that was so good, but . . . okay, if you say so." Rufus would only look at his big ol' boots, not meet Clewt's eye.

Clewt flinched. Here was a man who had just done his bidding but who it was quite obvious wasn't pleased at all with having done it. Now why was that? "Rufus? Look at me."

Again the tall man hemmed and hawed, swung that big horsey head to and fro.

"Rufus?"

Finally he looked up, to find Clewt smiling. At him. The biggest pie-eating grin he could muster. "Now see? That wasn't so bad." He draped an arm around Rufus's shoulder. The tall man shrunk even more in on himself.

"You see, Rufus, there comes a time when a man has, how

can I put this? He's fulfilled his earthly duties and there really is not much more he can do for the good of mankind. You follow me, son?"

"I . . . I can't say I do, no, boss."

"Well, let me put it this way." With a quick movement that surprised and pleased even himself, Clewt Duggins upthrusted a long, thin-bladed melon knife into Rufus's midsection, just under the point where the ribs joined in the middle of the tall man's breadbasket. At the same time, Clewt tightened his shoulder-draping arm and pulled downward on Rufus's frame, forcing the blade deep.

The tall man's eyes widened impossibly, matched with his O-shaped mouth. Red blood soon streamed in strings from his mouth, making his lips look grotesquely shaped.

"Now, son," said Clewt in Rufus's ear in a low, hoarse whisper. "Take no offense in this, and know that I take no pleasure in it. Well, maybe a little." He chuckled. "But it's really needed doing for some time. You are not suited to this life. Everything I've asked you has been a painful decision for you. And that's just not good. I need people who understand me, people who will snap to at a moment's notice and not feel as though what I have asked might or might not be a good thing. You see?"

Rufus's eyes began to glaze over. Clewt leaned close to the man's long, collapsing face. "What's that? You say you understand? You say you take it all back? You say you'll be more like the other boys, less apt to drag those big ol' feet of yours?" Clewt straightened, slid his knife free of the man's body, and pushed him backward.

Rufus wavered at full height, then slowly fell backward, like a fresh-chopped tree not yet aware that it had been cut through. His left leg buckled at the knee and he collapsed sideways, not raising his hands to stop his fall.

Clewt looked down at his right arm, coated in a sleeve of

glistening blood. "Oh dear, now that is messy. And unfortunate for you that you didn't speak up sooner."

The far-off sound of hoofbeats drawing closer pulled his gaze toward the hills to the southwest. A rider crested, then galloped down the last ridgeline before the ranch. "Looks like someone's headed back." But Clewt's smile faded. "Where are the rest of them?" He watched the horse's progress a moment more, his features darkening with each passing moment he did not see other riders trailing behind.

A gagging sound that turned into a long, final wheeze rose up from the man at Clewt's feet. "Oh, shut up," said the boss, driving his boot into the man's back. Rufus didn't move.

Clewt stomped off toward the barn and thrust his arm into the water trough, rubbing the blood from his arm, sluicing it off the knife blade. Every few seconds he glanced toward the approaching horse, his breathing coming faster and harder, his mouth setting into a tight, firm line and a growl rising from his throat.

He stood by the trough watching the horse approach. Water ran from his soaked arms, the long, thin-bladed knife still gripped in his right hand. Something was off about it. Was that shimmering heat? A rider? Could be, but the man looked to be fighting to stay in the saddle, swaying from side to side. Was it Paddy, with his Appaloosa, that dark coat, and wide-shouldered torso? Had to be. But why was he alone, and what in the heck was wrong with him?

"Whatever it is, he'd better hurry up," Clewt said in a low voice. "Have to trail the woman and her rescuer."

The horse finally slow-stepped to a stop just under the arch. And that's when Clewt saw there was no man in the saddle at all. He squinted, tried to see across the few hundred yards to the gate, wondering where Paddy was. Why? It's not like he needed the man, nor did he particularly want him around. He had planned on killing him anyway, as soon as he found the treasure. Maybe the crazy Irishman didn't make it through the task he'd sent them on. Maybe they'd run into some sort of trouble at Farraday's. He knew the rangy rancher hadn't been there the entire time because he'd been here, at the Double Cross, killing Clewt's snakes and getting himself tied up.

Clewt smiled, canted his jaw to the side. Maybe the second man at Farraday's place, whoever he was, was more than a match for his men. Hadn't he wanted them to die off anyway? Save him the trouble of having to gut them like ol' Rufus here. Clewt looked down at the man sprawled halfway across the yard. He'd not taken any great pains to hide the body, nor to kill him where he could easily be gotten rid of. Why bother?

Clewt knew that since he'd gotten out of prison, he had been pleasantly surprised by the lack of people willing to stand up to him and his newly recruited boys—new, that is, save for Paddy. There had been a time when loyalty to one of his men, such as the crazy Irishman, had been important to him. But that had been so long ago, was so far buried in his blood-slick past that Clewt could no longer recall when it had been that way. Or why, come to think on it.

The way he figured it, he owed nothing to anyone, save himself. The dragon needed no one and nothing—except maybe a fortune in stolen Mexican gold, a treasure that should have been his all along. The thought of it stashed somewhere, just waiting for him somewhere in the dark, not being allowed to glint and glisten in the sunlight, drew a groan of frustration from him. He'd follow through with his plans—arm himself, pack a saddle horse, and trail the woman and Farraday. They'd been gone long enough, anyway, for them to think they'd really escaped from him.

Clewt smiled and began to hum, not even aware he was doing so, mumbling out the ragged fragments of something his grandmother used to sing to him. If he'd been aware of what he was doing he might well have paused in his work, drifted back to a more pleasant time, back before that first dragon flapped into his life, belching smoke and flame and blood.

But he didn't give it much thought. To him the sounds he made were random, tuneless snatches, noises to make while he prepped his horses for what he knew would be his final ride on this long search.

Much of this quest had not gone the way he'd dreamed about it, from his dark, rat-crawly cell in Mexico. But then again, when in life did everything go according to plan? Not often, he was willing to wager. And all in all, considering the payoff in gold he was soon to find, it could all have gone so much worse.

"At least Alton had had the foresight to marry. Elsewise, I'd have killed him and would have had nobody to lead me to the treasure. Or whatever is left of it."

That had been the one flaw in his plan. He had no way of knowing just how much of the treasure that back-stabber had spent the years. Alton finished strapping onto a second horse a pack saddle with ample collapsed canvas panniers—they would hold a mighty amount. Then Clewt paused, brow furrowed once more.

He stood back, not feeling too worried about trailing the woman and Farraday. Not yet. After all, he would be toting guns and would be on horseback and they would be afoot, and unarmed. He fished a small dark cigar out of his shirt pocket and popped it between his lips, dragged a match head along a strip of canvas, and set the brilliant flame to the end. He pulled the smoke in deep, held it there but a moment, then blew it back out in two long, roiling jets from his nostrils. That always made him smile.

Now that he thought on it, the one pack animal didn't

seem enough somehow. What if Alton had spent even less cash on his land and home than Clewt originally had guessed he had? What if there was—dare Clewt dream it?—even more treasure than he had thought he might end up with.

The thought of finding the treasure had excited him, but the thought of finding even more than he had long dreamt of made him worried. He nibbled his bottom lip for a few more moments, then headed back into the barn for a third animal and packing outfit. It would definitely not do to show up poorly equipped and have to leave some of the treasure behind. I can't live with that, thought Clewt. No way, no how.

Chapter 30

It was the rasping, gravel-on-steel caw of the squabbling buzzards that dragged Hob from his stupor. He pushed himself upward, leaned on his one good, begrimed hand planted firmly on the ground, and swung his head slowly side to side, like a thin, dazed old bear, trying to piece together what had happened. It didn't take long, as the crazy Irishman lay close by, sprawled on his back, not looking too good. Hob didn't investigate closely, but it appeared from a few feet away that the man was dead. His face looked as if it had been stomped by a rogue stallion.

That's right, Hob thought as he stared at the Irishman. He shot at me, and his revolver must have kicked back and slammed him a good one in the face. Now it all came back to him, the horrible fight, the bum mashing his left hand. He cradled it to his chest, wincing at the sight of it more than the pain—the fingers had swelled fatter than they'd ever been in his life. There was a slight pain in his shoulder.

Hob looked down at himself, at a ragged, bloody knothole in his shirt, at the top of his left shoulder. The Irishman had only succeeded in grazing him. It was tender as all get out, but the wound had puckered and tightened and stopped bleeding. Good. One less thing to worry about. He'd have to get to his feet—ha! The one good foot, anyway, and see what he could do about finding a horse, then going to help Ty.

But for the moment, it was all Hob could do to rest up. He was too old for this crazy fighting business. How long had he been doing this sort of thing? Doing battle with rogue, wild dog-men? Why was it perfectly acceptable to shoot a hydrophobic dog, but not a man who was acting the same way toward his fellows?

Hob let out a low sigh that sounded like more of a moan. He was a scarred mess of a man, and as he lay there, propped on his one good hand, he wondered about his long, strange life. None of that mattered now, for he'd been stomped and shot—okay, grazed, but it still hurt like the dickens—by that foul Irishman, and would likely end up a worse cripple than what he was already. Or more to the point, he still might end up dead. Neither of the thoughts made much sense to him, but how much worse could his life get? He guessed the next few hours would reveal the answer to that.

He swung his gaze toward the house, expecting, even as he turned, to see a leveled smoldering ruin. What he saw was still a sad sight, but much better than he had a right to expect. Smoke spiraled upward from a dozen spots along the largely still-intact structure, but it appeared that the fire had burned out.

Even when it had been at its hottest while he'd been inside, then outside skirting this end of the house, the fire hadn't seemed all that menacing. Poorly lit—and he was glad of it. The Irishman had been too hasty, hadn't really stoked it in any one spot. And for that, Hob was mighty pleased. They would have a mighty amount of work to do to make it livable again, but he and Ty could manage it, he was sure of it.

And that's when another scrim of burlap seemed to have been pulled away from his eyes, from his mind. He thought of Ty clearly then, knew he had to get to him, had to help him save the girl, help him fight that Clewt Duggins. An evil character if there ever was one. He and his men had always been on dodgers at the top of the pile, fresh posters every month, it seemed, for terrible crimes for which they never were caught, at least not while Hob was a lawman.

It wasn't until he heaved himself upright, then kept going and fell over onto his less wounded right side that he saw the reason for this unexpected insult. The Irishman had shot all to pieces his best wooden leg!

Chapter 31

The main street of Ripley Flats was, it seemed to Henry, anything but flat. Or straight. The thing started out on a rise, then curved like a drunk snake's backbone to the left, even as it led a steady trickle of riders and wagons—and two cavorting dogs—downhill and straight to the first of three saloons. Henry had never been one for frequenting houses of drink, as he called them, but even he had to admit that the thought of a cold glass of beer and maybe a few slices of bread, some thick slabs of cold pork stuffed between, would hit the spot.

But he had no idea if Crazy Horse Ranch Woman was thirsty. He also had to admit that as they had drawn closer to their destination in the past week, he had begun to finally feel better, less fevered and stronger with each passing day. It was mostly due to her doting care delivered with a confusingly indifferent attitude. He had also begun to feel less and less inclined to follow through with the actual deed of hunting down a notorious killer and more and more like he wanted to go back home to Dane Creek and hug his wife and son.

If he had to guess—and he'd spent a lot of the trip doing that since Crazy Horse Ranch Woman wasn't much of a talker—he'd say that his shifting attitude had to do with her. He'd observed her for a couple of weeks now, had talked with her, albeit haltingly, throughout their journey, and he didn't want to end up like her. She was so bitter and resentful and intent on delivering harm to another that she was driven beyond all reason, beyond anything healthy, at the pure expense of her own life.

Henry wanted to live because he didn't want his wife and son to be confused, angry survivors like Crazy Horse Ranch Woman.

"What's wrong with you, Mr. Henry?" She had halted her horse a few paces before him, had turned in the saddle to regard him with that same cold look. He'd finally decided just a few days back why that look was so chilling. It was the same uncaring look he'd seen on the faces of the dead over the years. Too many of them to count, from the war on up through various peacekeeper jobs. And they all were final and cold and sad, so sad.

"Nothing. Nothing at all. I was just thinking about how nice it would be to sleep in a bed once again. To eat a hot meal with proper utensils and a plate. Maybe have a cup of coffee from a proper mug." He looked at her and smiled. "Come on," he said, urging his horse down into the town proper. "I'll treat you to a piece of pie and a cup of coffee."

But she hadn't moved. Just watched him, her eyebrows knitted tight. "You're backing out on me, huh?"

"What? Why do you say that?"

She ignored what he said. "And here I thought you wanted your own revenge as much as I did."

"Yeah, well, maybe I just want to live to see my family. Is that so bad?"

A fringe-top surrey carrying a dandified man in a spotless gray beaver bowler and matching jacket, accompanied by a short, plump woman tightly packed into a pink satin dress slowed at Henry's raised voice. The man clucked to the single horse pulling them and cut wide around them, off down the dusty lane at a quick *clop clop*. They both looked back with dismay on their fresh faces.

Henry looked from them to Crazy Horse Ranch Woman and saw, for the very first time since they'd met, that tears had pooled in her eyes and threatened to spill over and glisten on down her cheeks. It was the first time he'd seen her as a weak, sad, defeated woman who would be old far before her time. His comment had done this, and he felt terrible about being so thoughtless. But as quickly as that weakened state flashed itself on her features, it was gone again.

She reined Lilly around. "You go have your pie and coffee. I have to see a man about a ranch." With that, she was gone, the back of her dirt-lined duster wrinkling and bunching as her tired horse picked its way down the sloping main street into town.

He sighed and nudged his horses into a quick step behind her, any thoughts he had of pie and coffee pinched out.

She slowed, reading signs and assessing the various folks staring back at her from the sidewalks and in the offices and other places of business lining the surprisingly bustling street. From up on high, at the head of the lane, he had seen beyond the main street of Ripley Flats to a small sprawl of squarely laid-out streets, as if built on a grid. Henry guessed there were several hundred people as full-time town dwellers. Someone there might well know who Alton Winstead was and where he could be found.

And when she stopped her horse, that's just what Crazy Horse Ranch Woman asked the town marshal who'd been sitting on his porch, assessing the back of his eyelids.

"Hey, hey, what's that now?" He let the front feet of his chair come down hard on the porch floor. He dragged a knob-knuckled hand down his face, rustled his big walrus mustaches and shook his head like a wet dog. "What's that you say?"

"Alton Winstead," she repeated. "I'd like to know where his ranch is at."

The man stood, his stovepipe boots looking as if they were two sizes too large for his bowed legs, his vest two sizes too small, straining as it was on a perfectly round paunch that looked out of place on his otherwise thin frame. "Why?"

"My business," said Crazy Horse Ranch Woman.

Henry sighed inside and pasted on a smile. He touched his hat brim. "How do, Marshal? I am Henry Atwood, from Dane Creek. We are, as the lady says, looking for Mr. Winstead. He is an old friend and we would like to surprise him with a visit. It's been a long time on the trail, as you can imagine, and—"

The marshal cut him off. "Friend, huh? Well, why didn't you say so? Now you mention it, I expect the reason he ain't been seen in town of late is because he's been entertaining all these friends of his. Must be a big celebration out thataway."

The woman leaned forward, her saddle creaking. "What makes you say that, Marshal?"

Henry watched her—she was almost friendly. He decided she'd do anything to get what she wanted.

"Oh," said the old lawman. "A few days back a whole pile of men come riding in, claimed to be his friends, too."

"Claimed, you say, Marshal?" said Henry. "Did they leave room for doubt?"

The marshal's woolly eyebrows pulled together. "Why, you a lawyer?"

"Me? No, sir."

"Oh good, 'cause talk like that's unusual hereabouts."

"Those men, Marshal," said the woman. "What did they look like?"

"Look like? Heck, I don't know. They was a run-down lot, more interested in liquor than checkers, I can tell you that much, all but the ramrod of the outfit. Now he was a curious sort. Hard-looking character, all pocky-lookin', but you could tell he could impress the ladies. Had that curly hair, dark eyes, and mustache. Smoked black cee-gars that stunk to high heaven, and the smoke come boiling out of his nose like he was a locomotive or something. And I'll tell you another thing." He raised a finger, pointing not quite at them. "He looked to be the only one who bathed regular." He laid a finger aside his nose and nodded. "A man can tell these things."

"Well, thank you, Marshal. They're his friends, all right."

"Oh? Yours, too, I reckon?"

"Not hardly," she said.

"Well, any friend of Alton Winstead is a friend of Ripley Flats. He's a fine gent." He leaned forward. "Not much of a rancher, mind you." He winked a big wispy eyebrow. "But a good and generous gent."

Can't be too good, thought Henry, if he used to run with Clewt Duggins.

"Generous how? With money? Time?" said Crazy Horse Ranch Woman.

"Well . . ." The old lawman pushed his hat back on his forehead. "Now that you mention it, he ain't been into town in a few days. Not like him." He tapped his stubbled chin and cradled an elbow in one old knobby hand. "We often have a cup of coffee of an afternoon, talk of this and that. Maybe a game of checkers."

Even Henry had begun to grow tired of the old man's meandering, nonanswering demeanor. "Excuse me, Marshal. Which way to his spread?"

"Oh, take the middle road northward out of town. You can't miss it. Go about sixteen, no, eighteen miles out. Well, maybe not that far out, maybe only a dozen or more. Anyways, there're only two places out thataway. Second one's the Double Cross. That'd be Alton's. He's a great one for a joke—I reckon that's the story behind that ranch name. But the first ranch you'll come to, at about mile ten or so, now that'll be Ty Farraday's spread. A decent enough young man, but he's saddled with that ornery old one-legged coot, Hob. I don't know how he does it. I'd rather live with my wife than that crazy old man."

He tipped his hat again and raised a confiding hand to the side of his mouth. "And that's saying something." He winked. "Tell Alton I said hello. And he owes me a game of checkers."

Henry nodded and reined his horse down the street, trying to catch up with Crazy Horse Ranch Woman, who'd beelined toward the north road as soon as the marshal had confirmed the direction of the Double Cross Ranch.

Chapter 32

"Ty, I've never come to the falls this way."

"Me neither." He checked their back trail, wiped the sweat from his eyes, smelled the sickly stale stink of snake blood and flesh still stuck to him. He'd love to shuck these snake-bloody clothes and scrub himself clean. But that luxury would have to wait.

"Whew, Mr. Farraday. You are exuding a rank odor, I don't mind telling you."

Ty looked at her, eyebrows raised. "Let's go."

"Look, Ty. I'm sorry. I was trying to make a joke. I really do appreciate what you did back there. Killing those snakes. You saved my life. I mean it, Ty."

But he kept walking forward, showing her nothing but his back. He wanted to turn around and stick a long finger in her face and shout at her for everything he hadn't been able to say for all those years.

They walked on in silence for another few minutes, the occasional snapped twig and their hurried, labored breathing the only sounds.

"It'll be fall soon," said Sue Ellen. "I hope it's not a long, snowy winter."

She was making conversation, he knew. Trying to fill the uncomfortable spans of silence. He didn't care if she felt uncomfortable in his presence. She'd earned it. Then he heard something and held up a hand. She walked right into him. He gripped her shoulders and said, close to her face. "Shhh. Quiet now."

He scanned their back trail again, certain he'd heard the snort of a horse, far off, but still, such sounds only carried so far. He couldn't be sure it had come from back behind them. Maybe from the south? He looked that way, felt something on his cheek. It was Sue Ellen's breath. He looked down at her, their eyes only inches apart. Her upper arms were still gripped in his big hands, and she looked so innocent, so pretty to him then. As she always had.

"Ty," she whispered.

Her breath tickled his whiskered chin. Then he thought of the reason they were in this mess. Alton. Alton Winstead. Even dead the man had the power to ruin Ty's life. "No, no, no, no." He pushed her away, set his jaw and shook his head. "No. Not again." He turned, said in a low growl, "Let's go. We're almost there."

After a few seconds, he heard Sue Ellen's lighter footsteps following along. And the sooner he could make all this happen—assuming he could make it all happen—the sooner he could get shed of her, of the killers in their midst, and get back to life as a small rancher, a rawhider—the very name he'd long wanted to outgrow. He'd wanted to shed it like a snake sheds its old skin. But now, after seeing all this misery associated with Winstead's property, the only thing Ty figured he wanted was to be a small rancher, good at what he did and happy to be what he was. It wasn't much, but the Rocking T was his and Hob's. And he didn't have to share it with any woman. Ever.

"Shouldn't we have gone back to your place? We don't stand a chance fighting Clewt from the waterfall. We don't even have a weapon other than your pocket knife and these clubs you made from branches. There's nothing at the water-fall, Ty!"

"The treasure's there." He said it, but he didn't slow his pace, or turn around He kept right on hiking. "Besides, it's a whole lot closer to the Double Cross than to my place. And if we're lucky, Hob'll be along. But if we don't get a move on, we won't be there in time to do what I need to."

"And what is that?"

"Can't say just yet."

"Can't," she said, panting at the increased pace his long legs had kicked up. "Or won't?"

Ahead of her, a grim smile spread across Ty's face. One way or another, everything would change today. And he, for one, would be glad of it.

Chapter 33

It took Hob a while to make his way to the house. He had an old, professionally carved spare leg in the barn somewhere, stuck in a dusty corner, no doubt, but he'd be darned if he was going to rummage for it. So he opted for the padded crutch that Ty had made for him.

He used it only when he'd taken his rough-carved wooden leg off for the night, and sometimes early in the day when he didn't have the gumption to pull and twist and buckle on the leg first thing. The crutch was a bit singed at the bottom, and the padding on top was charred and crispy, but he quenched it in the water trough and it worked well enough.

He managed also to lure a lone long-eared mule over to the fence. Tulip, he called her. She was a decent sort, worked hard and rarely complained. But trying to saddle her had always been like trying to throw a saddle on a tiger. That took another thirty minutes. He also lashed on a pair of cloth panniers. Before mounting up, he washed his stomped-on hand, cursing the dead Irishman the entire time.

Then, knowing what dangers lay ahead, Hob went around to the dead men in the yard, and to the spot he had lain, and retrieved as many working firearms and bullets as he could find, plus his knife, still wedged under the Irishman where he'd fallen. He detoured into the still-smoking house and found an onion and half a loaf of bread he'd had in a cupboard for dinner, then filled two water canteens from the barn, then stuffed all this into the panniers.

The mule danced and kicked and made an awful racket, almost equaling the sounds that came from Hob himself. It didn't help the mule's demeanor that the panniers bounced in counterpoint to her rousing dance, slapping her on the rump with their heavy load of guns and ammunition. Hob managed to lash her tight, fore and aft, to the corral fence. Then he heaved himself up the rails, one at a time, an arm and a leg incapacitated, the others sore and in need of soothing remedies. But all that would have to wait for downtime. If that was something they would ever have again.

"Dad-blast it, Tulip! I ain't in no condition to deal with your shenanigans! Now settle down!" He landed a slap on her rump that only served to rile her further. It was all Hob could do to stay in the saddle.

He'd hurried as much as he could, knowing that each minute spent dallying was a minute that Ty was without help, and the girl Sue Ellen was that much closer to whatever foul plans Duggins had in mind.

Once he'd mounted up and secured the old beast as best he could, Hob took off for the Double Cross—he had to head there first. He knew Ty had said they'd meet up at the waterfall, but that didn't make any sense. That would only take him out of the way, slow him down. The ranch was where Ty would be if he'd had any trouble at all. And considering it had been a long while since Ty left the Rocking T, Hob had a gut hunch that the boy had run into trouble.

As he rode as hard as he could make the old mule step and clomp, wincing in pain with every jostling step on the rough ground, Hob did his best not to think about what could have happened to Ty.

The boy was everything to him, though he'd not admit it

to a living soul. Ty Farraday was the only thing that still connected him to Annette, sweet Annette, Ty's mother and the only woman Hob had ever loved. And he'd never told her so. Oh, he suspected she knew, but the boy had been her only focus in life. She'd never given any indication that there might be room in her life for anything or anyone else.

But the memory of Annette was why Hob had strapped on a cross-draw holster that he'd shucked off the gut-shot skinny man. His own left arm was far beyond useless with its purpled throbbing fingers. But his right could still draw, peel back a hammer, and squeeze a trigger. And he hoped he got the chance to do just that before the day was through.

Long minutes after Hob rode the mule northward out of the ranch yard, a low moan rose up, wavering from a bloodied mess of a man laid out on his back past the far end of the cabin. Shallow breaths convulsed with small, sharp coughs. Eventually one eyelid fluttered, then the other, and they both snapped wide open, revealing bloodshot brown eyes that stared straight up at a smoke-hazed blue sky. The moans grew into growls, the shallow breaths grew deep, and the Irishman pushed upright to a sitting position, looking around in a state of raw anger.

As he took in his smoking surroundings through bloody eyes, his breathing ragged and a whistling sound coming from his left nostril, Paddy wondered how in the name of all that was sacred he ever survived all that had dumped down on his head since he left Winstead's place. By all rights he should have expired after being shot at by that Farraday from up in the high rocks.

Then the old man had actually shot him right through the shoulder; then he'd been rammed into the barn, then dragged by a horse! But he'd lived. And then he'd braced those other two fools and shot them, even when they'd hauled iron on him themselves!

But the worst had yet to come—the old man refused to die, refused to give up, even after Paddy shot out his tree-stump leg. And just how could the skinny old man haul that thing around all day? Then just when Paddy had thought he'd finally get his revenge on the nasty old dog, when he'd stomped the life from the old man's hand, the vicious cripple had stabbed Paddy in the leg—the pain was excruciating.

And now here he was, sitting in a pool of his own blood, his leg a permanently gimped thing, much like the old man's. Paddy wasn't sure, but he might even lose the use of it, maybe lose the leg completely. He looked down at it, tried to move it, and noted the wound had puckered and crusted somewhat.

He would never forget that crazy old man's face. And as soon as he could wrap his own face and leg with a few rags, he would find himself a horse and head on back to the Double Cross, deal with Clewt, and then track down the old man. If he had to, Paddy would spend the rest of his days as drunk as possible, only sober enough to draw a sight on the old man's head, then pull that trigger. He couldn't be far, but Paddy wanted to find that blasted Clewt first. The "boss" would be the first to die, treasure or no.

As Paddy grunted and groaned and gasped his way up-right to stand, wobbly and woozy on his one good leg, he wondered if maybe he hadn't reached the end of his road after all. Waves of hot and cold rushed up and down him, from his head to his feet and back again. He felt suddenly ill and, before he could stop himself, the bubbling remnants of his last meal—a greasy wad of lard biscuits and near-raw bacon, topped with four runny eggs—all rushed upward, gushing out his bloody mouth and nose.

As he stood leaning against a wobbling stack of firewood, vomit dripping from his face, Paddy grew quite satisfied in his anger. It wasn't until he'd made his way around the front of the house and found Barn Cat, the string bean of the gang, sprawled on his side, dead and bled out, that he realized his own gun was gone. The old man must have snatched them all. Then he looked around. Maybe the old man was still in sight; maybe the old dog was preparing to draw down on him that very second.

And the thought struck Paddy as funny, so much so, in fact, that despite the pain of his cored leg, his shot-up shoulder, his broken ribs, and his bruised and bloodied face, he chuckled and chuckled as he used Barn Cat's own knife to hack strips of fabric off the dead man's togs. He fashioned a sling for himself, and wrapped a few tight lengths just under his knee to help stanch the flow of blood that had begun welling out once again when he'd started hobbling about the yard.

Paddy rummaged in Barn Cat's vest and found a few lucifers. He snatched out the man's makings from his shirt pocket and rolled himself a sloppy quirly. The smoke tasted good and helped clear the rattling sounds in his throat. "I feel like homemade sin, Barn Cat." He looked down at the dead man, one of the two he'd shot to death earlier. "But you, sir, look absolutely under the weather."

When he'd had his fill of the cigarette, he tossed it onto the dead man. Then he tipped his head back and sniffed the breeze, for no particular reason other than all he'd smelled for a long time, it seemed, was the rank tang of blood. This time was no different.

He limped his way around the far side of the house, found the other fool as dead as when he'd left him there, and, satisfied that the old man had also taken that man's guns, Paddy slowly made his way toward the barn, where he was pleased to find two things there, both appearing as if they were waiting for him.

The first was a flattened but still serviceable bowler hat,

the very one that had careened off his head when the old man had shot him. After a couple of false grabs, he managed to hook a finger under its upended brim and lift it up to inspect it. He punched a fist into it and plunked it on his head. A sigh marked its welcome return.

The second pleasing surprise was the sight of a somewhat short, rather fat pack pony standing close by in the corral, munching on a wispy stand of late-season grass at the base of a leaning, weathered post.

"You and me, pony, we're about to become good friends." He made his way into the barn and found a bridle and saddle just right for the small horse. It took him a few minutes to lug it all out to the corral, but he was pleased to note that the beast had been much-handled and so was of an even temperament.

He rigged it up, mounted, and headed northward, his savaged leg throbbing to beat the band. The only thing that kept him from giving over to the wash of pain pulsing all over his body was the picture he kept polished in his mind of Clewt Duggins—the man responsible for all the misery in Paddy's life—writhing in the dirt, screaming for mercy, and spurting his life out a little at a time from a dozen-dozen wet wounds.

Even in the midst of his own agonies, Paddy grunted in anticipated satisfaction and smiled.

"What are you doing?" growled Henry, making a quick grab at Crazy Horse Ranch Woman's reins. He held fast to them as her horse fidgeted.

"You unhand my horse, Mr. Henry Lawdog." Her face was tight, red with excitement. He knew why.

"No, I will not. You can't take off after him."

"Why in the heck not?" she said, still in a hoarse whisper, as they both watched the wrecked man in the bowler slowly depart from the ranch yard on the too-small horse.

"Because he can lead us to Duggins."

The two exchanged a silent look; then, as if rehearsed, they both looked back toward the retreating form. They watched a few moments more until the wounded Irishman on his little horse slowly rounded a corner out of sight.

"He was one of them," she said, so quietly Henry wasn't sure he'd heard her.

"I know."

"That Irishman. . . . I want to kill him with my bare hands. . . ."

"I know," said Henry. "I know. But that won't be enough. Let him work for us for a little while, then—"

"You won't let me kill them, will you?"

Henry shrugged. "Let's investigate this place while we're waiting for him to get on up the trail."

They rode, slow step by slow step, into the dooryard of the ranch house. "Lots went on here," she said.

Henry nodded, slipped down from the horse. He checked the man stretched out, gut-shot, before the house, but he was too far gone to be helped.

"Where there's one, there's bound to be more. Especially if Duggins and that Irish pig are involved." She looked down at the gut-shot man, sneered, and spit in his face. "He was another one."

A few minutes later, they found the man behind the still-smoking house. She repeated her greeting and said, "We should go. I don't want to lose him."

"He has to be going to Winstead's place. According to that old marshal there aren't any other ranches out here." He turned to her. "We'll find Duggins."

"We'd better." She climbed aboard Lilly and rested a hand on her thigh. "You coming?"

Henry nodded and climbed back into the saddle, more nervous than ever.

Chapter 34

As Ty and Sue Ellen approached the once-familiar chasm, he was struck, as he always was when he came upon it, no matter the direction, by how suddenly it always appeared, seemingly from nowhere, a long, ragged gash in the landscape. The next hundred or so yards would be tricky to navigate, because aside from a few small boulders the landscape was barren of anything they might use as cover from Clewt's approaching eyes. And he had no doubt the seedy rogue was on their trail.

He'd heard the hoof clacks, fleeting sounds, but there nonetheless. And the breeze, a light norther, had at times shifted and carried the whiff of tobacco, again a fleeting thing, but enough to tell Ty they were being trailed. The thought gave him grim comfort. Soon he would deal with the cur. And he could hardly wait. But first he had to get them to the waterfall. Its rock-jumbled, lairlike setting would afford them the most natural protection they were likely to get.

And if Sue Ellen was correct, and the treasure, whatever the blasted thing was, was to be found there, it might buy them time until either Hob showed his old, craggy face, or, if he were dead—a likely but horrible thought—then Ty would have at least gained the only somewhat safe point for miles around. And Ty was glad to have at least that slight bit of help, especially against someone as crazy as Clewt Duggins, and any other members of his gang still left alive and roaming the countryside like hydrophobic coyotes.

From what he'd seen of Clewt, coupled with what Sue Ellen had related to him, Clewt's behavior bore all the earmarks of someone becoming unglued from whatever it was that held him together. In Clewt's case Ty was sure the binding agents were mostly spite and greed, with a double pinch of mean to keep it unpleasant.

In the war, Ty had seen a number of men who looked fairly normal one moment—if a life of shooting men and men shooting at you, at all hours, in all conditions, can be considered normal—stand right up in the midst of a volley and walk right into a dozen bullets. Some of them had walked surprisingly far before whipping in circles like tossed rag dolls, before dropping to the bloody earth. That sort of behavior was what he was pretty sure Clewt was up to. Heck, the man might have been that way for years. The way he was behaving, he'd end up shooting at them even before they revealed where the treasure was, if there even was a treasure, and if they even knew where it might be. There has to be an easier way of living, thought Ty.

Sue Ellen seemed pretty sure of the treasure, and all the vague pieces had fit together—Alton had wandered into the region looking newly rich and acting like a fool with his money, spreading it around like it had no more value than water in a rainstorm. And then there were the buying trips he went on, rarely taking his new bride with him, where he'd be gone for weeks sometimes, only to come back puffed to the gills with money.

Sue Ellen had told Ty everything she knew that might be useful about the so-called treasure. Even then she'd seemed cagey to him. Seemed to Ty she was keeping something back. As long as it wasn't something that might get him or Hob killed, he didn't really care.

"You hear it?" He gestured with his chin, not caring if he sounded like an excited kid. "The falls." He loved the place.

She paused, her eyes narrowed. There were lines around her eyes, accentuated by the grime they both wore as evidence of the previous few rough days. She was still a beautiful woman, but there was something else about her now. Something almost cold, maybe even with a hint of ruthlessness about it. He hoped he was just imagining things. But living with a money-minded man such as Alton Winstead was sure to taint anyone's way of acting.

"Mmm, no, I don't hear it yet." But she kept staring toward it. "What do we do once we get there?"

"We get that treasure, use it as ransom—our lives in exchange for the treasure—and then we'll see what he does."

Sue Ellen's eyebrows rose. "We'll see what he does? He'll kill us, Ty. That's what he'll do. That's your plan? We've come all this way and that's what you plan on doing to him? Ty, he tried to kill us. Not just kill us, but . . . kill us with snakes! Oh, I don't believe this." She held the sides of her head and slumped to the ground.

Ty shook his head. "Did I say that was my entire plan?" He offered a callused hand. "Come on. We have to get across that open patch without stopping." She refused his hand, pushing to her feet with a knee-popping sound. She looked tired. Heck, so was he.

He'd forgotten how bloody belligerent she could be. That was one thing he'd always wondered about—how that sort of trait would age on a person. Apparently he was finding out, at least for a little while. If Sue Ellen was any indication, that stubbornness hung over her like an old wash rag, weighing her down and making her bitter.

Chapter 35

As he gently steered the horse through the petering trees, for the most part letting the beast pick its own path, Clewt mused on the past few days. He hadn't reckoned on feeling so confused. It felt to him as if nothing had gone right since he got out of that Mexican prison. Of his entire gang, he and Paddy were the only ones to survive the experience. All the others—Manny, Roger, Shanky, Bulleit, and Garvin—died inside the walls.

Two were beaten to death—Manny by a guard, Roger by his cellmate. Shanky caught TB and coughed up little chunks of his lungs until there was nothing left to cough up. Bulleit went crazier than a hatter and tried to force his own head through the bars one night. He was partially successful—he pushed his skull halfway through the bars, but that's as far as he got. Poor Bulleit was found the next morning with his eyes bugged out of his misshapen skull, and his lips pooched as if he were trying to kiss someone on the other side of the bars. And ol' Garvin, he just plain died in his sleep.

Of all the boys, Clewt envied Garvin's way of passing the most. How pleasant that would be, he'd often thought, to go to sleep one night and that, as they say, would be that.

Clewt caught a glimpse of a bird rising out of the stunted pines up the slope before him. The woman and Farraday had doubled back on themselves, then changed course from their initial direction east, where Clewt assumed they were headed to circle around the Double Cross, maybe pick up mounts that he assumed Farraday had hidden in the woods. But in that, he'd been wrong. They'd changed course and headed northward, then west. What was their game?

"Where're you headed, my little treasure hounds? Gonna lead Clewt the Dragon to his earnings?" He mumbled this in a low voice, raspy from tobacco, then tweezered a fresh smoke out of his shirt's breast pocket and thumbnailed a match head alight. He could feel the treasure filling his hands, stuffing his pockets, overflowing the panniers on his pack animals.

Certainly Winstead had spent much of it in buying and setting up this ranch, but the ranch was a hollow thing, no cattle and only enough horses to keep the man's buggies moving. So what had he spent the rest on? Nothing, there was no other answer. The fortune was still here, somewhere, squirreled away, safe from the world. Yes, Clewt could just see Alton Winstead roving into these woods to his hiding place—still on Double Cross property—and counting his wealth, maybe sliding free a piece now and again to keep on living like a king.

Clewt blew a cloud of smoke at the back of his horse's head. The beast's ears twitched. Had to be a whole lot of treasure left, though. All those gold chalices, crosses, candlesticks, goblets, plates, platters, bowls, saucers, and who knew what else, all waiting for him. Over the years, he had envisioned the hoard as encrusted with jewels. Now he was unsure if it had just been his fancy recalling that, or were jewels really stippling the surface of a good many of the looted Mexican valuables?

Before he realized it, he'd crested out atop a mostly treeless ridgeline. He was sure he'd been following their trail. He was also pretty sure they didn't know he was dogging them. He just knew he'd guessed right—let them go, but make it look like they were breaking out, and they'd beeline right to the treasure. What he had in mind for them would serve their asses right. That sort of greed had to be punished, had to feel the wrath of the dragon! Ha! Clewt loosed a low, wet laugh, spat, and sucked on his cigar, pulling the hot smoke deep.

In truth they'd made it pretty easy for him—good thing, as he was no tracker. Not like ol' Paddy. Now that Irishman could follow a trail. Clewt wondered where he'd got to. "Send a man to do a job and you are bound to be disappointed." He said it as he scanned the gradual slope of the land before him, a wide-open patch littered with a giant's handful of gray boulders like children's marbles. Beyond that the land seemed to drop off into a wide declivity that narrowed far below, the base lost in a vast and long jumble of gray rock, scree slopes, and a dark thatch of trees running like a shadowed green-black scar, north to south.

Far below, beneath that rocky, treed darkness, a river wormed its way through the valley, tumbling from on high to Clewt's right, upslope at the height of land, through what he guessed were layers of stacked chasms and rocky corridors that looked to grow deeper and darker with more severity, falling away as they progressed toward the south, far to his left.

But it was a quick, dark flash of movement at the edge of the golden-grassed span between him and the chasm, at the far edge of it, that caught his eye. There was no sound save for a stiff northerly breeze soughing across the spot, whispering in the trees back behind him. Had he seen the woman? Farraday? He was nearly sure of it. What else could it be? His eyes scanned the yellowed thatch before him, saw nothing for a few moments, then detected a faint trail of bent grass—they had come through. What he'd seen must have been them. Maybe one of their heads.

Clewt smiled, puffed on the cigar sending smoke breezing away, and nudged the horse forward.

Trudging on his slow but surprisingly steady packhorse on his way to the Double Cross, Paddy looked to the northwest and his breath snagged in his throat. He saw a man skylined for a few fleeting moments atop a ridgeline, just above that river chasm. That wouldn't necessarily be an out-of-place sighting except that something about that silhouette was familiar. Then he nodded and grinned. Only one man he knew sat a horse all slumped and curve-backed like that. And then he saw something that verified it—a long stringing cloud of black smoke bloomed from the man's head, then as quickly swirled away.

Only one man could sit a horse like that and spout thick smoke like that—Clewt Duggins. The boss. For a moment longer Paddy watched the spot, now vacant, where the man had been, then tugged the short horse's reins straight toward it. What Clewt was doing up there was anyone's guess—unless he'd found where the treasure was hidden. Had to be the case.

A quick needle of anger drove through Paddy. That would be just like the boss—wait until everyone was gone from sight, then backstab them. Well, now, boss, how about a nice surprise? How about ol' Paddy shows up when you least expect it and he takes everything from you, beginning with your treasure—so you can see it happening—then following up with your life?

All those years being the one to take the guff, the one to say, "Yeah, boss . . . Okay, boss." All those years of listening to him in that foul stink pit of a Mexican prison, dragging chains and mixing adobe, making bricks, gouging rock, listening to the boss yammer on and on about how we'd get even, just the two of them. And then, when it seemed like they'd never live through it, never get to try to hunt down the man who put them there, they were released.

Just like that, one day they were being gnawed on in their sleep by rats, the next morning they were called before *el jefe* and told that they had paid their dues and they were free to go. After ten long years that Paddy was sure would end only with their deaths, they were told they would be free men once more. Their ankle shackles were chiseled apart and with the sound of steel still ringing in the air, Clewt and Paddy were pushed out the front gate of El Diablo Prison. Just like that.

But the time in prison had warped Clewt, made him into something darker than he had been. All that talk in prison about getting revenge on Alton Winstead hadn't been just talk. It had been the very thing that kept Clewt alive. And everything he did once he left the prison had been with one goal in mind—to find and kill Winstead. Paddy had no one and nothing in the world save for Clewt, so even though the man wasn't much like he had been, he was better to stick with than going it alone.

Clewt still had that edge of boldness to him that the Irishman both feared and revered, so Paddy followed along. All the way up from Mexico, stealing what they needed, and much more that they didn't, but that they just plain liked. And along the way, Clewt insisted that they build up a gang again. As far as Paddy could tell, Clewt had no grand ideas like he used to about robbing trains or looting banks. But still, he wanted a gang.

And the men he chose . . . Paco, the brutal Mexican, was untrustworthy and vicious. His compadre, Juan, was skittish but slow. Barn Cat, the only man who could stand Paco, had been tall and stupid. Then there was the quiet, dark man with hateful eyes and an impulsive streak that Paddy had enjoyed putting an end to at Farraday's ranch, and the sorry squealer Paddy had to shoot after Farraday blinded him. No one ever knew his name. Lastly, Clewt had hired on Rufus, a dumb, overgrown boy with a face like a mule and a brain to match.

Nothing Paddy said could stop Clewt from adding to the gang, a gang that made up not a tenth of the usefulness of their old gang. What a shame. And now Paddy had to kill Clewt for being so much less than what he used to be. And for causing Paddy so much misery. He'd almost done for him back at that fine horse ranch, but it had not been the right time.

Paddy's little horse stepped hard, slipped off a rock, and nearly went down on a foreleg, almost unseating Paddy. He strapped the struggling beast on the neck and it righted itself, responded with a lunge uphill to the one leg hammering its sides, the boot's heel jabbing its barrel of a belly.

"No time for games, little horse! I have a man to save. Save him from himself, that's it. Yes, that's it. And maybe get ol' Paddy himself a handful of this cursed treasure I have heard of day and night for eleven long years. No time for faltering now, little horse!" Another vicious strapping and the beast dug in hard, nostrils distended, and plunged on up the hill. It didn't matter to Paddy that he was suffering from a dearth of weaponry. He'd find a way to do for the boss somehow. . . .

Emerging from the tree line on the flat far behind, Henry Atwood and Crazy Horse Ranch Woman watched their quarry wind his way uphill, toward the spot where they, too, had seen the skylined rider.

Chapter 36

Since leaving the ranch, Hob had kept up a fairly constant burble of chatter to Tulip the mule, his only companion. And now they had reached the western bank of the Olefine River, really not much more at that spot than a twenty-foot-wide flowage, though deep at times. But upstream, at the falls, the Olefine was a mighty brute, a roiling, thrashing thing that Hob knew had tripped up more than a few beasts, wild and otherwise, in its time. And even though it was somewhat subdued, a bit tamer, downstream, he knew better than to fall prey to the river before him. She was an unforgiving wench.

"No, no, Tulip." He shook his head. "Should have crossed sooner, closer to the ranch." Why did I not? He half smiled and nodded, knowing what he'd done even before he'd become aware of it. He suspected, somehow deep inside, that he had been headed to the falls all along. Yes. That made sense now. That was the place that he and Ty had agreed to meet. And somehow, too, he knew that's where Ty would be. Not at the ranch. Hob took comfort in the knowing of this. Even in this grimmest of times, he believed in it, had to.

Even had Hob been the sort of man to think long and deep about a thing, he would have come to the same conclusion, but he wasn't a thinker in that sense. He was a doer. But it all amounted to the same thing. When a man has raised another man as a son, they form a bond, get to know each other in the way that only a father and son can.

Many times over the years, Hob and Ty had shared unspoken thoughts, known what the other was doing, had done, or would be doing. Sometimes they'd saved each other's bacon in a pinch during roundup, branding, or on a drive. Or even just setting posts or clearing land.

But on this day, Hob knew the stakes were raised. He felt somehow that he had just enough time to either head to the Double Cross or to the waterfall. In that eye-blink of time that it took to make the decision, Hob chose to follow that kernel of truth seeded deep in his brain, that kernel of knowing that told him to head to the waterfall. That's where the boy would be.

He nudged Tulip into a lope uphill, on the western edge of the Olefine, headed northward. The mule responded in kind with extra effort, as if she knew just what was at stake for the man astride her. "Got to stop calling him the boy, Tulip. Ty Farraday's a full-grown man. A good man any fool like me would be proud to call his own son."

The only response was the faint but increasing roar of the waterfall's drumming roar, upstream of them, a sound as constant and certain as the fact that the day could only end one way—with more death.

Chapter 37

Ty had Sue Ellen creep forward on her belly beside him toward the tumble-down edge of the chasm. "Hob?" he shouted, though he knew his voice would barely be heard over the constant rush and roar of the water.

He waited a few seconds, tried again. He very much doubted that the old man would have gotten here before him. Maybe he wasn't even coming here first. But somehow Ty suspected that though Hob's mind would tell him to head to the Double Cross, the old man's gut would tell him to go to the waterfall. But he wasn't there yet. If he were, he'd have already made his presence known. Of the many things that could be said of him, Hob was not shy.

The second call went unanswered, and Ty knew for certain they were the first ones there. It wouldn't do to sit and wait for Hob, hoping the man was going to show—and with weapons. He had to get Sue Ellen to safety. "Let's get down there, to the falls."

"I'm not even certain this is where he hid his treasure, Ty. It was a guess, you know?"

"Sure, but we have to start somewhere. Besides, I need to show you something."

"What?"

"You'll see." He gestured with his head, and they began

the slow, switchback trail toward the waterfall. Halfway there they stopped, felt the mist rising up out of the cascading spume.

"I'd forgotten how beautiful it is here."

Ty nodded, but inside he was thinking that he'd never forgotten. Finally, he spoke. "How did Alton really find out about this place, Sue Ellen?"

"I . . ." But she didn't continue.

Ty faced her.

She sighed, looked away. Even in the dappled shade of the trees, he could tell her face had reddened. "I wrote about it. In a secret diary. I thought only I knew of it."

"And what did—"

But she turned to him and cut him off. "It said how much I still loved you. Okay? Is that what you want to hear? Is it?"

He said nothing, watched the water roar down the chasm. Finally he looked back over at her, standing slump-shouldered just a foot away, looking as forlorn as anyone he'd ever seen. It would be so easy to gather her into his big arms, pull her in. . . . So he did.

They fit together as easily as if they'd been made for each other. They stood there on the spot they'd hugged so many years before, together again, but not the same people. After a few long minutes, she said close to his ear, "Oh, I've made such a mess of things, Ty. There's no going back to the past, is there?"

"No there isn't, Sue Ellen." He pulled away from her, held her at arm's length, and looked into her eyes. "But there is always the future. You understand that, don't you?"

"What are you saying, Ty?" A glint of hope sparked in her green eyes.

"Oh, isn't this so very special!" The voice thundered down on them, from the moss-slick rocks above. Ty and Sue Ellen looked up, eyes wide, to see Clewt Duggins smiling down at them. A thin black cigar jutted from one side of his mouth, and smoke roiled out of the other and from his nose as if from a half-clogged chimney. His mouth itself stretched in a wide grin. His eyes sparked with the devil's own light, his dark, curving brows topping them like the wings of a malevolent bird.

But it wasn't the man's face that worried Ty. It was the Winchester, thumbed back and aimed right at them, that set Ty's teeth to grinding. "Step back, Sue Ellen," he whispered. "Closer to the rock face behind you."

"But he's—"

"He won't shoot us. Not yet, anyway. Now do as I say." Ty urged her backward, all the while keeping his eyes on the killer above.

"My many thanks for leading me here, Farraday!" shouted Duggins, still smiling. "Now where's my treasure?"

"What treasure would that be, Duggins?"

"Funny, sir. And an unacceptable answer."

Without breaking eye contact with Duggins, Ty spoke in a low voice to Sue Ellen out of the corner of his mouth. "Follow the trail to your right. It leads to the waterfall."

She didn't move.

"Trust me, Sue Ellen!" he growled.

"What are you saying down there?" Clewt's tone was not a happy one.

"Shut up, Duggins! I'm fed up with you!" Ty knew responding in such a manner was a risk, considering Clewt was as close to a madman as Ty had ever hoped to get. But it was a risk worth taking. He had little else to rely on, save for his pocketknife, a wooden club, and this scant, rocky overhang. Hardly enough, but it had to be, for they'd run out of luck.

Ty had just made it under the slick rock outcropping when Clewt's first bullet *spang*ed off the wall. Ty snugged up beside the unmoving Sue Ellen, not taking time to stop, but nudging her toward the waterfall, two dozen feet away.

"What are you doing?"

"Saving our hides. Now get going!"

"But . . . it's the waterfall!"

"I know—head for it, but stick tight to the rock face. And do it fast. Duggins will shift around up there, get a better sightline on us. Now move!" To hasten her drag-footed departure, Ty pushed her from behind. As he suspected, no matter the danger she was in, Sue Ellen didn't take kindly to being forced to do something. He didn't care. He pushed harder, and she relented, edging forward, her bloodied hands gripping the rock, scrabbling for fingerholds. The sight of her cracked fingernails sent a twinge of sorrow into Ty's throat.

Another bullet careened close by the back of Ty's head in a buzzing line, which he felt sure would slice right through the rushing torrent of water that grew louder with each halting step forward they took.

"Sue Ellen, for the love of Pete, get moving!"

"Why?" she shouted. "It's just water we're headed for!"

"No! There's a cavern!"

"What?"

"Just go, go!" He thrust his chin forward, indicating that she should keep on moving.

She must have still held enough trust in him to believe, because she continued onward toward the rushing water. Two more bullets, closer than ever, whizzed by. Ty was sure the second shadowed his shirt. Move, girl, he willed her. Move!

From above came a garbled shout from Clewt. He didn't care what the man had to say; it was all trash and of no consequence to their survival.

Soon they grew wet with the froth and spume whipping outward from the torrent. Sue Ellen halted once again, in the worst spot imaginable—they had rounded the rocky curve by the waterfall. It left them exposed to the killing shots of Clewt Duggins. And much as Ty hoped the man would have taken to the trail and tried to find a way to head them off—a route that Ty knew did not readily exist—Clewt once again disappointed him by holding his high ground and waiting them out. He rained round after round down on them. He must be feeling confident that they had led him to the spot where Alton Winstead had stashed the remainder of his glorious treasure.

Ty didn't know or care just what the treasure really consisted of, nor how much was really left over after Alton's decade-long spending spree. But he did know that Duggins believed it was a vast hoard and that, at the moment, was all that mattered.

Sue Ellen stopped once again, right before the waterfall. Ty knew the only thing saving their miserable lives right now was the obscuring effect of the mist rising from the fall's pounding flowage. But that wouldn't slow Clewt for too much longer. Ty gripped Sue Ellen's waist and drove forward with her, much as he would tackle a rogue calf thrashing free of a sloppily thrown loop.

One second they were being pounded and soaked by pummeling water; the next they lay sprawled on a slick, wet floor of smooth stone, a blinding curtain of diamond-brilliant water cascading before them.

They lay flopped on the stone floor, Ty atop Sue Ellen, both of them heaving hard breaths, their faces inches from each other's. The sound, too, had slightly diminished, giving way to an almost soothing rushing noise, as if they were listening to it underwater.

"What . . . what is this place?" Sue Ellen pulled her gaze from Ty's face, mere inches above her own.

"Why, it's what I like to call a home away from home!" The voice came from behind them, in the dark recess of the cave, and it was followed with a cackle of a laugh.

"Hob?" Ty rolled from atop Sue Ellen. "Is that you?"

"Darn tootin' it's me."

"You're okay?"

"I'm alive, but I've been in better shape, boy."

"How long have you been here?" Ty ran a hand through his damp hair, walked toward the sound of Hob's voice.

"Just barely got here myself. Imagine my surprise to see you two stumble on in. And then, well, seeing the way you two landed, I figured I had better say something sooner than later. I'm not used to such shenanigans."

Ty heard a scraping behind him, and spun to see Sue Ellen struggling to her feet, sliding on the slick floor. He offered her a hand, but she refused it.

"How you farin', girl?" Hob's voice softened.

"Hob, I'd say it's good to see you, but I can't. Where are you?" She smoothed her dress, pushed her hair away from her dirty face.

"I'm back here in the shadows. It's drier and—"

"Hob," said Ty. "Much as I'd like to find out what you've been up to, we have Clewt Duggins hard on our trial."

"I figured something like that was happening, that them shots weren't just some farmboy out target-shootin' at cottontails."

"You happen to bring anything we might return a few shots with, Hob?"

The old man chuckled, but he sounded to Ty as if he were tired. A match bloomed and Hob's dim outline grew brighter as he lit an oil lamp. He lowered the glass globe, and Ty saw how haggard he looked. "Hob, what happened?"

Sue Ellen went to his side. "What did they do to your hand, Hob?"

He tried to pull the arm aside, but the move drew forth a groan from his tight-set mouth.

"Never mind about it now," said Hob. "We have bigger

fish to fry, and I suspect one of them's looking for a way on in here. Ty's right—let's palaver later. Ty, take this rifle, revolver, and gun belt, and, Sue Ellen, you take this revolver and some bullets. Good, now let's us see what we can do about Duggins. Ty, I suggest you go over there; Sue Ellen, you stick to that side, yonder. That's the way I come in. Far as I know Duggins is the last of his lot, so we should be able to make quick work of him, call it a day."

"You got the rest, Hob?"

He chuckled again. "In a manner of speaking."

A muted popping sound erupted from in front of them, and something sizzled through the watery curtain, pelted and pinged off the rock walls of the grotto. Sue Ellen shouted and staggered back into the wall, the revolver clattering to the stone floor.

"Sue Ellen," shouted Ty, rushing to her side. She staggered forward, fell into his arms, her right hand clutching her left forearm.

"I'm okay—just my arm," she said through gritted teeth. "Oh, look out!" she said, looking past Ty's shoulder, but a roar and a flash erupted from right behind them.

"I get him?" said Hob, stumping forward on his crutch and holding a smoking shotgun, the butt tucked tight under his armpit, his finger ready to test the second trigger.

"Wait, wait, Hob—" Ty was reluctant to leave Sue Ellen, despite her efforts to show that she was fine. He knew better—that bullet had likely shattered the bone in her forearm. He helped ease her back to the drier recess of the grotto, sat her on the floor, and laid the pistol on her lap. He leaned close and said in a low voice, "Shoot anything that isn't me or Hob, okay? I'll be right back."

Before she could protest, he low-walked over to Hob, jerked his head toward the far left side of the space, then made a few hand motions that they obviously knew the meaning of. The old man nodded, Ty quickly blew out the lamp, then scuffed low to the left side, advanced beyond Hob, and inched closer to the waterfall.

As he held there, waiting, crouched in the darkness, he felt the cold dampness of the stone floor. He had intended to tell Sue Ellen about this cavern all those years ago, but wanted to surprise her. They'd had such good memories and good times at the falls, in the dappled sunlight, swimming and drying in the sun on the rocky slopes of the magical pond below. He'd often been on the cusp of telling her about the grotto, about finding it in the old days of a few years before, when the Paiutes had been a real threat.

Somehow, every time he had wanted to tell her, the timing seemed off, or he'd thought she might laugh, tell him that he and Hob were behaving like schoolboys, with a secret club. He had finally determined he would tell her about it, show it to her; maybe she'd think it was as fascinating as he did, but then she'd left him for Winstead, and he'd rarely come back since.

He had gone to the waterfall a time or two to brood. One day, months after she'd married Alton, he chanced to go by there while looking for strays. He'd seen a flash of color among the trees. It was Sue Ellen's dress. She looked so sad standing there. He'd almost called out to her, but bitterness stopped his tongue. Instead he'd ridden back to his life, back to trying to forget what might have been. He'd rarely gone there since.

But a couple of years ago, Hob had confided in Ty that he'd ride up there sometimes and sit in the cave, puff on his pipe, and think.

"About what?" Ty had asked.

"Nothin'. Nothin' at all. Why?" The old man had stuck out his jaw. "I need a reason?"

"Nope," said Ty, turning to hide his grin.

A few minutes later, Hob had said, "It's a . . . a soothing place. That's what it is."

Ty had nodded in agreement, not a hint of a smile left on his face. Hob was right, of course. In the grotto, the watery sounds had a way of hushing the worries in a man's mind.

"You, in there! I'll let you live, but I want my treasure! I am not leaving until I get it—so you all better make a decision pretty soon. In fact, I'll give you two minutes. No, no, make that one!"

Then, not surprising anyone, Clewt began firing through the wall of water.

"Man's watch must be broke," shouted Hob, shuffling away from the water a few feet.

Instinctively, Sue Ellen slid lower down the wall, Hob flattened against his wall, and Ty used the opportunity to drop low and thumb back the hammer on the pistol Hob had given him. Already the rancher was on the move, gauging the location of the shooter from the direction the shots had come. There weren't many options for escape, but even so it would be foolish of Clewt to think he could hold them off for long single-handedly.

Ty hoped the madman had no other members of his gang riding to assist him. But he didn't know for certain. Hob had said he'd done for the rest of them, but who knew? Until he had positive proof, he'd consider each shot a gang-led attack.

But at least now he had an idea of where Clewt was shooting from. Ty peeled off four rapid rounds in that direction. And he was rewarded with a clipped groan followed by a shout—considering he'd heard it through the waterfall's noise, Ty hoped it meant he hit pay dirt.

He figured that might be enough to slow the man down, catch him off guard, even for just a few seconds. Ty low-crawled, all but belly to the floor, and angling tight to the jag in the rock that marked the edge of the waterfall, he pushed on through until he rounded the edge, peering toward the thin-ledge trail that he and Sue Ellen had scrambled along to get to the waterfall.

He saw no sign of Clewt, dropped his head lower, and peered up, toward the overhang. He'd been convinced that the killer had been on the ledge, but then a bullet drilled into the rock just above his head, sending splinters of rock down at him, burning trails into his scalp, flecking his face with needles of pain.

Ty recoiled and crawled back around the rocky edge.

"I think you got him, boy," said Hob.

"Not good enough."

Ty scooted back a few feet. "Sue Ellen, you okay?" he whispered.

"I'll live, but I'm a fair distance from all right."

Hob chuckled. "That's one of the things I always liked about you, girl. You are an honest woman."

She couldn't stop herself from laughing a little. "Hob, you never change."

"Hate to break up the chatter," said Ty. "But we have a whole lot of mess and I need to get out there and take care of Duggins or . . ."

The crack of a gunshot stopped the words in Ty's mouth. In the dim space they held their spots, frozen, listening, straining to hear beyond the dull roar of water. Seconds later they heard another crack, followed by the tell-tale *spang* of bullet-on-rock.

"Sounded like a sidearm. What's Clewt Duggins carrying? You know, Ty?"

"A rifle. But I doubt he would shoot two rigs at the same time."

"What are you saying?" Sue Ellen asked.

"I think someone else may be out there," said Ty. "Hob, how many did you get?"

"Well, when I left the Rocking T, the Irishman had killed two of his own men; then I did for him. He was a tough nut, though. Nearly had me. You?"

"Yeah, similar situation. I was up on that ledge above that rocky pass. You know the one, up by the hoodoo?"

"Yep, sure do."

"The Irishman, I believe they call him Paddy, he finished off one of his men. I did one, but missed the Irishman as he rode toward the ranch. I'm sorry I didn't get him before he got to you."

"Nothing to worry about, Ty. I enjoyed that whuppin'."

Another exchange of shots between two different guns again barked and ricocheted beyond the water, but closer this time. "You both stay here, back in the shadows, and defend yourselves. I'll make it plain if it's me coming back."

Without another word, he crouched low, headed to the opposite side of the waterfall, and without stopping, snaked on through.

"Ty!" growled Hob, but got no response from the rangy younger man.

"He'll never change," said Sue Ellen, a trace of bitterness tainting her words like a mouthful of bad food.

"For our sakes, you'd better hope he don't never change, girl." Hob kept an eye on the side of the falls, expecting Duggins to burst in at any moment, trying to figure out how many more men Duggins had in his employ. Could be a dozen, for all he knew. "How many more men does he have, Sue Ellen?"

"I've been trying to figure that out. As near as I can tell, not counting Duggins, there are six men."

"That leaves at least one man unaccounted for. I hope Ty keeps his guard up."

When Ty returned fire through the water wall, what felt like a hundred needles bored straight into Clewt's belly and right side. The bullets had hit the edge of the rocky fissure behind which he had partially hidden. He didn't think he'd been shot, but it didn't matter. He didn't imagine getting shot in the side could feel much worse.

He tried to suppress his howl, but breathed hard through his clenched teeth, biting clean through his cigar. The end dropped down into the roiling water. He pulled back and gathered himself, wondering who'd shot at him. He was still waiting for Paddy and however many of the others were left alive—though he doubted any were left—and while that didn't bother him overly much, he did half-wish he had a hand in killing the vermin holed up in that cave behind the water. Heck, all he really wanted was his rightfully earned treasure.

And that's when it hit him—the cave had to be where the blasted treasure was kept. Made sense—especially since that's where the woman and Farraday had beelined for. Clewt cursed himself, daring to look down at his rock-shard-peppered side, stippled with dozens of angry, oozing wounds. None would be fatal, but every dang one hurt as much as it ever would.

And then another bullet clipped in close, same direction. Good thing he had tucked himself in tighter to the crevice or he would have had lead for lunch. "Hey!" he shouted. "Who's there?"

He hoped it was one of his boys.

"That you, Clewt?"

No mistaking that Irish brogue, and Clewt had to admit he was glad to hear it was his oldest friend, even if he knew he'd have to kill him when this was all through. He'd be darned if he was going to share the treasure, not when he'd gone through this much to get to it, and much of it on his own. Paddy had probably been lazily picking through the ranch house, looking for scraps. Well, let him have them, for that was all he would get.

Another round worked in closer. "Paddy! Leave off that shooting! I'm in that rock!"

"I'm not shooting at you! I'm over here!"

As Clewt looked toward where the voice came from, he saw a dirty, battered bowler pop up across the narrow chasm like a damaged mushroom.

He looked pretty bad to Clewt, bloodied all over, and his nose looked as if he'd been unlucky enough to get a hoof to the face. But he still wore that foolish Irish smile.

Paddy held up both hands, one hanging lower than the other, no weapon in either. "You stay there," shouted the Irishman. "I'm coming over. Got something to tell you!" He smiled the entire time he said it.

"Tell me?" Did this situation look like a Sunday social to him? What was Paddy playing at? "You drunk?" said Clewt over the roar of the water.

"No, but I am thirsty—can't wait to buy me some liquor with my share of the treasure!"

Keep on dreaming, thought Clewt. Then, as he watched, Paddy's hat whipped off the surprised man's head, spinning through the air before finally arcing down far below into the mists of the cascading water. Clewt flashed his eyes back to Paddy in time to see the man's uneven smile droop like something melting. His hands did the opposite, and shot up to the top of his head where a furrow of blood had been carved, from side to side, across the top of his skull.

The blood welled as if slowed in time, seemed to bubble up, then slipped down like a curtain that soon masked Paddy's already-battered face. The lower half of it opened wide as the Irishman's screams rose in pitch and echoed across the roaring canyon, sounding, for a few seconds, louder than the waterfall's constant thunder.

For a few horrifying moments, Clewt lost all sense of himself, and his own protection. He couldn't quite understand what was happening. He saw movement across the chasm, upstream to his right, turned to look at it, and saw that cursed Farraday just peering up from behind a rock, drawing another aim at Paddy. The man's first shot hadn't done the job.

Clewt could shoot at the rancher—all he had to do was to aim his rifle. But in the time it takes for a man to change his mind, Clewt stayed his hand. He watched as Paddy, through his bloodred mask, returned his stare, accusing him, as if to say, "Why not save my life?"

Clewt held his *segundo*'s gaze, shook his head no, side to side, as Farraday's second shot dropped Paddy. The Irishman crumpled to his side even as his head burst like an overripe melon. Clewt took advantage of the grisly distraction and slipped free of his paltry hiding place. He didn't stick around to watch Paddy's lifeless body collapse into a pile, hidden in the gray jumble of rock.

Clewt reasoned that though he could have shot Farraday, it was worth it to him to take the trade-off, to let the fool rancher kill Paddy for him and provide him with a way to wiggle out of the spot in which he'd been pinned.

It wouldn't take much to get himself to the waterfall. He just had to keep one eye on Farraday, and one eye on the entrance, lest that woman snipe at him. He'd reached a point in the rocks where he could remain concealed. He could also risk being seen by Farraday, who he'd lost sight of, as well as risking exposure to the woman. Clewt climbed.

Chapter 38

"For a wounded man, he sure can move like a jackrabbit," said Henry Atwood, squinting toward the spot where he'd just seen the battered bowler-wearing member of Duggins's gang hopping along and dragging a bloody leg, one arm looking nearly useless.

"I don't care what he moves like." Crazy Horse Ranch Woman slipped from her saddle and pulled a rifle from its sheath. She reached inside her duster, slid a revolver free, and stalked in the same direction the man had gone.

Henry sighed and slid from his horse, tied it off, then did the same for Lilly, whose reins Crazy Horse Ranch Woman left trailing on the ground. He retrieved his own rifle, checked ammunition for that and for his revolver. "Well, horses, I do hope if I don't see you again that someone takes good care of you. You surely deserve it."

Henry felt a wave of guilt splash over him, convinced he hadn't done enough to ensure his wife and son would be taken care of. And then he heard shots up ahead. Thoughts of his family shrank in his mind as fast as they had bloomed. The randomly spaced shots and shouts grew louder the further up a narrow trail he loped. And there was another sound, too, more constant than any others—a rushing roar that soon overpowered all other noise. A waterfall—he knew what it was even before it came into sight.

Henry came upon a forlorn-looking mule that didn't even glance at him as he passed. A dozen yards up-trail, just before he reached the river, he nearly tripped over Crazy Horse Ranch Woman. He dropped to his knees beside her, and was about to flip her over to see if she was hurt, when she reached up with a surprisingly strong grip and dragged him down. "Get under cover, Mr. Henry Lawdog," she growled. "You'll get shot stumbling around like that."

He looked at her, but she jerked her chin toward the river in front of them. At first Henry didn't see a thing, but as he looked upstream he saw, too far out of rifle range, a figure slowly making its way across one side of the rocky formation that seemed to encase the source of the waterfall, above which sat a natural stone arch spanning the flow. The river gathered much of its force here, where it poured down. All the rocks lining the edges of the river through this stretch looked to have been carved by great gouging fingers, more out of one great mass of rock than a collective of tumbledown boulders.

"That's him." Crazy Horse Ranch Woman nodded.

"Who?"

"Clewt Duggins." As she said it she sneered, gritted her teeth, then spit.

Henry nodded, kept his gaze pinned to the man scrabbling across the rock, and making slow progress of it with one stiff, bum leg. What was he up to? Henry squinted and craned his neck a bit more, not that it helped much. The man was out of range of anything other than a decent Sharps with a nice scope.

He did notice that Duggins looked haggard, had lost his hat somewhere, and . . . was that blood on the man's face and side? Still, the killer was armed, as Henry had expected.

Crazy Horse Ranch Woman crawled away.

"What are you doing?"

"What do you think?" she said. "I'm going to get him."

"We need a plan."

She wagged her rifle, and without looking back, said, "This is all the plan I need."

It was then Henry knew she hadn't needed him in the least. So why bring him? Maybe she did it for him, knew without her he'd just wander, unsure of his goal, and never make it back. Maybe she did it to make him realize how much he had to lose? Maybe, he told himself, you should get your sorry backside up there and help her.

Duggins looked to Henry like a stiff-legged spider. He and Crazy Horse Ranch Woman were too far to shoot at the villain with any accuracy. Henry scanned the landscape. What was the murderer so intent on? And that's when Henry saw the man in the rocks to the left of the waterfall. He was clearly in danger—as Duggins was stalking him. Any man stalked by Duggins had to be someone at least deserving of a warning.

Henry considered shouting, but that could distract the man, divert his attention in the wrong direction. He lifted his rifle, thumbed back the hammer, aimed it, and touched the trigger a whisker of a second before Crazy Horse Ranch Woman growled and pushed it down to clunk against a rock. But Henry's shot had taken flight, straight and true.

Henry saw a puff of rock dust erupt beside Duggins. The killer dropped to his belly, swiveling his head, and shouting, "Who was that? You know who I am?" His voice carried loud enough over the roar of the waterfall.

If Henry didn't know who the man was or how evil he was, he might have found Duggins's genuine dismay to be funny.

"Why'd you shoot at him?" Crazy Horse Ranch Woman looked about ready to bite Henry's face.

Henry nodded upstream to their left. "Him. There."

Crazy Horse Ranch Woman followed his sightline and saw a slight movement as a man shifted position in the rocks, looking down toward them, then up again at where they shot.

"Looked to me like he's on our side. Didn't want Clewt to get the drop on him."

"He shoots Duggins before I do, I'll kill him, too."

"What's it matter who shoots him?"

She looked at Henry with a scowl, shook her head, looked back to the stranger in the rocks.

"What if I shoot him?" said Henry.

"Then I'll shoot you."

"Not hardly," said Henry, but when she didn't respond, he knew he was as wrong as could be.

"Look!" Crazy Horse Ranch Woman seethed as she pointed. "He's heading back the way he came."

Henry spotted Duggins again, and sure enough he was backing upward, keeping an eye on their location. Soon he disappeared down behind the rocks from which he'd emerged.

In the distance, they saw the man Duggins had been stalking stand up, then stare in their direction. Obviously he didn't regard them as a big threat. Henry saw he was a tall man, wide-shouldered, and appeared much tattered and blood-ied. He also didn't look very impressed with them, though he did look confused as to what they were doing there.

That makes two of us, thought Henry. Crazy Horse Ranch Woman stood and, as if she didn't even see the stranger in the distance by the waterfall, she resumed barreling up the path.

Henry cut ahead of her, led the way this time, walking right on up the path toward the strange, tall man. He heard her behind him. They both carried their rifles, cocked and at the ready as they trudged. The man appeared to be waiting for them.

"Keep a sharp eye for that rascal Duggins," said Crazy

Horse Ranch Woman to Henry. "We get up there I'm crossing over the top, going after him."

Henry nodded, said nothing.

They were within a few yards of the tall man when he spoke, though still keeping an eye toward where Duggins had been hiding atop the waterfall. "Hold your ground. Who are you? What are you doing here?"

Henry and Crazy Horse Ranch Woman stood as ordered. But they didn't lower their rifles. They didn't know him any better than he knew them. "Easy, friend," said Henry. "We're hunting someone."

"And who would that be?"

"What's it to you, stranger?" said Crazy Horse Ranch Woman. "My business is my business. If you're a friend of Clewt Duggins"—she glanced right again—"you'd best prepare to die. If not . . ." She shrugged.

While they spoke, Duggins dropped down to the opposite side of the waterfall, edged down beside the flow. He slid back into the crevice in the rocks where he'd hid earlier, so close to the cave's entrance, so close to his treasure. He was sure of it, could feel it hidden in there. There must still be a lot of it left. Why else would they work so hard to defend it?

Out of sight, across the river, and out of hearing range due to the pounding rush of the waterfall, Crazy Horse Ranch Woman pushed past Henry, and advanced on Ty, her rifle still held before her.

Ty brought his rifle to bear, trained on her. "I said to hold your ground. You will not pass unless you give me your guns. Now what's it going to be?"

"Shut up, mister. I have come a long way for my prize, and I will not be robbed of it."

What she said made little sense to Ty, but her determined look told him she was probably telling the truth somehow.

"Hold there!" shouted Ty again.

But she kept on advancing, so he bolted forward, pushed the barrel of her weapon aside, surprising her with speed just in time to avoid being shot. She growled an oath at him as he wrenched the rifle from her and threatened to swing it at her, but she put her arms up. Ty glanced briefly across the waterfall, but didn't see Duggins yet.

The strange man came up behind the woman on the trail. But this man had his arms up, his own rifle held in such a way that he couldn't swing it into action easily. "Relax, mister," said the stranger. "We're hunting Duggins too. He's killed people we each know and love. Been on his trail a long time, from way down south of here."

Ty gave him a hard stare, alternated his gaze between the two surprise visitors and the opposite side of the waterfall. Still no sight of Duggins.

"Prove it. Step around the lady here and hand me that rifle. Then keep your hands up high."

He looked at the woman, who said nothing, just stared him down with a mean look.

"Lady," said Ty. "I've been through more in the past day than your ugliest stare can do to me. I suggest you get those hands up and keep them up."

She did, with prodding from his rifle barrel's business end. Her duster opened slightly and he saw her revolver in its holster. He kept his rifle trained on her and shucked it.

"Mine, too?" said the strange man behind her.

Ty looked at him. "No, but don't test me, stranger. I mean it."

Henry nodded. Ty glanced over across the river again. Still no Duggins. He didn't like that. "You two, get ahead of me. Walk that path there; we're going behind the falls."

"What?" the woman said. "No, no, no." She shook her head in defiance. "I'm going after Duggins."

"Don't tell me what you're going to do," said Ty. "Besides, he'll come to us."

"Come on," said Henry, gently pushing her along.

"Trust me," said Ty, hustling them before him.

Minutes before in the cave, Hob had rummaged in his outdated sack of meager supplies. The best he could turn up was an old shirt, which he ripped into lengths of rag. "Sue Ellen, you doing okay, girl?"

"Just like before," she said through gritted teeth. "I've been better. But I'll make it through. This arm might be useless by then."

"Pshaw! Don't talk that way, girl."

"So, I got her, eh?" Clewt Duggins burst forth in a shower of spray, a revolver drawn on them.

"You!" said Hob. He wobbled from his awkward crouch beside Sue Ellen, clawing for a sidearm and grunting in pain from every movement he made.

"Eh-eh-eh, don't move so much." Clewt wagged his weapon at them. "This pistol's liable to go off. And, yeah, it's me. But tell me, old broken man, just who are you?"

"Don't tell him anything, Hob. He's a killer."

Clewt was about to respond when scuffling noises from the opposite side of the waterfall drew their attention. "Oh, now look at this," said Duggins as soon as all three newcomers walked out from behind the water.

"You two." Clewt waved his pistol in their direction. "You look familiar. Not that I care much. You all are in my way. I am here for one thing and one thing only. I need you to give up that treasure. You!" He thrust the pistol at Hob. "Old man! Get away from her."

Hob crabbed away from Sue Ellen, edging toward the dark, a strange look on his face.

"You filthy animal," said Henry, staring at Clewt Duggins. "I came all this way . . ."

"Yes? And?" Duggins smiled wide, threw his head back in a laugh. "I remember you now! You're that pathetic milksop of a lawman from way down yonder—am I right?"

While he spoke, Hob angled closer to his shotgun, half hidden in the shadows. Ty saw what he was up to and created a diversion by making a show of helping Sue Ellen.

"What are you doing?" said Clewt. "Get away from her! Now!" He raised the pistol and aimed it at Ty's head.

"Nothing doing. I'm helping her—or do you want the one person who knows where your precious treasure is to bleed out right here in front of you?" He winked at Sue Ellen, who took the hint and sagged closer to the wall, looking suddenly as if she might fade away any second.

"What?" Duggins advanced on them, fear and anger warring on his blood-flecked face.

He didn't get two steps when a dark shape arced down behind him and clubbed him in the side of the head. He weaved on his feet, his head wobbling, and collapsed to the floor, still conscious but clearly dazed.

Crazy Horse Ranch Woman made a move toward him, but Ty grabbed her arm, pushed her toward Henry. "Hold her still."

Henry nodded.

By then, Hob had struggled upright, his crutch tucked under his arm, the shotgun held, barrel down, in the other.

He rapped Duggins with the crutch. "Hey, wake up. You hear me? Now, what I want to know is . . ."

"Yeah, what?" Clewt's sneer waxed and waned with his heaving breaths.

"I want to know how you lost your leg." And then, to

emphasize to the point, Hob thunked the man's wooden limb with his crutch.

"Oh, for the love of all that is still right in this foul world!" It was Crazy Horse Ranch Woman, and as she said it she spun on Henry, wrenching free of his grip. Her dirt-colored duster flared wide and she drew free a fresh long-barrel Colt Navy. The handle butt met the side of his head with a thud, and Henry collapsed. But she was already ducking low and pivoting.

"Look out!" shouted Sue Ellen, but the darkness of the grotto prevented anyone from seeing much of what they should be looking out for.

Hob turned to see what the commotion was behind him and Clewt lashed out, snatching at the old man's crutch. That's all it took for Hob to topple. Duggins rolled onto his left side, snatched at the shotgun in the dark, a pleased look on his face as he wrenched it free of the old man's flailing clawhold.

"Gaah! Ty! Duggins is armed!"

But Ty was already on the move, keeping himself between Sue Ellen and this fresh ruckus behind them. He already had his pistol drawn, but in the dark and with everybody scrambling, it was difficult to get a fix on what was happening.

"Stay low, Hob!"

He saw a single form still upright—the crazy woman—saw the man she'd come with laid out on the floor. He saw Hob struggling to get back against the far wall.

"Where's my treasure!" barked Clewt. It wasn't a question, more of a screamed demand. And no one answered him.

In the few seconds it took for all this to transpire, Ty saw that Clewt Duggins had the shotgun. The woman advanced on him.

Clewt used the wall to push himself to a standing position, holding the shotgun poised before him. He knew it was a two-shot gun, but couldn't recall if Hob had shot, reloaded, or not.

"Where is my treasure? I earned it and you are robbing me—robbing me!"

Ty swore he could see spittle fly from the man's mouth as he raged.

"Where is it—it's mine, I earned it!" He spit a mouthful of blood, advanced a step, turning, and Ty saw him skylined against the lighter wall of water behind him.

"I will ask one more time!" Clewt brought the weapon to bear, holding it almost to his shoulder, and worked it side to side slowly, like a snake's mesmerizing head just before it strikes. "Where . . . is . . . my . . . treasure!"

The crazy woman stepped forward, brought the Colt up with a confident sweep, cranked the hammer back slowly, and aimed it at Clewt Duggins's chest. "You filthy killer, I got your treasure right here." But she didn't pull the trigger. She merely stared at Clewt Duggins.

With the shotgun's barrel pointed at her chest, Clewt fingered a trigger and . . . nothing happened. His smile drooped.

Crazy Horse Ranch Woman's smile broadened and she nodded. "My husband, Jay," she said, and blasted him in the chest. Clewt staggered backward.

"My son Billy," she said.

Duggins took another hit, which whipped his torso to the right, one arm flapping at the elbow. He staggered backward one, two steps.

Crazy Horse Ranch Woman advanced on him. "My son Little Tully!" Another shot to the chest.

"My sweet horses!"

Clewt began to buckle at the waist, but still he stood, staggering backward into the sheeting water. It looked as if he were caught in a raging downpour, but somehow he stayed upright under it.

Crazy Horse Ranch Woman advanced another step. "And my broken heart that can never be mended!" she shouted, triggering a last shot.

Duggins's face, under the pounding water, was a mask of disbelief, his chest a welter of wetness and seeping pink. Then he simply slipped backward, disappearing from sight.

In that instant, they heard a thundering boom and a blast of lead bees drove through the wall of water and into the grotto—the second shot from the shotgun. Crazy Horse Ranch Woman's arms whipped upward as if she were overcome with the spirit of the moment, breaking into a revival-tent dance. Her Colt Navy flew from her grasp, clattered to the grotto floor. Her head whipped backward on her taut-muscled neck, and she fell straight back, arms outstretched. Her head slammed into the rock floor, bounced, and wobbled side to side.

Hob dragged himself the few feet over to her side. "Ma'am! Hey, you all right?"

She looked up at him, then at Ty, who'd hustled to her side as well. But he saw her chest and gut had been savaged by the thick slugs from the shotgun. She was bleeding badly, bleeding out right there. And she was smiling, even as blood bubbled and ran from her mouth. She tried to speak, coughed, said, "Thank—" Then her eyes filmed over and her head slipped to one side.

From beside Ty came a soft rush of pent-up breath; then a voice said, "Oh no. . . ." Henry Atwood sobbed quietly, held one hand to his bleeding head, rubbed his eyes with the other grimy hand.

"How many more rats you figure are in these rocks, anyway?" Back outside in the fading afternoon light, Hob scowled at the embankment to each side of the falls, his old whiskered mouth arched in a sneer, as if he'd been told a lie by the very river itself.

"I believe we've cleaned them out, Hob," Ty said, draping an arm across the old man's shoulders.

A week later, with Alton's savaged remains buried properly on his ranch, along with those of Duggins and his gang, Ty and Hob had left Sue Ellen alone for a couple of days, at her insistence, once she convinced them that she would be fine. She needed a little time to figure out where it was she was bound for.

They had sent the stranger, Henry Atwood, back the way he'd come, with the sad woman's remains bundled and encased in salt and lime in a plank box, the seams sealed with pitch. Hob assured him it would be sufficient to get her back to her family's plot so she could spend eternity with her husband and sons.

Before he left, Henry had found a bittersweet surprise waiting for him in his saddlebags. Crazy Horse Ranch Woman, family name of Dunderson, had written out a last will and testament, leaving Cuthbert Henry Atwood, should he be lucky enough to survive, her vast horse ranch, provided that he bring his wife, son, and his wife's family there to live and work. She also asked that he tend her family's graves.

The day had begun cold, with a stiff norther blowing in, but by the time midday rolled around, the sun had reared its head from behind the dwindling cloudbank. Ty and Hob labored at dismantling the charred wreckage of the house. Both men were shirtless, one well-muscled and coated with a sheen of sweat, grime, and sawdust, the other a bony old chicken of a man, his stringy muscles keeping up, one arm in a sling, the hand bandaged.

They'd managed to work without stop for hours, but finally Hob called a halt and dragged out the water bucket and a sack of biscuits he'd baked over the outdoor cook fire.

They'd been staying in the bunkhouse, enjoying themselves despite the work that lay ahead for them.

"You know, Ty," said Hob, "that girl is gonna up and leave the area if'n you don't stop being angry. We all make mistakes in life. Some bigger than others. Why even I've made a few in my day, hard as it is to believe."

As Ty sipped his dipperful of water, something caught his eye over Hob's shoulder and he stood, nodded toward it. "She hasn't left just yet."

Hob turned to see Sue Ellen riding in a buggy toward them.

"Now how do you suppose she managed to rig that up, what with one arm lame and all?"

"Hob, that woman has more grit and fire than any ten men."

The old man swung his head up to look at Ty. "Well, it's about time you admitted it."

"Admitted what?" said Ty as he pulled on his shirt.

"Oh, nothin'. Nothin' at all." Hob shook his head, smiling as he donned his own shirt.

The two men stood a half minute waiting for her, fidgeting and trying to not look or feel awkward. She pulled to a stop before them, and Uncle Hob edged past Ty, wobbled forward, and offered her his hand as she stepped down from the buggy.

"Thank you, Uncle Hob."

He grinned and nodded. "What brings you to our fair abode, Sue Ellen?" He winked at the irony of his assessment—the charred building behind them was anything but fair at present.

"Sue Ellen." Ty nodded, not smiling as he greeted her.

"Hello, Ty."

As Hob's head swiveled from one to the other, his look one of expectation slipped into one of pity. But he kept his tongue.

"I know you're both busy," said Sue Ellen. "I'll get right to the point. Alton wasn't the sort of man most people would have liked if he hadn't come around here with money. But at least they pretended to like him, and I think somehow that was enough for him. Or at least he pretended it was. I hope that makes sense." She looked right at Ty and continued. "He wasn't a bad man, really. I know you won't ever believe that. But it's the truth." Her voice hitched a moment. She crossed her arms and looked across the long, sloping vista of rippling hills stretching to the west, the sun lighting the tops a golden color.

"There's one more thing I wanted you both to know about Alton, and after I've said my piece, I'll leave you to your work."

Ty continued to stare at the ground at his feet, his jaw muscles bunching, no indication of what he was feeling written on his wind-burned face. Hob scowled at him, but Ty never looked his way.

Sue Ellen continued. "I was going through things at the house. When I looked through Alton's office, I came across a burlap sack. Even after Duggins and his men rooted in there like pigs, they never found it. It was wedged behind a hidden backing in a cabinet I'd never looked in—it was always filled with Alton's papers, important things. It seemed like it wasn't any of my business."

"Well, what was in the sack, girl?" Hob's bottom lip pooched out and his brows knitted, telegraphing his eagerness to hear what she had discovered. He glanced at Ty, and could tell that even the big rancher wanted to look at her, could tell he was listening intently too. Hob almost smiled.

"I found a pair of gold candlesticks."

"Gold, you say? That the fortune that weasel was after?" Hob rubbed his good hand on his stubbled chin.

Sue Ellen nodded. "That's what's left of it, apparently.

There was also a letter to me in Alton's hand that said a number of things."

Ty looked at her. "Why are you telling us this, Sue Ellen?"

"Because it's important to me that you know what sort of man he was. He was certainly all the things you think he was. For that matter, he was so much more—and less—than I thought he was. Some of the things Duggins said about him, I know Alton wasn't capable of. I'm convinced Duggins was talking about things he himself had done. But none of that matters now."

Ty slowly nodded, but didn't look convinced.

"Well, just because this galoot isn't interested doesn't mean I don't wanna know what that letter said. Out with it, girl!"

Sue Ellen nearly smiled. "In short, he wrote that last year he began to feel guilty about what he'd done to Duggins and the others all those years ago, leaving them to pay for their crime while he made off with the stolen items. So he made some sort of deal with the Mexican government to return the rest of the treasure in exchange for the release of Duggins and the others."

Both Ty and Hob looked at her.

"But by then, only Duggins and the Irishman were still alive. Duggins almost died a few years before when he got a wound in his leg that went septic. They amputated it in prison, and he lived."

"Curse that doctor," said Hob, and spit on the ground at the memory of Duggins and his killing ways.

Sue Ellen nodded. "Alton's motives, I'd guess, were to help himself sleep better at night, but I wish he had let them rot in prison."

All three stood in silence for a time, staring at the ground, watching cattle graze on a close pasture.

Finally, Hob pushed himself upright. "Well, I got to go

work on my new leg. I found a nice piece of stove wood that might do the trick." He hobbled with the crutch over to Sue Ellen, patted her shoulder and said, "Don't be a stranger. I'm nearly back to my old cookin' self." He winked and made his way toward the woodpile, his crutch making an uneven sound in the dirt as he went.

Ty and Sue Ellen continued to stand in silence for another minute or so. Then Sue Ellen said, "I should be getting back. Lots to do before I—"

The tall, rangy rancher interrupted her. "Let's walk," he said, avoiding her gaze. He nodded toward the narrow horse trail that wound around past the barn and up into the close-by hills.

Sue Ellen nodded, and they headed on out of the barnyard, side by side.

Hob watched them walk away, and it was soon apparent from their slowed pace and slight head movements that they were talking. He rubbed his chin and kept watching. Just before they rounded the corner of the barn, Ty's big hand reached over and touched Sue Ellen's. As they walked out of sight, Hob could have sworn those hands folded over each other.

"That's my boy," said Uncle Hob, smiling as he hefted the drawknife and set to work on an improved leg for himself. Soon, he was whistling.

Read on for an excerpt from

DEMON'S PASS

A Ralph Compton Novel by Dick Vaughn

Available now from Signet in paperback and e-book.

North Kansas, spring, 1868

The boy's name was Parker Stanley, and he had heard all the jokes about having a name that was backward. "Putting the horse before the cart, and so forth." Now, as he sat leaning against the broken wagon wheel, he tried to hang on to his name . . . to hang on to anything that would tell him that he was still alive.

He wasn't sure how long he had been watching the approaching rider. Heat waves shimmering up from the sunbaked earth gave the rider a surrealistic appearance, bending the light in such a way that sometimes the rider was visible and sometimes he wasn't. Parker wasn't that sure there really was a rider. If so, was he human? Or, was he an Angel of the Lord, coming to take him to join his mother and father?

Parker looked around at the burned wagon, and at the scalped bodies of his mother and father. A few of the arrows the Indians had shot at them were still protruding from their bodies.

There was very little left of the wagon's contents. The Indians had taken all the clothes, household goods, food, and water. They had taken his older sister, too. Elizabeth hadn't cried, not one whimper, and Parker remembered how proud he had been of her bravery.

The Indians hadn't found the little leather pouch, though. It contained all the money from the sale of the farm in Illinois, and was to have been the start of their new life. Parker saw his father hide the pouch, just before the attack began.

How long had it been since the attack? No matter how hard he tried to think, Parker couldn't come up with the answer. Was it an hour ago? This morning? Yesterday? He had been sitting right here, at this wheel, for as long as he could remember.

The rider reached the wagon, swung down from his horse, then walked toward Parker, carrying a canteen. Parker watched him, almost without interest. When he felt the cool water at his lips, though, he began to drink thirstily, gulping it down in such large quantities that he nearly choked.

"Whoa, now," the rider said gently, pulling the canteen back. "Take it easy, boy. You mustn't drink it too fast. It'll make you sick."

The rider wet his handkerchief, then began rubbing it lightly on the boy's head.

"You took a pretty good bump on the head," he said. "They must've thought you were dead. You're lucky you still have your scalp. They generally prize blond hair like yours."

The water revived Parker's awareness and, with it, the realization that both his parents had been brutally killed. He managed to hold back the sobs, but not the tears.

"Your folks?" the rider asked softly.

Parker nodded.

"Cheyenne, I expect. I'm real sorry about this, son," the rider said.

"There was a white man with them," Parker said.

"What? A white man? Are you sure?"

Parker thought of the big redheaded man who had cursed when they found no money in the wagon.

"Yes," Parker said. "I'm sure. He was a big man with red hair and a red beard. I'll never forget him."

"There's nothing worse than a white man who has gone bad and thrown his lot in with the Indians." The rider looked over at the bodies of the boy's parents. "You stay here. I'll bury them for you."

"I want to help," Parker said, stirring himself to rise.

The rider smiled at him. "Good for you, lad," he said. "In the years to come it'll be a comfort to you to know that you did what you could for them." He looked toward the wagon and saw part of a shovel, the top half of the handle having been burned away. "You can use that. I've got a small spade on my saddle."

They worked quietly and efficiently for the next half hour, digging only one grave, but making it large enough for both his mother and father. They lowered Parker's parents into the hole, then shoveled the dirt back over them.

"You want me to say a few words over them?"

The boy nodded.

The rider walked back to his horse and opened a saddlebag. Parker watched as he took out a small leather-bound book and returned to the graveside. With his own survival now taken care of, and with the business of burying his parents out of the way, Parker was able to examine his benefactor closely. He saw a tall, powerfully built man, clean-shaven, with dark hair. Parker wasn't old enough to shave yet, but he knew the trouble it took to shave every morning, and he thought the rider must be a particularly vain man to go to such trouble on a daily basis, especially when on the range like this.

"What are their names?" the man asked, interrupting Parker's musing.

"What?"

"If I'm going to say a few words, I need to know their names."

"My ma's name is Emma. My pa's is Amon. Amon Stanley."

The rider cleared his throat, then began to read:

" 'I am the resurrection and the life, saith the Lord; he that believeth in me, though he were dead, yet shall he live; and whosoever liveth and believeth in me shall never die.

" 'Oh God, whose mercies cannot be numbered: Accept these prayers on behalf of thy servants Amon and Emma Stanley, and grant them an entrance into the land of light and joy, in the fellowship of thy saints; through Jesus Christ thy Son our Lord, who liveth and reigneth with thee and the Holy Spirit, one God, now and forever. Amen.' "

"Amen," Parker echoed quietly.

The rider closed his book and looked down at the mound of dirt for a long moment; then he looked over at the boy and smiled, and stuck out his hand.

"I'm Clay Springer," he said. "How are you called?"

"Parker. Parker Stanley. Parker is my first name."

"Parker Stanley . . . that's a fine name for a man," Clay said. "Well, climb up on back of my horse, Parker. We can ride double."

"Wait," Parker said. "Can I tell my ma and pa one more thing?"

"Of course you can, son. Take all the time you need."

Parker cleared his throat, and looked down at the pile of freshly turned dirt.

"Ma, Pa, if all your teachin' about heaven and all that is right, then I reckon you can hear me, 'cause the Lord has, for sure, taken you into his arms. So, what I want to say is . . . don't worry none about me. I aim to live the kind of life you would'a both wanted me to live. And I figure, the way things are now, why, you'll both be watchin' over me even more'n you would'a if you was still alive.

"And you can set your minds to ease about Elizabeth, too.

I aim to find her. It may take a while, but I promise you, if it takes twenty years, I'll keep lookin' for her.

"I reckon this is good-bye for now, but, if you don't mind, I'll be talkin' to you from time to time. Oh, I prob'ly won't be comin' back out to this place anymore. But, then, I don't think your souls will be hangin' aroun' here anyway."

Clay stood a few feet behind Parker as he said his final words. He was glad he couldn't be seen. It wouldn't be seemly for the boy to see him wipe the tears from his own eyes.

"I reckon that's it," Parker said.

"You'll do your folks proud, Parker, I know you will," Clay said,

Parker started toward the horse; then he remembered the hidden pouch of money. It was under a loose board in the front of the wagon, a part that hadn't been damaged by the fire. He started toward it.

"What're you going after?"

Parker looked back toward Clay. The man had saved his life, helped bury his parents, and even read prayers over their graves. But a sudden cautiousness made him hesitate to tell Clay of the money. What if all the help this man had given him had only been a ruse to see if there was anything of value left? He felt almost ashamed of himself for being suspicious, but he thought it would be better to be safe than sorry.

"Just some letters," Parker said. "I want to keep them."

"All right."

Parker moved the board to one side and picked up the small leather pouch. He could feel the hefty wad of bills inside. As he had overheard his mother and father talking about it, he knew they had one thousand dollars left over after buying the wagon and supplies.

Parker slipped the pouch down inside his waistband, then

walked back over to the horse. Clay was already mounted, and he offered his hand to help Parker climb up.

The air was perfumed with the smell of rabbit roasting on a spit, while Clay and Parker drank coffee. Parker hadn't been a coffee drinker before. His ma told him she'd as soon he not drink coffee until he was an adult, and that was what he told Clay when Clay offered him a cup.

"Well, Parker, some folks become adults before other folks," Clay said. "Seems to me like that time has come for you."

Clay was right, Parker thought. He was on his own, now. As far as being an adult was concerned, that sort of sped things up. He accepted the coffee. It tasted a little bitter to him, but he was determined to acquire a taste for it.

Clay sipped his own coffee through extended lips and studied Parker over the rim of his cup.

"How old are you, Parker?"

"I'm sixteen," Parker said.

Clay raised one eyebrow.

"All right, fifteen . . . and a half."

"Where were you folks comin' from?"

"Illinois."

"You got any relatives back in Illinois that you want to go to?"

Parker shook his head. "No, all my ma's folks live in England and I don't even know their names. My pa had a brother, but he got killed at Antietam."

"Bloody battle, Antietam," Clay said, shaking his head. "Any close friends or neighbors?"

"None I would want to be a burden to," Parker replied. He took another drink of his coffee. It seemed to him that it went down a little easier this time. "Anyway, I don't want to go back. I've got to find my sister."

"Older sister? Or younger?"

"Older. She's eighteen."

Clay studied the boy for a long moment before he talked. "Boy, you have to face the fact that you may never find her. A group of renegades like that . . . especially if they have a white man riding with them . . . will sell her to the highest bidder."

"I'll find her," Parker insisted. "It may take me a while, but I'll find her."

Clay started to caution him against false hope; then he checked the impulse. Instead, he smiled at Parker. "I'm sure you're right," he said. "If anyone can do it, you, my stalwart young lad, can."

"What's a stalwart?" Parker asked.

Clay laughed. "It means resolute, courageous, determined," he said.

"Determined. Yes, that's what I am. I am determined."

"Well, now, the question is, what are we to do with you?"

"Do with me? Why do you have to do anything with me? Just get me back into a town somewhere and I'll be grateful."

"I can't just turn you out on your own," Clay said "You're too young."

"I thought you told me I was an adult."

Clay cleared his throat. The boy was trapping him with his own words.

"Well . . . you are, as far as I'm concerned. But there're other things to consider. Your schooling for example. You being only fifteen, you're going to need another couple of years of schooling, and I don't think you can get that on your own. Tell you what. I'm going into Independence tomorrow. Suppose we go see the judge and let him decide your case."

"What do you mean, decide my case?"

"Decide what to do with you," Clay said.

"Oh." Parker was quiet for a long moment. "Mr. Springer, will the judge put me in an orphanage?"

"He may," Clay admitted. "I believe there is an orphanage in Independence."

"I don't want to go to an orphanage."

"Why not? There will be people there to look after you. You'll be fed and clothed, and you'll go to school," Clay said, trying to paint as attractive a picture as he could.

"I don't need to be looked after. I can feed and clothe myself."

"Parker, I don't know how much money there is in that pouch you've got stuck down in your waistband, but I'd be willing to bet there isn't enough to take care of you until you are full-grown."

Parker gasped and instinctively felt for the pouch.

"You were right not to tell me about it," Clay said. "I'll give you credit for that. But this should prove something to you, I hope. If I were the type person who would rob you, I could have already done it. So even your attempt at secrecy wasn't enough. See, you'd be better off going to an orphanage." Clay pulled a blanket from his saddle roll and tossed it over to Parker. "Here," he said. "Wrap up in this and get some sleep. It's been a bad day for you, but you'll see things more clearly tomorrow."

Black thunderclouds rumbled ominously in the northwest at the next morning, but they held off long enough for Parker and Clay to reach their destination.

Independence was laid out like a giant cross, with Liberty Street forming the north-south arm, and Independence Avenue cutting across it, running east-west. Independence Avenue continued on as a wagon trail running west, out of town.

Parker looked at this town, which was to be his new home. It was a very busy town. There was a lot of wagon and buggy traffic, and dozens and dozens of people walking along the plank walks that lined both sides of the streets. At intervals there were boards stretched all the way across the dirt streets to allow people a way to cross when the roads were full of mud. This was the first town Parker had seen since his family had stopped for a few days in Sedalia, Missouri, some six weeks earlier. Despite the unhappy circumstances under which he was now seeing Independence, he found it very exciting to be in a town again.

At the intersection of Liberty and Independence, Clay stopped in front of the Morning Star Hotel.

"Why don't you take my horse on down to the livery and get a stable for him?" Clay suggested, handing Parker a coin. "Tell the hand to feed him oats and rub him down. Then come on back to the hotel. I'll be up in my room."

"Where will your room be?"

"I don't know yet. I haven't registered. You can check with the desk—they'll tell you."

"What's the desk?"

By now Clay had slipped down from the horse to allow Parker to move up into the saddle. Clay looked up at him and smiled.

"Are you serious?"

"I've . . . I've never been in a hotel before," Parker admitted.

"Believe me, from the condition of some of the ones I've been in, you haven't missed much," Clay said. He removed his saddlebags and hung them over his shoulder, then pointed through the door. "Look, when you come back, just go inside here. There will be a man behind a counter. Ask him what room number Clay Springer is registered in, and he'll tell you."

"All right," Parker said.

Parker watched Clay go into the hotel, then started riding toward the livery, which was about three blocks down on Independence. He reached down and patted the neck of the animal he was riding. His father had never owned a horse.

Back in Illinois, he had farmed with mules, but he sold those when he made the decision to take the family West. He had then replaced the mules with a team of oxen.

Parker thought it would be nice to have a horse, and the freedom to go wherever a horse could take you. What if he just kept this horse? With a good mount and a thousand dollars, he could get a start somewhere.

And he wouldn't have to go to an orphanage.

But even as the thought crossed his mind, he knew he wouldn't do it. No matter how he might justify it to himself, it would still be stealing . . . and worse, he would be stealing from a man who had helped him.

By now Parker's slow ride down the street had brought him to the livery barn. Turning in, he climbed down from the saddle and handed the horse over to the attendant who met him, a boy not much older than himself.

"This your horse?" the boy asked.

"It belongs to a friend."

"Looks like a good horse."

"He sure is," Parker said, almost possessively.

"I ain't seen you around here," the livery attendant said as he took the horse's reins.

"I've never been here."

"You 'n your folks gonna live here?"

"I . . . I don't have any folks."

The boy looked around in surprise. "You an orphan?"

"Yes."

"I'm only half an orphan. I got me a ma, but she sure ain't much."

Parker gasped. He had never heard anyone speak so freely of their own mother.

"You think that's evil of me, don't you?" the boy asked.

"I would never say anything like that about my ma. If she was still alive," he added.

"Yeah, well, most mas is good, I guess. But my ma is what they call a whore. She works down at the Crystal Palace 'n when she's not layin' up with some man, she's more 'n likely drunk. But at least havin' a ma . . . any kind of a ma . . . means I ain't a orphan, so I don't have to go live up on The Hill. Any ma's all right if she keeps you offen The Hill."

"What's The Hill?"

"You kiddin'? You an orphan 'n you ain't never heard of The Hill? It's the orphanage. It's run by Ol' Man Slayton. Jebediah Slayton. They say he's the meanest man ever lived. He works the orphans till they're 'bout ready to drop, 'n he beats 'em when he don't think they're workin' hard enough. Just you wait. If you're a orphan like you say you are, 'n you're movin' here, you'll find out soon enough."

"Maybe I won't go to the orphanage," Parker said.

"If you stay here, you'll more'n likely have to. Seems like that's the law or somethin'." The boy looked at the sky. "It's fixin' to rain somethin' fierce. If you ain't got a place to get out of it, you can stay here for a while."

"Thanks," Parker said. "I've got a place."

"Better get to it then," the stable boy said as he disappeared into the barn.

At that moment the thunderclouds delivered on their promise, and the rain started coming down in sheets. Parker dashed across the street and up onto the wooden sidewalk. Many of the stores had roofs that overhung the sidewalk, so though Independence Avenue was already turning into a river of mud, Parker was able to return to the hotel without suffering too much from the weather. He stomped his feet just outside the door to make certain he had no mud on his shoes; then he went inside.

The hotel lobby seemed huge to him. There were a dozen or more chairs and sofas scattered about, several potted plants, mirrors on the walls, and a grand, elegant staircase rising to the second floor. Parker looked around for a moment, taking in all the images of this, his first time in a hotel. Then he saw a counter and a man behind it looking at him.

"Boy, what you doin' in here? This isn't a place you can just come in out of the rain," the man behind the counter said, gruffly.

"I'm looking for Mr. Clay Springer."

"Springer. He just check in?"

"Check in" wasn't a term Parker had ever heard used, but he reasoned what it must mean.

"Yes, just a few moments ago."

"Yeah, thought that was his name. He's in room 212."

"Where's that?"

"Well, if it's 212, it must be on the second floor," the man said in exasperation.

"Oh."

The man sighed, and pointed to the stairs. "Go up these stairs," he said. "It's the first room on the left."

"Thank you."

Parker climbed the stairs; then when he saw the right door, he opened it and went inside. Instantly, he heard a metallic click, and he turned to see Clay holding a cocked pistol leveled toward him. Parker gasped in surprise and took half a step back.

"Boy, don't frighten me like that," Clay said, sighing in relief. He released the hammer and lowered the pistol. "Most people knock before they come into someone's room."

"You told me to come on up," Parker said.

"So I did," Clay said.

"Well, that's just what I done."

Clay was in the midst of changing his clothes. He had already put on another pair of trousers, but was bare from the waist up.

"I had some bathwater brought up," Clay said. "I've already taken mine, and the water is still warm, so you can take yours now. I'll be back later this afternoon. Then we can go downstairs to take our supper. I'll bet you've never eaten in a restaurant either, have you?"

"No, I haven't," Parker admitted. "But, listen, I don't need a bath. It hasn't been that long since I had one."

Clay smiled at him. "It's been long enough," he said. He pointed to the tub. "Take a bath." Clay started toward the door.

"Mr. Springer?"

"Yes?"

"Are you going to check on the orphanage?"

"Maybe."

"I already did," Parker said.

Clay stood there with his hand on the doorframe. "What did you find out?"

"It's like you said. They've got one here," Parker said. He didn't say anything else about it.

Clay nodded. "That's good to know," he said. He let himself out, then closed the door behind him.

After Clay left the hotel room, Parker got undressed for his bath. He held the pouch of money for a moment, trying to decide what to do with it. Then he saw the bed. Hiding the pouch under the mattress, he returned to the tub and slipped down into the still-warm water.

Don't forget to wash behind your ears, Parker, his ma's voice came back to him.

"I won't, Ma," Parker said, quietly. "I won't."

S0464